The SERPENT House

Bea Davenport

BEA DAVENPORT

First published in 2014 by Curious Fox,
an imprint of Capstone Global Library Limited,
7 Pilgrim Street, London, EC4V 6LB
Registered company number: 6695582

www.curious-fox.com

Cover designed by Richard Parker
Illustrations by Orinthia Tyrell (Beehive Illustration)

ISBN 978 1 78202 085 1

18 17 16 15 14
10 9 8 7 6 5 4 3 2 1

A CIP catalogue for this book is available from the British
Library.

Typeset in Palatino

Printed and bound by CPI Group (UK) Ltd,
Croydon, CR0 4YY

Huge thanks to Jackie Kay and Kim Reynolds, my supervisors at Newcastle University, for their help and their wisdom during the writing of *The Serpent House*. Thanks also to all my fellow students who were so generous with their time and advice. Irene Allen from the charity Lepra helped enormously with my research. Editors Vaarunika Dharmapala and Penny West at Curious Fox improved the work more than I like to admit. And as always, all my thanks to Mark, Naomi, Patrick and Mary for their unending love, support and faith in my writing.

Chapter One

From the private diary of Lady Eugenia Hexer
Hexer Hall
27th November, 1898 (Advent Sunday)

*This morning at church, the fresh scents from the
wreaths and bundles of greenery decking the building
masked its usual musty smell; they did nothing to help
the chill in the air. The ladies nodded at me politely
because they must. I own so much of the land around
here. But my family's name is not a good one, even
after all these centuries. Bad reputations can last down
many generations. Mr Pocklaw, the minister, wore
purple robes. He spoke of deliverance and the coming
of the one who ends the dark times. For once, I paid
attention. No! It is not that I have seen the light all of a*

sudden – it's more that, at long last, revelations seem to be happening in my own life.

Afterwards, the coach rattled back to the Hall. It was as we drove into the courtyard that I saw him. The winter sun was dazzling and I could make him out only in silhouette. His lean body, a young man not quite fully grown. That wild hair. My new young gardener, reputed to have a magic touch with plants. When I approached him, he jumped to his feet and made a clumsy sort of bow. He is completely untrained in how to address his betters, but this is of scant importance. In his hands, he was twisting plants and stalks into some kind of ball shape. I asked him what he was doing and he told me he was making a tussie-mussie for his younger sister, who is ill. He held it out for me to try its scent. It was eye-wateringly strong. Rosemary, mint and thyme, he said.

Something compelled me to ask him more about this sister. It seems they are orphans and since the mother's death the child has been unwell. He truly dotes on the girl and is heartbroken to have left her behind. The picture he painted of her, with her cropped hair and her penchant for boy's clothes, is so like the prophesy that I almost gasped aloud.

"The lost and sorrowful child, the sometimes-boy and sometimes-girl, will make your journey and bring you knowledge." For a number of years I have lived with this unfathomable prediction.

I was filled with a wild impulse and told the lad

that he must bring his sister to live with him. I have offered him the use of an old outhouse on the edge of the grounds. I told him I'd heard of his reputation, that he could grow plants that no one else can bring from the soil. He actually blushed, which made me smile. The reason I brought him here is because I need his help in creating a healing garden in my grounds. It will take his special talent to make it happen. When I talked more to him about this, he smiled so wide, his face a picture of such hope and gratitude, that I had to pull my cape around my shoulders to stop myself reaching out to him.

"We have many more plans to make," I told him. "As it is winter, you have less to do in the gardens than usual. If you keep up your duties, you may work on preparing the cottage for you and your sister to live in. She may join you at Christmas, one month from now, and I will find work for her in the Hall. Ask my housekeeper if there is anything you need." I made my way across the courtyard and into the house. I was shivering, my eyes full of tears, although it may have been the cold.

So at last, my journey feels as if it is truly beginning. Perhaps now is the time to record it all, as one day students may wish to know every step of it. Unless I write it all down, I fear it will never be believed.

I was not expecting Christmas to be a happy one. It is hard to feel peace and goodwill when your mother is just two months dead. When she passed away, I was sent to live with my Aunt Catherine and my cousins, James and Hannah. The cottage was cold and they were colder. My aunt was not cruel. But nor was she kind. All the time, I missed my Mam and most of the time I missed Tom, my older brother and my best friend.

Tom was sixteen years old and becoming a man. He had a special talent for growing things – our vegetable patch back home was fit for the queen. Soon after we came to live at my aunt's, a very rich lady hired Tom to turn his skills to her new gardens. The trouble was, it was too far away for him to visit me very often. Writing is not his talent, although our mother taught us both, so I didn't get letters from him. I was left behind here with no one to talk to. It was a hard eight weeks.

Late on Christmas Eve, I sat shivering at the kitchen table, scraping at some spuds for the Christmas Day dinner. The knife was newly sharpened and I cut my fingers twice. Each time, Hannah spotted it and screamed at the pinkish cloud that stained the cold water, and each time Aunt Catherine cuffed me across the ear. She couldn't understand why I was so clumsy, she said.

"Your mother had fingers so deft they could do anything," she told me. It sounds stupid, but I hated the way she said "your mother", through her pinched mouth. "Your *mither*." As if she could hardly bear to squeeze out the words. I never called her "my mother". Tom and I called her "me Mam". It rolled off our tongues as if it was one word: Me-Mam.

I put up with "your mither" for weeks and suddenly – perhaps because I was tired and my fingers were sore – something burst out of me. "She's not my *mither*," I found myself shouting. "She's Me-Mam. Me-Mam!" I beat my fists on the table as the words drummed out of my mouth. "Me-*Mam*, Me-*Mam*, Me-*Mam*!" Hot tears burned the back of my eyes and I fought as best I could to keep them in. Aunt Catherine picked up a wooden spoon and rapped my fingers, hard. She caught me twice – oh, the pain in my cold, wet fingers! I snatched my hand away but I stopped talking. Aunt Catherine turned her back on me. Hannah and James were supposed to be placing the wooden figures in the crib in the corner, but they kept watching me and grinning.

"That's you," said James, waving one of the shepherd figures at me, one with his smooth round head bent, the better to look at the carved baby Jesus. "You're a wooden-top."

I was about to say something back and I would surely have got into more trouble, but then I heard footsteps coming up our path towards the door. I jumped up, hoping, hoping ... and it was, it was my Tom, come back to see me for Christmas. His face and hands were pink and shiny with the cold. He seemed so much taller and broader than I remembered, even though it was just a few weeks since I'd seen him. His soft hair had grown down past his ears and it made him look like a big, shaggy puppy dog.

He laughed and hugged me. Now I felt those tears starting to come and this time I couldn't stop them.

My aunt stood up and greeted him, stiff and stern as usual. She's never cared for Tom, and since Mam's death he's talked back to her far too often. But it was Christmas, so she tried to smile, a small crack that caused other tiny, angry lines around the edge of her mouth and her stony face.

"See what I have," Tom grinned and plunged his hands into his bulging coat pockets.

"Oranges!" yelled James and Hannah, lunging towards him. They made me think of the pigs running for their swill. Tom handed them one orange each. "From Lady Hexer's own storeroom."

My aunt gave a tiny grunt. "I hope you had permission to take them, Tom Cotterill. I don't want any stolen fruit in this house, Christmas or no."

"Of course I was allowed," Tom replied, raising his eyebrows. I sighed to myself. They were squaring up like fighters already. "Lady Hexer told me to take some home for the children. In fact, she made a point of saying I had to give the biggest one to you, Annie."

He held out the last bright fruit, which seemed to light up the whole dull, cabbage-smelling kitchen. I took it and pressed it to my face, breathing in its wonderful smell. And what a smell; a feast on its own. I held the globe-shape, warm from Tom's pocket, towards the candlelight and watched how it made my fingers glow like flames around the fruit.

Hannah looked put out. "Why should she get the biggest one?" she whined. "*I'm* the oldest."

Tom added: "I would never steal, Aunt. You ought to know that. Why would I need to? Lady Hexer's the most generous employer I have ever known."

My aunt gave another grunt. "So you say. Of course, I don't know much about this employer of yours, but I have heard worrying stories about her, for all her great wealth. I don't know what kind of habits you have taken up since you went to work over there, but you will find we still go to the church service every Sunday. Tomorrow, too, with it being Christmas Day. If you want any dinner, you'll come to church with us."

Tom looked at me for a moment, then back at his aunt. "Of course I'll come, Aunt. I never said I wouldn't. I want to walk with Annie and hold her hand. After the service we will visit our mother's grave."

I smiled up at him. If only Tom was here all the time. He always stood up for himself so well. I could never think of clever or brave things to say to my aunt and cousins, not until it was too late.

Aunt Catherine served up some ham broth for supper and afterwards we were allowed to eat the oranges. Tom used his sharp knife to cut mine into quarters. The smell made me blink. It made my mouth feel suddenly parched, as if I would choke if I didn't get a taste of that sunlit juice. I sucked the first chunk so happily it made a loud slurping noise. Tom and I giggled and Aunt told us not to be so disgusting.

13

Oh, the sweet and sour taste of it. You could close your eyes and imagine yourself in some faraway, picture-book country where there might be trees laden down with fruit and brightly-coloured birds flapping around them. I used my teeth to wring out every last drop of juice, sucked my sticky fingers and ran my tongue around my mouth to enjoy it all as long as I could.

Later, Tom and I sat together on my small bed.

"I got your letter," he told me. "I like you sending me your news. I'm sorry I don't write back."

Tom is proud of how clever I am. Mam always said it was because my father was a man of letters. I never really understood that, though. He never wrote any letters to me. Or to her.

Tom looked at me. He had worry in his eyes.

"How have you been?" he asked. His voice was more gentle than any I'd heard lately. His eyes flicked up to my headscarf and back to my face. "I think about you all the time, left here with no one to care about you. It's so miserable here. I don't know how you put up with that woman."

"Aunt Catherine? She's worse with you, Tom. Because you argue with her. I don't argue, I just do what she says," I said with a shrug.

Then I added: "Usually," and Tom gave me a wink. "But I know she doesn't care much for men. If I wasn't her sister's child ... well. But I do miss you. And Mam."

Tom squeezed my fingers and winced. "You and your cold hands. Is there no blood in them, my boggle?"

He's always called me names like that. Everyone says that when I was born I was an ugly little thing, a cross, red-faced bairn with a nose like the cap of a mushroom. But Tom looked after me, from the start, Mam said. There'd been other babies – after Tom, before me – but none had lived very long. Tom, at around six years old, had told our mother that I would be all right, because I was no human child; I was some sort of boggle or goblin. I'm no prettier now. Especially now.

"Anyway," Tom went on, "I have a kind of Christmas present for you, but it's something to tell, not something to give. You must wait till tomorrow."

"Tell me now," I demanded. "Please."

Tom laughed. "No. All I will say is this: it will cheer up your Christmas Day. I know it. I'll tell all tomorrow after church." I couldn't imagine what could cheer up a Christmas Day without Mam. But I trusted Tom more than anything.

The Christmas morning mass seemed to go on for ever and ever. It was a cold walk of almost two miles to the church and we shivered our way joylessly through the carols, bobbing between the unforgiving wooden benches and the damp-smelling kneelers. The priest droned like a fly woken up mid-winter. When it ended, at last, Aunt Catherine, James and Hannah went on ahead of us, while Tom and I stood by our mother's small headstone. It was the newest and cleanest in the churchyard. We hadn't been able to buy it ourselves, of course, but the stonemason had a soft spot for Tom and everyone had loved our gentle Mam. So he carved the headstone out of kindness and Tom paid him in what he called bagies, or turnips, and bags of spuds.

Aunt Catherine told us to say a prayer for our mother, but when we got to the grave, neither of us knew what to say. The silence felt heavy, broken only by the birds cawing through the chilly air. It was so still, the air seemed stopped and weighed down with cold. I didn't really care. The sad, grey weather felt right. On the day Mam died, there was the brightest blue October sky I had ever seen and it felt like an insult.

Tom looked at me. "Do you want to say a prayer?" he asked me, blowing on his fingers and shifting from foot to foot.

I shrugged. "I know I should, though if I'm being honest, I ran out of prayers after Mam died. I know I shouldn't say that, right here in a churchyard and just after mass on Christmas Day and all that.

"I prayed so hard that she'd get better, Tom, because that's what everyone told me to do. But she died after all, didn't she. I don't see what's left for me to say to that God."

Tom gave a small smile. "I know what you mean. So instead of a prayer, I'm going to tell you my news now. If Mam can hear us, I think it's something she'd like to know."

I felt my heart starting to beat harder.

"I've told you how good Lady Hexer is to me," Tom started.

I nodded.

"I've been so lucky," he said. "She's made me quite a favourite. She says I'm the only one who can help set out her new gardens. I sat with her at her own grand table – you should see it, it's this long," and he waved his arm into the distance. "She asked for my advice about it all. The plants, what should go where and whether some of the rarer ones will grow. And we've talked. She asked me about my family and I told her all about you and your..." he stopped and I could see him trying to find the right words. "Your health."

I frowned and put my hand up to my head, wrapped up in its grubby woolly scarf. I did not like the thought of strangers knowing that since our mother's death, my hair had fallen out in clumps, leaving me uglier and more odd-looking than ever. Tom was beside himself with worry about it. Aunt Catherine said she didn't have the money to spend on quacks and medicines, so I would just have to put up with it, shameful though it was. Shameful to her, she meant.

"Just listen to this. Her Ladyship has given me an old cottage in the grounds. It hadn't been lived in for a while and there were holes in the roof and all sorts of places where the rain and wind came in. But she sent one of her men to help me fix it up and now I have my own home to live in. She's said that I can bring you to live with me, Annie. To live with me!"

His words came out faster and faster, as if they were running down a hill.

"When I told Lady Hexer how much I missed you and worried about you, she said it simply wouldn't do. That's how she said it: *it simply will not do*. She said she would like to help. She seemed so interested in you. So I'm to bring you to stay with me, where I'll be able to look after you and make sure you're healthy.

"You can do some work in the kitchens and some cleaning to earn your keep. But we'll be together and you'll be away from this miserable place. We'll be right beside the sea. The air smells so clean. When you take a deep breath, I swear it seems to wash out your insides. I will make sure you eat the best food we can grow. You will get better and those curls will grow back again faster than we know it."

I couldn't remember when I had last seen him grin so widely. "What do you say, hobgoblin? Will you come?"

I jumped up and threw my arms around his neck. I would have squealed if we hadn't been in a churchyard. I squeezed Tom as hard as I could.

"Oh, Tom," I yelped. I could hardly speak at all because I found myself laughing and crying both at once. "You were right. This has been my best ever Christmas present."

We knelt down and each gave the frosted headstone a quick kiss. "When we next come back to visit, we'll bring a bunch of spring flowers," Tom promised, to the stone and the earth. Out of nowhere, a bitter breeze made us shudder. Then we began our walk back to the house, faster and faster, giggling to think what our aunt and cousins would say when we told them our plans.

Aunt Catherine was awkward about it, as we'd guessed. "I promised my sister I'd look after Annie," she said. She looked as if she was searching around in her mind to find a reason to stop me from going. "I can hardly let her go off to somewhere I know nothing about, with a brother hardly more than a child himself."

Tom hated that, of course. "I'm a working man now," he said. "I have a home for my sister and a way she can earn her keep. You know I can take care of her, Aunt."

"She's too young to be working," said Aunt Catherine. "Your mother would be furious. She wanted better for Annie. That's why she took the time to teach her her letters. You want to pull her down into the scullery again. Think how your mother would feel, her Annie skivvying—"

Our cousins sat watching, their mouths open.

"She skivvies for you," Tom replied and my aunt's face went red-purple. "She'd do better to get paid for it. She'll be in the house of a fine lady and yes, she can read and write. So she'll do very well, I promise you that. What can you offer her that's better?"

Aunt Catherine narrowed her eyes at Tom. They are blue like Mam's but they are the wrong blue. "You think far too much of yourself," she hissed. "Will you make sure she goes to church? Will you make sure she says her prayers? Or will this grand lady take care of that?"

Tom stood up tall like a hero from a storybook. "Perhaps we will go to church again some day," he said. "When we both forgive God for taking our Mam away."

Our aunt and cousins drew in their breath and my aunt crossed herself in prayer, as if to rid the air of Tom's wicked words.

"But for now, Aunt," Tom went on, "I want to give Annie a chance of being happy. You're welcome to come and visit us, to make sure I'm looking after her as our Mam would want. But you won't stop Annie from coming with me."

My aunt turned away and instead of more angry words she slammed pots and plates about, as loud as she could. James and Hannah kept out of her way. I was shaking. But when I caught Tom's eye I gave him the widest grin I dared.

Later, James pulled my ears and told me that I'd spoiled Christmas Day. Everyone was now so angry with us that we wanted to leave as soon as we could. We planned to go the very next morning. It would be a long walk and the weather was bleak. I found I had a churning brew of feelings inside me. I was both excited and scared. I knew that if Tom said things would be well, then surely they would. Yet there was a small part of me, somewhere deep down, that was fearful, although I was unable to say exactly what made me afraid.

Chapter Two

Early the next morning as we prepared to go, James and Hannah laughed at me and told me I was off to be a skivvy.

"Got yer scrubbing brush? Got yer mop?"

I was surprised when their mother told them to stop it, with real sharpness in her voice. Then, as I made for the door, Aunt Catherine suddenly grasped my hand and pressed two copper pennies into it.

"Annie," she said. "Come back if ever you wish. I know this is not your home and I am not your mother. But there is always a place for you here. That's all."

I stared at her in surprise. Her face was hard, as usual. It did not seem to match her words.

"She won't need to come back here," said Tom. Aunt Catherine looked at me and gave a tiny nod, then turned away. The door shut behind us and we left.

It was so early it was still black-dark. As we walked, it started to snow. Nasty, spiteful globs of freezing wetness spat in our eyes and soaked our clothes. After a few miles, my legs were aching with cold and weariness. I barely had any feeling in my feet. Tom picked me up and carried me on his back for a while, but I knew that was too hard on him. And then, suddenly, as it was beginning to get dark again in the late winter afternoon, a horse and trap came past and Tom flagged the driver down. He agreed to take us most of the way and I managed to sleep for some of the journey, in spite of the bumps and jolts.

When he set us down we were in the village of Hexendale, and to help keep me awake Tom pointed out the grocer's shop, the ale houses, the ironmonger's and the church, although of course all were in darkness at this hour. We had just over a mile left to walk, down towards the sea, which Tom said would be in sight if only it wasn't so dark. But we could smell it. The air filled our lungs with salt and ice.

It stopped snowing and, though I could still barely feel my legs or my feet, soon we trudged into a long road which was the entrance to the Hexer Hall estate. It seemed to go on for many a step and to either side there were dark, dark gardens, all black shapes that were hard to make out. As we walked, with our path marked out only by the white of the snowfall, I was overcome with – what? A feeling I could not quite explain. I stopped and stood still, shivering, afraid, and my head swam. I heard a voice as if it was calling from a long way away. It said something like my name, but it wasn't quite right.

"What's wrong? We're almost there," Tom urged me on and I forced my legs to step one in front of the other, although it felt like a huge effort to do it. I couldn't see a thing either side of the roadway. It was all dense shrubs and trees. But I thought I could hear things – I don't know what – moving about, making dry, whispery noises. Did I hear someone give a soft whimper, a sob? Or was that just me?

"Tom, I'm scared," I whispered to him. "I don't know why, I just am."

But then Tom said: "Look. See that little cottage?"

I could just make out a small stone building with a tiny light in the window. "Who's in there?" I asked as we hurried towards it, forgetting my sick feeling of a moment ago. "Why is there a light?"

Tom pushed open the door, which smelled of fresh, new wood, and stood back for me to walk in first. I thought for a moment I was asleep and in a dream. I entered a warm room, with a fire chuckling in the grate. The air was scented sweetly with wood and coals. On a table was a candle in a glass jar and two plates set with big chunks of pie. There was bread and a jug of something. It felt like a scene from a fairy tale. My fear seemed to slide away to nothing.

"Where is this?" I breathed. "Whose house is this? Should we be in here?"

Tom laughed, setting down our bag and putting his arms round my shoulders. "This is our new home. Do you like it?"

23

"But the fire, the food – who's done all this?"

"That'll be Lucy. She's my friend who works in the big kitchens. I had a feeling she would do something like this. She was longing to see you. You'll meet her tomorrow and I know you'll like her. She'll take care of you when you're working in the Hall."

I sat down by the fire and sighed as the warmth began to make my feet and fingers tingle and ache. The pain was sweet. Tom handed me the food and a drink, which turned out to be milk. My eyes started to close long before Tom blew out the tiny candle.

I can't remember when I last slept so long and so well. I woke up warm and muddle-headed. My blankets felt heavy and after a few minutes I realised Tom must have laid his own bedclothes over mine. He wasn't in the cottage. I could tell it must be quite late in the morning because there was brilliant white sunlight outside. I sat up, blinking at this new place. It still felt unreal. The fire had gone out, but I pulled a blanket around me and went to the tin jug to splash some water on my face. Then I walked around the tiny room, my whole body still aching from yesterday's long trudge. There wasn't much here: a small table, newly carved, two wooden chairs, the fireplace with a pot strung over it, and the bed. But I knew I loved it. Tom and I could be happy here, I thought.

There was a tapping at the door and I opened it just a tiny crack. Outside was a girl of about seventeen, the like of whom I'd never seen before. She was smiling so wide I couldn't help smiling straight back.

"Annie? Can I come in? I'm Lucy. Tom said I might bring you some breakfast."

I held open the door to this peculiar creature. She kept on smiling and her face was soft and round, pretty as a toffee apple. I couldn't take my eyes off the colour of her skin and her tight-curled hair, black as midnight. I wanted to reach out and touch her, to make sure she was real. She handed me some bread, still warm, wrapped in a cloth. The smell made my stomach growl, so loud I had to excuse myself, and Lucy just laughed.

"Tom's told me so much about you," she said. "I'm so glad he's brought you here."

She gave me a long look and I wondered if she was surprised that a boy as handsome as Tom could have such an ugly sister. But then she shook her head and said: "Just look at you. You remind me of a wee doll."

I thought that was a nice thing to say and I kept remembering it all day. It made me feel warm inside.

Lucy had a beautiful voice. Her words came out as if she was mixing a sweet and spicy pudding. "I love the way you talk," I blurted out and she laughed.

"A Scottish accent. I can't believe you haven't heard one before. Lots of people talk like this around here," she said. "We're right on the border, you see."

Lucy had been brought up near Edinburgh, she said, and that was a place I'd heard about. She laughed again when I asked if everyone in Edinburgh looked like her.

She told me her father had sailed to Scotland from a land far over the sea. She told me the name of the country but I'd never heard of it, which made me feel a bit stupid. Lucy has never been to see her father's country, though.

"I wish I lived in Edinburgh," I said. "I wish I talked like that."

I suddenly thought my own voice sounded flat and rough compared with Lucy's music. "But I love your voice too," Lucy told me. "And Tom's."

I guessed almost straight away that she was sweet on Tom. I liked that idea.

After we'd eaten and I'd dressed, Lucy offered to show me the Hall. We stepped out, my boots still damp and snow-stained, into a bright, white day. The cottage was well set back from the gardens, but as soon as I got into the Hall grounds, the sick, dizzy feeling from last night came over me again, as if I was about to fall over. Was that a whispering in my ears? Was someone saying my name? Or was something rustling somewhere nearby? I stopped walking and Lucy looked at me. Her eyes were all concern.

"I expect you're still worn out. Such a long way you had to walk last night," she said, so kindly. "But look, just a few more steps and you'll see the big Hall. It's quite a sight."

So I forced my feet forwards again and as we rounded a corner, a tall building reared up at us like a wild animal. We stopped to take it in. Hexer Hall was built from a pinkish-grey stone and all over the front of the building were elaborate carvings, which made it look as if the house was squinting and frowning at me. The sick feeling in my stomach grew stronger. I still thought I could hear that whispering, but it was too distant to make out words.

"What a place, eh?" laughed Lucy. Without meaning to, I clutched at her arm. She pointed to the carvings on the stonework. "Can you see what they are?"

I screwed my eyes up at them, wiping the sunlight-tears away.

"Snakes," she explained. "The Hall was rebuilt in the last few years, after Lord Hexer died. Everywhere you go there are these coiled-up snakes. They're in the stonework, in the banisters, the tiles on the fireplaces. Absolutely everywhere."

"Why?" I asked. "Why snakes?" I'd only ever seen a harmless grass snake. But they made my flesh crawl. At home, I couldn't even look at the picture under S for Snake in our Alphabet of Animals. Tom used to fold the page down for me, so I wouldn't see it.

Lucy shrugged. "I'm not sure. Mrs McKinnon says Her Ladyship comes from a very old family and that the snakes were once part of their coat of arms. But no one really knows if that's true or not." She linked her arm through mine and kept me walking towards the side of the Hall and the kitchen door.

The kitchen was huge and warm as a hug. It felt safe, just like the cottage. No whispering noises, no dizzy feeling. I stared around at the enormous fire, the high shelves of plates and copper, and at the pans hanging from the ceiling, clanking gently in the draughts. Bright sprays of holly, ivy and sharp-scented eucalyptus were still hanging up, left over from Christmas. Two other women were there. One was Mrs McKinnon, the head cook and housekeeper, who said her name to me as if I was someone important. She said how pleased she was that I had come. The other was a sharp-faced, fair-haired girl around the same age as Lucy, sitting bent over some sewing at the kitchen table. She looked up but did not smile.

"This is Becky," Lucy said. "Becky, here's Tom's wee sister."

Becky muttered something and bent her head down over her work. Lucy shrugged and shook her head. Then I was ordered to sit at the table while Mrs McKinnon served up a bowl of soup, all steam and heat. It was early for lunch but the smell of it made me feel suddenly starving.

As I ate it, quite greedily I think, I gazed around the kitchen. This one room was bigger than our entire old house. I hoped I wouldn't be asked to fetch a plate from the dresser because I would never be able to reach those high shelves. And I would be truly terrified of dropping the pretty blue-patterned china. My favourite shelf was lined with jars of jams and preserves, all jewel-coloured. I tried to take in their names. Raspberry, strawberry, redcurrant, quince. Blackberry, loganberry, apricot, orange. I will never want a row of fine silk dresses as much as my own kitchen shelf with all those bright jars and their mouth-watering names.

"Becky is sewing your maid's dress," Lucy told me.

"Tom told us how you like to wear your funny old clothes. Trousers and leggings and a skirt all at once. How does anyone tell if you're a boy or a girl? That may be fine for playing back at home. But when you're working in this house, you'll have to wear a dress and an apron, like me. Becky sews better than any of us so she's altering one of my old dresses. It'll look perfect when she's finished, you'll see."

Becky looked up at me, with eyes pale as sea-glass. She put the end of her thread in her teeth and bit it sharply. "What about her head?" she asked Lucy. Then she turned her light gaze back to me. "You can't go round in that, whatever it is," she added, staring hard at my headscarf.

I clutched it without thinking. "I have to keep it on," I said.

Lucy gave me a troubled look. "Well, now. I'm sure Becky can make you a cap. Becky, you can make a pretty white cap for Annie, can't you?"

Becky glared. "Why should I? Why should I be put to more work for someone who's lower than me? Why is everyone making this fuss over this– this scruffy little–"

I never got to hear what name she was going to call me because suddenly a bell jangled on the wall and everyone gave a jump. Becky leaped up and dropped her sewing on the table. She straightened her own dress and left the room in a flurry.

"Lady Hexer," said Mrs McKinnon. "Calling for something. Becky likes to wait on Her Ladyship herself, as much as possible. She is a hard worker, I'll give her that.

29

But she hoped to bring her own younger sister to work here and she can't understand why Tom was allowed and she was not. She's grumbled ever since she heard about you. But she'll get used to you, my pet."

I knew, from living with Aunt Catherine and my cousins, how it feels to stay somewhere you're not wanted. So I hoped that Becky would forgive me more readily than James and Hannah. Truth be told, I myself couldn't understand why this rich lady had singled out Tom and granted him such great favours.

A few minutes later, Becky opened the kitchen door and walked in with a pink flush to her cheeks. "Lady Hexer wishes to see you," she said in her thin voice. "I've said you're not fit to see anyone at the moment. That you are dressed in boys' rags and not washed. But she insists."

Both Lucy and Mrs McKinnon started to fuss around me like pecking birds. "Is that dress ready?" Mrs McKinnon asked.

Becky just pushed it across the table towards her. I found myself being hurriedly stripped of my outer clothes and the black dress being pulled down over my head. I tried to smooth out my headscarf but Becky's sharp fingers gave it a tug.

"This won't do," she snapped and pulled it off my head. There was a moment's silence as everyone stared at my patchwork scalp. I felt my face go hot. Lucy gaped helplessly around for something to cover my head, but nothing showed itself.

"I'm not going up there like this," I said, firm as I could, though I heard my voice shake a little. "Give me my scarf back."

Becky looked at me with raised blonde eyebrows and then, without a word, she flicked the scarf onto the kitchen fire. It went straight to ash. Lucy gasped and Mrs McKinnon said sharply: "Becky! Really! There was no need for that. It – it wasn't kind."

"The thing was filthy," Becky said. She looked straight at me, with her water-coloured eyes. "It smelled," she added, flicking her fingers like she was trying to rid them of dirt.

I couldn't speak. My hands flew up to my head and I tried, hopelessly, to cover over the patchiest parts of my scalp, wishing I had a dozen more fingers. Lucy looked tearful, but she said, "Annie, my love, you mustn't keep Her Ladyship waiting any longer. I am sure she will understand about your ... appearance." Then she added, "*I* will take you upstairs." She shook her head at Becky.

As I left the kitchen and went up a flight of stone steps that led to the upstairs rooms, with Lucy holding tightly to my hand, I heard the housekeeper begin to tell Becky off. We went through another heavy door and then we were in a wide, chilly hallway with a grey-green marble floor.

"Never mind about her," said Lucy, very quietly. "Let me tell you something good. We get paid better here than anywhere I've ever worked. It's because not everyone will work for Lady Hexer. Some people think she's a bit odd. When the old Lord died and she started changing the Hall, lots of servants left. She does have some funny ideas, I

31

suppose, and they say she came from a long line of ... well, never mind. You see, not everyone will employ people who look like me, so I am glad of my job here. She's the kindest person I've ever worked for, I promise. So don't be afraid."

Lucy was gently pushing me towards a staircase with a wrought-iron banister that seemed to spiral upwards for miles. On the first steps, I began to get that sickly feeling again and tried to say so, but Lucy bustled me up and up so fast I soon became out of breath. Then I was outside a tall door and Lucy was knocking on it. I felt a sudden sharp pain in my side and winced. Then another sharp jab in the shoulder. I realised what had happened – Becky had left pins in the dress. But it was too late to say anything, because Lucy was pushing open the door and steering me into a large, heavily-curtained room. I looked up to see a woman sitting on a couch, quite still. She looked like someone in a great painting, with her folds and folds of silky dress and her fine-china skin. She smiled faintly and beckoned me forward. Lucy nodded at me and I gave a sort of a bow, because I felt I should do something, but had no idea what. Lady Hexer asked Lucy to wait outside. Then she beckoned me again and I shuffled forward a bit more. I found I was trembling hard. I have never met anyone so wealthy or grand and I had no idea what to expect.

"You are Annie? Tom's sister?" she asked. Her voice was as cool and flowing as the silk of her skirts. I nodded. My throat felt as if it was closed up and I still felt faint.

"Child," said Lady Hexer. "You seem afraid. Please

don't be. My name is Lady Eugenia Hexer. I have been looking forward to meeting you."

"Why?" I blurted out. Then I thought that it must have sounded very rude. "Madam," I added, as a bit of an afterthought.

Lady Hexer's eyes seemed to flicker with a tiny light. "That is a very good question. Sit," she said, waving at a chair with her hand. I sat down quickly and winced as another pin scratched my backside.

"Tom has told me all about you," Lady Hexer went on. "And about your unfortunate... " Here she glanced at my bare head and I felt myself flushing again. "Your health problem. I would like to see if we can do anything to help. I have an interest in matters of health."

I looked down at my hands and realised they were very grubby. I tried to hide them in a fold of the new dress. Her Ladyship watched. "This is your new maid's outfit?" she asked. I nodded.

"Tom tells me that you are often to be found in an unusual mixture of clothes," she went on. She leaned forward and looked at me more closely. "That it can be hard for people to tell whether you are a boy or a girl."

I nodded again. As soon as I could walk, I tried to be as much like Tom as I could, following him around and pretending to be a boy. His old leggings were easier for climbing trees and scaling walls than any skirts. Sometimes, the kids in the village laughed at me, especially the other girls. They couldn't understand why I didn't want to dress like them. The grown-ups tut-tutted at me and shook their heads. Aunt Catherine said I was a disgrace. But every time Mam put me into a dress, I wriggled back out of it as soon as her back was turned, until she gave up trying.

"People have sometimes said that I look like a boy," I said. "I don't really care though." I paused. "Madam."

"Well, now," she went on, with another small smile. "I believe we can find a good use for you here. What do you think of the Hall?"

I didn't know to reply. Was I really being asked for my thoughts by this grand lady? "I, er, I think it's very strange," I found myself saying. "But I haven't been here very long."

"Well. Quite," Her Ladyship nodded. I couldn't tell anything from her face, which was beautiful in a way that I wasn't used to. She looked more like a statue than a real person. "We will get to know each other better soon. Bring Lucy back in here, will you?"

Lucy came back in with a curtsey and took my hand.

"Take this child downstairs and give her a hearty meal," Lady Hexer commanded. "She seems quite pale and light-headed. And tell Becky to finish off the dress properly. This poor girl is being tortured by pins."

She turned to me. "You will begin working for me tomorrow morning at eight. Come up to this room and we will discuss what you are to do."

I tried to curtsey like Lucy. But with no idea how to do it, I must have looked like a duck. Then we went out of the room.

It was as we were walking back down the wide stairs

that the feeling of dizziness got worse, as if I'd breathed in some sort of poisonous gas. I thought I heard someone calling my name, or something like it: it sounded more like Anya, not Annie. The voice was inside my head, but far away, in a way I could not explain. I stopped a few steps behind Lucy and clutched at one of the shaped iron decorations along the spiral banister. When I put my fingers around its snake-like curves, it felt cold as metal should. I stopped to take a breath and as I did so, I thought I felt the shape warm up and move, like a ripple through my fingers. I tried to scream, but nothing came out.

CHAPTER THREE

For a terrible moment I wondered if I'd suddenly died. I couldn't see anything. But I could hear my own panicky breathing. As I blinked away the blackness, I saw I was no longer holding the stair rail. I was leaning against a stone wall in a corridor that I had never seen before. I breathed in a mix of smells, of damp and cold and of something else much sweeter, something that I thought I knew but could not place.

I took a step forward on shivering legs. I could see a tiny glow of a light, much further along the passageway, so I started shakily to make my way towards it. And then I realised, in the gloom, that a shape was also making its way towards me. It was a small shape, perhaps a child near to my age or younger. As the figure came closer, I saw that it was a girl. She was wearing a long plain shift dress and she was staring at me open-mouthed. She spoke, but I couldn't understand what she was saying and I tried to tell her this. She shook her head at me, as if she couldn't understand me either. She pointed towards my head and repeated her words again and this time I thought I caught one or two of the words. I thought she was saying, "Where is your hood? Where is your hood?"

Her fingers reached out to me and they curled into wisping black shapes that I tried to push away. Then the light became blinding and I blinked again and again, my eyes sore and watering. When they finally cleared, I was lying on Lady Hexer's stairs. Lucy was fanning me and Mrs McKinnon was trying to push a cup of water to my mouth.

"She's coming round," I heard someone say. "Oh, Annie, pet! Are you all right?"

I sat up slowly. I had no idea what had just happened.

Hexer Hall
27th December, 1898

When I heard about Annie's experience, it pulled me sharply back to something from my own past. Hearing the girl's confused and childish account of what had happened, I suddenly saw myself at that age, or perhaps slightly younger. The memory tugged at me and I want to recount it here, as I now know it was the first sign that I was destined for great things.

It was a cold, dark day like this one and, forbidden

to play outside, I was sent to the library to study. Tired of my usual books, I climbed the library ladder and ran my fingers along the dusty spines of those great tomes on the top shelves, the ones of such age that they were almost never moved, let alone read. My girlish fingers traced along their faded patterns and titles, looking for something to relieve the boredom of the dull afternoon, until they landed on a leathery cover bearing my family's coat of arms. A history, I thought. I determined to read it. It might answer some questions that my governess would not. But something happened as I touched it: a dizzying sensation, one that almost caused me to lose my balance and fall from the ladder. I clutched at the shelf to steady myself and carefully edged the book further out. Something told me, even as a rather reckless child, that there was something of great import here. Breathing deeply to stop my head spinning, I edged my way down the ladder, the book weighing almost as much as I did myself.

I dragged it into an alcove and tucked myself up with it. The pages were thick but mottled and dog-eared, and I had to flick away the tiny silverfish that scurried across the writing. To my young eyes, the language was hard to follow, and I turned the page with a loud crackle onto one with a picture. I stared at this for a long while. It was a map, I believe of Hexendale, and around the edge of this map was the most beautiful illustration of a snake, its scales in all rainbow colours that seemed to glow with their own light in the darkening corner of the room. As I stroked it, following the length of its magnificent body around and around, I felt myself being pulled. It was as if I was being swallowed by the book, and yet I was not afraid. I gasped for breath, at the sensation of being sucked in down a long, black passageway.

The next moment, I found myself staring around a room I'd never been in before. The figure of a small man was hunched over a desk, writing by the light of a flickering candle. I crept up to him from behind, eager to see over his shoulder. Suddenly I heard a terrible scream and I found myself back in the library, being roughly shaken by my wretched governess. The woman claimed to have found me in a faint.

It was then I did something I have always regretted. In my excitement, I tried to tell her what happened. I could see, as I gabbled at her, that a frost was forming over her face, and yet I kept going until she marched me along to see my father, who was furious. He would not listen to my tale and warned me that if I did not cease my prattle, he would give me a whipping. I ran to my room and stayed there for the rest of the night, with nothing to eat, listening to murmurings about the "family madness" outside my door.

The next day, the library was locked – and the day after that, and the day after that. When I finally managed to persuade a new maid to let me inside, I found nothing but a gap on the high shelf where the magical book had been. My governess told me my father had destroyed it, by throwing it on the fire. She warned me to forget about it, unless I wanted to bring more shame on my family. "Lord knows, your family can do without it," she said, although as usual, she would say no more.

Never again did I manage to find that doorway into the past, nor did I forgive my father for closing it off to me, even though I understand why he did it. I now know that the open mind of the right child is needed to make a new opening. And I am ever more certain that Annie is the one who possesses it.

Lucy and Mrs McKinnon took me back to our cottage and there they built up a fire and nagged me to eat all sorts of broth and bread and cake until I thought my belly would burst. When Tom came back from the gardens they scolded him and told him he had to take better care of me. When they'd gone, he put a strong arm around my shoulders. "I'm so ashamed. I can't bear it that I might have made you more ill," he told me.

I elbowed him gently. "Of course you haven't. It's just..."

I thought about telling him that parts of the house and grounds made me so afraid I felt sick. But I just could not bring myself to do it. And I couldn't explain what happened on the stairs. So I said, "Lucy says I'm probably still tired from the journey here. That's all."

My fainting fit, if that's what it was, had caused such a fair old panic in the household that they made me spend the next day resting. Rest was a new idea to me, though. We spent many months looking after Mam when she was ill. Then, when I moved into Aunt Catherine's house, she made certain I earned my keep. So after sleeping for longer than usual in the morning, I felt unable to sit still. I found my comfy old trousers and woollens, wrapped a woolly scarf round my head and went out to find where Tom was working in the garden. The grounds were too big for me to take in. They were like a dozen different gardens, but all part of the same one. There was a woodland, with tall, bare trees that looked as if a thousand witches had left their broomsticks there. Beyond this was a grander part, where great hedges had been cut into tall, twisted shapes, all wearing hoods of snow. In the centre of this was a fountain, completely still and frozen. I couldn't help running my fingers down this once-water, but they almost stuck to it and I had to blow on them to stop the ice-burn. I felt like the Snow Queen wandering through her castle grounds. There was also a huge building made entirely of panes of glass, like a grand palace on its own, but with only plants living in it. I felt as if I had walked for miles before I found Tom, in a wide, bare patch of ground. He was walking around with a ball of string and wooden pegs, marking something out. He looked pleased to see me.

"This is Her Ladyship's new garden," he told me. "I'm in charge of it. It needs to be planned out in a special way and then we'll try to grow plants for medicine. It'll be the only one of its kind. Imagine that!"

He told me how it would be marked out with hedges of green box and something with a silver leaf called cotton lavender. Then he listed all sorts of flowers and herbs, some of which I'd heard of before and some of which sounded to me like a foreign language. As he described the plants and how they could be used to heal all sorts of illnesses, he waved his hands and his eyes lit up. I thought how happy he seemed, happier than he'd ever been, since before Mam got ill. This made me feel good too. Tom's chatter seemed to warm up the frozen air and fire up the pale, weak sun.

"If I'd had some of these medicines when Mam was ill," he said, "who knows how I could have helped her?"

I linked his arm. How firm and manly it suddenly was!

"You tried," I reminded him. "You really did your best. You fed her as well as you could, until she wasn't able to eat."

Tom frowned around at the hard earth, where scraps of unmelted snow lay like torn-up pages from a storybook. "But I know so much more now. Lady Hexer gave me a book all about healing plants. I looked at it last night while you slept, until the candle gave out. I couldn't read all the words but I knew some of the pictures. Some of the plants we had around us could have helped her. Borage and mallow and violets. They work for coughs and bad chests. We had them growing so near us and I never knew to try them out. I wish I could go back and have that time over again."

I put my arms around his waist and squeezed. "There's no point in thinking like that, Tom."

"No," he agreed. "But I still have a chance to make you better. You'll see what magic I'll grow here. I think plants have the answer to everything, if we know what to do with them." I laughed at him. But of course I believed him.

I had to report to Lady Hexer first thing the following morning. Tom walked me through the breezy blue-blackness of the early morning grounds and Lucy met me at the huge kitchen door. I thought I heard the creepy whispering sound again as I walked, and it gave me a chill inside, but I didn't want to tell Tom about it. If I told him I could hear my own name, and yet not quite my name, coming from nowhere, what would he think of me? I hoped it would soon just go away, perhaps when I got used to the Hexer estate.

There were some places where the whispering was stronger than others, where the dry, eerie sound made my skin pinch and prickle with fear. But I made myself keep walking. This was something I could force myself to do, like when I walked behind Mam's coffin even though my legs didn't want to. If I kept going, I told myself now, there were other places where the horrible sounds and feelings simply seemed to stop, like inside our cottage and in the warm kitchen of Hexer Hall, which I'd already grown to love.

As I went through the door, the breeze made the hanging pans chime like bells and I noticed Becky glancing up at me without a smile. Lucy rushed over to give me a soft hug. Mrs McKinnon produced a spotless white cap and fussed around me, trying to fix it into place on my head and clicking her tongue when she couldn't find enough hair to grip the pins. I noticed there was a bad feeling in the air, hovering around like the lingering smells from breakfast. At first I thought it was because I was there, needling Becky with my presence. But then Lucy blurted out: "Why did she have to come today? Fancy making wee Annie go up there with that old witch! I hate to think about it!"

I stared at her. "Do you mean Lady Hexer?"

She shook her head and sighed. Mrs McKinnon looked at me. "Lady Hexer has a regular visitor and, well, none of us have really taken to her. Not that it's our place to comment on Her Ladyship's company. But she is a peculiar one, this Miss Haggstone."

"Peculiar?" Lucy snorted. "She gives me the creeps. I don't like even being in the same room as her. I don't know what they get up to with those cards and all that jiggery-pokery, but it makes me shiver."

Becky chipped in. "The last time I went in there the room was all dark. The curtains were drawn, in the middle of the day. They had some sort of a black bowl on the table and they were staring into it." She looked straight at me and I could tell she was enjoying herself. "Witchcraft, I thought it was. Perhaps they need you to practise their spells on."

Lucy shifted from foot to foot. "Stop it, Becky. Don't make things worse." She took my hand and squeezed it.

44

Her brown hand was warm and softer than you'd expect. It didn't feel like a hand that had already carried buckets of coal around the huge house, cleaned out grates and made fires, all before eight o'clock this morning.

Mrs McKinnon clicked her tongue. "Of course she isn't a witch, there's no such thing. She just looks a bit odd and–"

"Smells a bit odd," added Becky.

Mrs McKinnon glared at her. "You think everything smells odd," she said, in a voice that cut like scissors. "Your nose is wasted here. You should be making perfumes in Paris or some such thing."

She turned back to me. "She looks unusual, this Miss Haggstone. A bit frightening, perhaps, if you're a silly goose like these two here. When Miss Haggstone arrives, Lady Hexer seems to be ... well, things are different. Let's hope she isn't staying too long this time."

It was time for me to climb up the back stairs towards Lady Hexer's rooms. Lucy walked up with me, but had to leave me at the door to see to all her other work. Birds to pluck and herbs to chop and spices to grind, she told me. When I stepped inside, just as Becky had said, the heavy curtains were drawn, leaving the room very gloomy with just small slices of daylight slipping in at the edges of the tall windows. Two figures sat at the long, polished table. One was Lady Hexer, of course, who told me to come in. The other was at the head of the table, with a large book in front of her. Lady Hexer beckoned me forward and I realised Becky had spoken the truth when she said Miss

45

Haggstone smelled funny. As I came closer to her, I caught the mixed scents of sweat and gin, not very well hidden under some heavy, spiced perfume. Like the others, I found myself afraid of her, for a reason I couldn't work out.

She moved her wide head slowly to look at me. As I got used to the half-darkness, I took in a plump, middle-aged woman with grey hair piled on top of her head. Her eyes were lined, not just with deep wrinkles but also with some sort of inky black paint. She seemed to have painted over her eyebrows in the same ink, giving her a fierce expression. She was covered in swathes of shawls and scarves, although without the daylight I couldn't make out their colours. She gave me a slow smile, not a welcoming one, and her fleshy lips seemed to strain to do it.

"This is the child?" she asked, her voice deep as a man's and oddly accented, as if she had come from another world altogether. "This is your Iannua?" It sounded like Yannua. I wondered whether I should tell her my name was Annie, but I was too nervous. I remembered how I thought I'd heard the name 'Anya' being whispered. This sounded almost the same. What was a Iannua?

Lady Hexer, who looked to me like the very picture of grace and beauty next to this ugly old crone, gave a brief nod. "Annie, my dear," she said, silkily. "Come and say good morning to Miss Haggstone, my very good friend and confidante." (It sounded like this: *con-fee-dawnt*.) "She has been looking forward to meeting you."

Why? I wanted to blurt out again, but my throat was

46

stopped up with nerves and, anyway, I guessed this was not the way to speak to a lady in front of guests. So I stayed silent, hearing my own heart beat like a door banging in the wind.

Lady Hexer turned to her guest. "Annie is, of course, still unused to the house and to myself. But I see signs of great intelligence, given her low background. I have told you of the ... *incident* on the staircase. I feel sure that already the girl is responding to the atmospherics of the house and that she will be able to use the symbols."

I stared at Lady Hexer. What was she talking about? What could I have to do with all of this? What were *atmospherics*? What were *symbols*? Why did this woman call me Iannua?

Miss Haggstone narrowed her eyes at me, still with that false smile on her lips. "Let's see, shall we?" she said, in her low voice. "Let's have a little experiment."

I thought a tiny frown crossed Lady Hexer's face, but she turned to me.

"Annie," she said, and her voice sounded as if it was stroking me. "I know your brother is a very talented young gardener. I think you also are a child with great potential. Do you know what that means? It means I think you could become something very special. I believe that, with training, you could become my own personal assistant."

The Haggstone woman made a noise that I thought was a grunting laugh, but she was only clearing her throat.

"What I want you to do, my dear is ... is ..." Her Ladyship glanced around, "is to show me where you can see a serpent, somewhere in this room."

I looked at her for a moment, wondering if I'd understood her right. It seemed a silly thing to ask. Everywhere you looked in Hexer Hall, there was some picture or carving of a snake. But Her Ladyship gave me a nod, in the direction of the huge stone fireplace. It was built so that it looked almost like another room, a kind of cave, where a fire burned in a metal basket. As I got nearer, still blinking in the dimness, I could see carvings of coiled-up snakes in the thick tiles all round the hearth. I went closer, shivering in spite of the heat from the fire, and then in my head I began to hear the whispering sounds again, getting louder and louder. I could hear that word 'Iannua' again. I shook my head to try and rid myself of the noise. I reached out, unable to stop my arm trembling, and pointed to one of the snake pictures on the tiles.

"That's right," said Lady Hexer and I knew, somehow, that I was supposed to step closer. I put my finger in the groove of the carving and, without quite knowing why, traced it around the serpent's coils. It felt, somehow, as if I was turning a key. And that is when it happened again.

Chapter Four

There was a moment or more of total blackness. My head spun, like when Tom used to lift me and swing me round and round in the air, when I was very small. I opened my eyes and recognised the same freezing stone corridor from the other day. My fingers were no longer touching the thickly painted tiles, but raw, sandy stone. It was still gloomy, but ahead of me was the set of steps leading to the archway. I started towards its light. Then I heard soft steps heading my way and I ducked into the side of the arch. A man's figure came towards me and I squinted at it, trying to work out what was wrong with his shape. The figure wasn't very tall, for a man, and he had something bulky around his neck, like a thickly-wound scarf or a bunched-up cloak. It wasn't light enough to tell. Scurrying a few paces behind him, carrying a plate and a jug, was the girl

I met last time. She spotted me and her eyes widened. She nodded at me and the pair disappeared through the arch as if they'd been swallowed up. I glanced around it at their back views and could swear that the thing around the man's neck moved, on its own. It made me jump, but then I thought it must have been a trick of the light.

I waited for a few minutes, pressed against the rough stone wall, trying to work out what had happened. Had I fallen into some kind of cellar under the Hall? But how could that happen twice, in two different parts of the house? It hurt my head trying to work it out. After a short while, the girl put her head back around the arch, as I hoped she might. Again, she gabbled at me. Her words were like mine and yet different and very hard to follow. I shook my head at her. She looked cross for a moment and then beckoned me to follow her. We scuttled along the narrow corridor and I kept close on her tail as she turned down two more passageways, each as dark as the first. Every minute or so I heard voices and, once or twice, the sound of someone crying. It didn't seem to bother the child at all. She was a tiny, skinny thing but she moved fast as a rat. I wondered how I would ever find my own way back.

The girl pulled back a heavy cloth over an opening and I followed her into a tiny cell-like room, where a thick candle burned in a heavy jar. I stared around. There was a mat on the floor, which had the look of somewhere to sleep. A shelf cut in the stone wall held a few things – a pot, another candle, a bundle of cloth. She started speaking again, this time more slowly, and my ears caught the odd word. I had to try really hard to make it out. After a few moments, her language started forming in my ears, like when someone plays you a tune a few times until you know how it goes.

"Who are you?" she demanded. "Where have you been hiding? What is that on your head? Where is your hood?"

I couldn't help grinning at her pale, fierce face.

"Which question do you want me to answer first?" I asked.

She stared at me, trying to work out what I'd said. Then she started to laugh too.

"This is going to sound silly," I told her. "But I've no idea how I got here. What is this place?"

"Hospital, you fool," she said, shaking her head at my stupidity. I caught the words "lazar-house". She glanced up at my head. "You are sick."

"Oh, no," I said. "I'm not ill."

I fingered the white maid's cap and decided I would trust this girl. "It's just that some of my hair came out. I'm not actually ill, not so that I need to be in a hospital."

The girl sighed and her eyes were all pity, the way people used to look at me when I told them Mam would get better. She just shook her head again.

"What's a lazar-house?" I asked.

"This is," the child said, unhelpfully. She told me, slowly, as if I was a fool, that I was in St Bartholomew's leper hospital. When I asked if I was in Hexendale, she frowned and shook her head.

"I don't even know how I got here," I said. "One minute

I was in Hexer Hall and the next minute I was here. That's what happened the other day, too."

It was clear she didn't understand. But then she gave me a big grin and said, "Bet you're hungry. I have food." She rubbed her skinny tummy and pointed to her mouth.

I shook my head and tried to tell her I'd done nothing but eat for the last two days. And that I didn't need to stay here, I just needed to get back to my brother and Hexer Hall. I didn't say what I was thinking, which is that I wouldn't dream of taking food from someone who looked as if she needed it so much herself. She reminded me of the sad, starved chicken who used to peck around for scraps in our yard back home. I'm small and skinny too, but I felt big and clumsy next to this waif of a child.

She shrugged again. I could tell she hadn't grasped most of my words.

"Hexer Hall?" she repeated. She looked around and opened her arms. "Not here." Then she pointed at me. "What's your name?" Then pointed to herself. "I'm Meg."

I smiled at her. "Annie."

She smiled back. I held out my hand but she gave me an odd look and shrank back. Just then, somewhere in the distance, I heard a voice call, "Annie!" and I jumped.

"Who was that?" I put my hand to my ear.

Meg listened for a moment and shook her head. She started miming with her hands, pulling at her skirts and acting as if she was going to sleep.

"I don't need a bed, I'm not staying," I tried to explain, again, although Meg kept motioning for me to shut up.

"Really, you must stay. But listen." She glanced at her makeshift doorway and lowered her voice. I strained to make out her words, which sometimes sounded like she was talking through deep water. "We don't just take care of the lepers here. We want to rid them of the illness! I'm helping the doctor here. Perhaps he will cure you! Stay," she said again, waving her arm at the ground, then placing her hands, palms together, on the side of her head to show she wanted me to sleep here. She gave me her widest smile yet, showing a gappy set of teeth.

"Was it the doctor who was walking with you in the corridor?" I asked, pointing and miming.

Meg nodded. "His name is Huksor," she said.

"What was he wearing around his neck?" I asked her. "I couldn't tell in the dark. It looked like some great thick roll of cloth or something."

Meg gave a shiver. "Melusina."

I repeated the name. "What is Melusina?"

"The master's serpent," Meg told me. "He carries her around his neck."

I gulped. "He carries a snake with him?" I repeated, patting my shoulders to show Meg what I meant. "But won't it bite?" I made my fingers into fangs.

Meg shook her head. She pulled a face, to show me she did not care for the beast either. She chattered at me and, from the words I picked up, I gathered the thing was very handy for catching mice and rats. Give me a cat any day, I thought, shuddering.

Meg's words floated at me and sometimes I caught

them, sometimes not. She told me that Doctor Huksor was kind to her and that she stayed at the hospital because her father was ill. Or he may have been already dead, I couldn't quite work out which. She did jobs for this Huksor, she said.

I was about to ask more questions but then I heard a voice again, calling my name, more urgently this time.

"Someone's calling for me," I said. It came again, louder: "Iannua! Annie! Come back!" I poked my head out of the cloth covering the entrance to Meg's cubby-hole and suddenly seemed to fall, the blackness coming over me like a dark hood. I heard voices saying my name over and over and puffs of air being blown at my face.

Colours were swimming about in front of my eyes. I could see greens, blues, pinks. They began, very slowly, to form shapes. For a moment I thought it was Melusina coming towards me and tried to bat it away with my hand. Then I realised it wasn't the serpent – it was leaves, deep-green leaves against a pink and blue sky. The sky was shining as if it had been varnished. There was a figure like a beautiful goddess looking down at me. My fingers rubbed against carpet; I was lying on the floor of Lady Hexer's drawing room. She was kneeling beside me, fanning me and looking pale and frightened. I screwed up my eyes and started to sit up, noticing an aspidistra plant right next to me, in a pot painted with scenes from old stories. The words underneath read: Goddess of Spring.

Lady Hexer gave out a long breath. "Child!" she said,

softly. "I had begun to think you would never come back to us."

Behind her I was aware of the dark figure of Miss Haggstone and as my eyes made her out more clearly, I saw she was looking at me with surprise, mingled, I thought, with something else. She wasn't pleased with me, this much I knew. Lady Hexer led me by the hand to a one-sided sofa covered in a deep red, stiff material. She made me sit and handed me a glass of water. I sipped it carefully, the glass feeling heavy in my fingers, which were trembling and slippery with sweat.

"Where did I go?" I asked her. She looked at me carefully, as if she was unsure how to answer.

"Go?" she asked.

"You said you didn't think I would come back," I said.

She thought again, for a moment. "Why, I rather meant that you were not conscious. But perhaps ... well, now, perhaps it did not seem that way to you. Can you tell me what you think happened?"

I wondered how to explain this without sounding as if I belonged in the madhouse. "It felt like I fell," I began. "But I ended up somewhere else. Not in this room. I think perhaps it was somewhere under the ground. Is there a hospital near here?"

Her Ladyship stared at me, right into my face. Her eyes seemed full of an eager glow. "A hospital, my dear? What kind of hospital?"

I frowned. "I don't know, I didn't understand. What's a– a lazar-house?"

Lady Hexer looked as if a bolt of lightning had gone right through her elegant body. She grabbed both my hands. "Is that where you went? To a lazar-house?" She shook my hands hard in her need to hear my reply.

"That's where the girl said I was. But I don't know what it is."

"Haven't you read your scriptures, girl?" came the low voice of Miss Haggstone. "Don't you remember a story about someone called Lazarus?"

I thought for a moment. "Did he come back from the dead? In a Bible story?"

"That is correct," answered Miss Haggstone, shifting her bulk around in her chair and frowning at me.

"You mean, the people in the hospital came back from the dead?" I asked, feeling properly fuddled.

"They didn't come back from the dead, my dear," said Lady Hexer. Her voice had a tremble to it, like a musical note. "But they were as good as dead, or that is how people thought of them. Lepers. Do you understand what I mean?"

"Lepers? That terrible illness, that means you have to stay away from everyone else? I've heard of it, but–"

Lady Hexer nodded. "It seems you dreamed of a leper hospital. Am I right?"

"No one told me there was a leper hospital around here," I said.

"There isn't," said Lady Hexer. "But there used to be. Hundreds of years ago. It used to be right here, where the Hall is now. St. Bartholomew's leper hospital, it was called."

"That's the name the girl gave me. It's still here," I insisted.

Lady Hexer shook her head. "This is very hard for you to understand. What you have just done is something quite extraordinary. In your head you have seen the past. You have glimpsed what was here, once, but isn't any more."

I almost laughed at her. "That's not possible," I said. Then I remembered who I was talking to and added: "Madam."

Her Ladyship gave me a smile. "Not impossible. It just takes a special kind of person. You. I thought you may be the one."

I shook my head. "No, it *is* still here, the place where I went. It was solid stone. I touched the wall. I talked to a girl who stays there. I saw the, erm, the doctor and I thought he was scary. They were real."

At the mention of the doctor, Her Ladyship sat forward and again squeezed my fingers hard. "You saw a doctor? Tell me – tell me all about him."

I told her I'd only caught a glimpse of him, walking through a doorway wearing a huge kind of a snake around his neck. I told her his name: Huksor. At this point, Lady Hexer let go of me and sat back, heavily, onto a chair. She picked up the fan and started flapping it in front of her face, which was white as swans' feathers. She muttered, as if to herself: "It's true. It's true. It is happening, just as it was foretold. She has used the symbols and turned the key. It is all becoming…"

Miss Haggstone shambled out of her chair and waddled

towards me like a great over-fed turkey. Her wraps and shawls rustled and swished. She leaned down and stared into my face with her bulgy, reddened eyes.

"You had better not be telling stories, girl," she hissed. Her breath was sour and I held mine so as not to breathe it in. "I'm not sure if I believe this tale of stones and snakes. If this is an invention then you will be sorry, girl, and so will your brother."

I was too afraid to hold her gaze and stared at my shivering hands in my lap. "It's not a story," I mumbled. "It's what I saw. That's all."

"Leave her, Agatha, don't frighten her," came Lady Hexer's voice. "There is no other way she could have described these things. I need the child now. We will work together."

She came over to me and actually knelt down beside the sofa. It made me blush and squirm, to see her down in this position, with me sitting like a queen on the chair.

"My dear. What has happened to you today is of immense importance. You have seen into the very history of this house. You are, as I said, an exceptional child. You will not be wasted on cleaning and household duties – your role will be to help me in my research. Together, we will discover great, important things that will help the whole world – what do you think of that?"

I stared at her face, which was white and bright as a winter star. Miss Haggstone made her small snorting noise in the background. Suddenly, and for no reason that I can explain, I started to cry. The full feeling in my throat and the heat on my face seemed to make me melt. The crying turned into hard, deep sobs. I had no idea what had happened to me. I didn't understand what I was expected to do.

Hexer Hall
31st December, 1898 (New Year's Eve)

I can hear preparations for tonight's revelry downstairs and I do not mind it, though Mrs McKinnon knows that on this day I prefer to be alone. It was on such a New Year's Eve as this that I tried to nurse my beautiful daughter through her fever, waiting for a doctor who was so busy celebrating that he failed to turn up in time to help. I mopped her burning face and stroked her tiny fingers and I begged her to get better. But as the clock struck midnight, her panting breath slowed to a stop. They say they heard my screams as far away as Hexendale.

How? How can we be in this age of science and invention and medicine and yet we cannot free such a beloved girl from the clutches of disease? There were some, no doubt, who thought my family cursed. In a sense, they were. We are all cursed by fear and superstition that stops our progress. But I will not accept that. I will not say that is how it must be. I will turn it around.

For here we are, on the final day of the year, leading to the last year of the century. I think I am allowed to feel a sense of history taking place! The predictions about the child Annie have proved so accurate it is quite unnerving. She is my Iannua. She has travelled back in time to my ancestor's hospital and has even conversed with some servant girl, some child who has in fact been dead for centuries. Quite, quite astonishing. It is more thrilling than I can possibly convey in words. I believe things will now move quite fast. The only problem is the poor child is quite overwhelmed by the experience. I have had to tell her she is having some special kind of dream. I was most reluctant to send her back to the hut in the grounds, where she stays with her brother, but it would have seemed odd to do otherwise. I thought the housemaid was going to collapse with shock when I insisted on sending a large food hamper and warm bedding to the cottage. I have given Annie the strictest instructions to tell no one, not even the brother, what she has seen and done. I didn't have to make any threats, in spite of Agatha's advice. The girl is aware of how much her brother needs his position and that they are being treated in a way which is far above their station.

I will now oversee Annie's journeys and she will bring me back, at long, long last, the great work I believe my ancestor was working on: his book of cures. My family's secret knowledge will not be lost in time. I will dispel the disgrace that has shadowed us over the centuries. Huksor's genius will live again.

Chapter Five

Tom woke me on the morning of the last day of the year by bouncing around like a big overgrown baby and clattering the pots. He said he was making breakfast. I said it sounded more like he was trying to wake the dead. Then I realised what I'd said and shuddered.

"New Year's Eve," he told me. "The end of a terrible year and the start of a new one. Here we are with more food than our stomachs can take and a warm fire and a home of our own. We've hit luck at last and we deserve it."

I couldn't help smiling at him. He set two eggs to boil in the pot over the fire and broke chunks off a loaf of bread. He patted one of the chairs and I went to sit on it. Lady Hexer and the horrible Haggstone woman had told me not to tell Tom what happened yesterday. It was hard, because I tell Tom everything. I almost blurted it out last night when he'd asked me what I'd done all day. But then again, I wasn't sure if he would understand. He might start to worry that my brains had started falling out along with my hair. There'd been more dark strands lining my white cap when I took it off last night.

"How are you feeling today?" he asked me, in a softer voice. "Lucy was so worried when she heard you'd fainted again. But Lady Hexer says you're to do no more cleaning and hard work! She's going to take you on as a pupil and teach you things. I can hardly believe it. Think how proud Mam would be. Oh!"

His face turned into one huge, glowing grin. "Why don't you write to Aunt Catherine and tell her? That'd show her how wrong she was! It'll knock the silly smiles off James and Hannah's faces too, eh?"

I said I would. I started planning a letter telling Aunt Catherine that I was to be taken on as Her Ladyship's special pupil. But it felt like I wasn't quite telling the truth. It is a peculiar thing that missing out something important can feel just as bad as telling an outright lie. In my mind, it was just as if I was lying to Tom too. I hated that.

Again, I was supposed to spend the day resting, but I followed Tom around the silvery, frozen garden, pestering him as he marked out plots for planting in the spring. There were other gardeners there, some much older men. Somehow Tom had become their boss and they had to do what he told them. I thought they gave him some funny old glances. After all, he was young for such a task. But they were civil enough when they talked to him.

At dusk, Lucy caught up with us. We saw her scurrying along the whitened paths wrapped in a cloak and carrying a lantern, her breath like tiny ghosts on the winter air.

"Hogmanay, Annie! Hogmanay, Tom! Come along to the kitchen after we've served Lady Hexer's supper and we'll all have a feast to celebrate!"

So we did. The kitchen was golden and warm and scented as a bowl of chicken stew. It was crowded, as all the servants had got together for the party. I tried to take no notice of the way people stared at my head whenever they talked to me.

Lucy spotted it and squeezed my arm. "People look at me in a funny way too," she said. "It happens to anyone who looks a bit different. You get so used to it, you end up taking no notice at all."

Lady Hexer, as Tom said, was generous to her workers. The long pale table in the centre of the kitchen was laden with so much food you might have thought it would collapse. There was a strong-tasting soup which made my eyes water. Lucy said it had a bit too much garlic in it. There was hodge-podge, so hot it burned my mouth, and chunks of veal and ham pie in pastry thicker than the soles of my boots, and cold chicken patties with glistening bowls of pickles and chutneys. There was an orange batter pudding which tasted like something out of a dream: a dream of Christmas Eve and summer too. I spotted Tom using his finger to clean the bottom of his bowl, until he saw me and remembered his manners. I was too full even to taste the sponges and seed cakes. Best of all, though, there was a fruity cake in pastry that Lucy said was called 'black bun', something she used to eat at home. She'd made it herself for the first time, she said. I said I thought black bun was a poor name for such a wonderful thing. Just one mouthful tasted like all the riches of the East.

We waited until the big hall clock chimed midnight and everyone cheered. They sent a muscly, black-haired farrier out to knock on the kitchen door and come back in bearing coal, salt and whisky. I'd never heard of this before. First-footing, Lucy told me: the first man through the door will bring good luck for the year, as long as he's the right kind of person. I laughed at that, it seemed such a daft idea. Someone played a fiddle and someone else beat time with the spoons and, even though we were all a bit squashed, we managed to dance. As I sat down and got my breath back, I thought back to the chilly quiet of Aunt Catherine's house. She didn't believe in celebrating New Year's Eve. She said it was for pagans. James and Hannah would be in their beds now as if it was any other night. And here were Tom and I feasting like royalty. Tom looked as if he would burst with happiness as he danced Lucy round and round the table. She somehow kept her eyes fixed on his, in spite of all the bobbing about. So, I thought, whatever happens, I have to keep this happiness for Tom. Even if it means I have to do things that seem wrong.

Tom and I had both been granted a day's holiday for the New Year, which was just as well. We woke up late and bleary-eyed after all the celebrations. It was a grey, chilly morning and Tom banked up the fire. I jumped about to keep warm while I waited for the flames to lick their way through the sputtering coals, which Lady Hexer had sent us in a big bucket. Then I cooked some sausages. I couldn't believe how my stomach was rumbling with hunger after all I'd had to eat the night before. Tom rubbed his head and groaned.

"That's the last time I drink punch," he said. "My head feels like it's full of mud."

Lucy had warned me not to drink the punch so I just laughed at him. "What shall we do today?"

Tom grinned. "Lucy and I have planned a picnic. We thought we'd all walk to the sea."

I stared out of the tiny window. "In this weather? It's freezing."

But soon afterwards, Lucy arrived, with a basket and a woollen hat and heavy cape for me, and we started off through the woodlands and out of the estate. We followed a steep and sandy pathway towards the shore, long grasses whipping at our limbs. Then we saw it. I'd never been this close to the sea before and it took my breath away – and I mean really! I found myself panting and my eyes smarting in the strong breeze. The sea here was grey as washing water and it roared and leaped at me like an angry old wolf. But I thought it was the best smell in the world. I stood for a few minutes, just staring. It went on for ever and ever. The thundering waves made me gasp and just when I thought I'd seen the biggest crash possible, there it came again.

"This'll wake me up all right," Tom laughed. We found a spot in a sand dune that had some shelter from the winds, blinking the grit from our eyes, and settled down to enjoy the view. I had no idea the world was so big. Lucy snuggled up close to Tom, wiping wiry black curls like fronds of seaweed out of her eyes. Lucy has the kind of hair that makes you want to twirl your fingers around in it.

"So," she said, squeezing my hand. "Lord, those fingers are cold! How do you like your new home? We can't believe how Lady Hexer's taken to you."

I shrugged. "She's strange," I said. "I don't know what I mean, really, but she is. She makes me do—" I stopped.

They both stared at me for a moment. Then Tom took my other hand. "You know what's strange? People being good to us. You're used to that old misery, Aunt Catherine, and being in the wrong all the time. So now when someone says you're clever and wants to help you, you don't understand it."

Lucy nodded. I guessed Tom was probably right about that.

I had to report to Lady Hexer again the very next morning. The Haggstone woman was still there, glowering at me like some evil old pet cat. Lady Hexer was all gentle words and smiles.

"My dear," she said, beckoning me to sit with her up at the polished table. "I have used the change of year to think long and hard about your future. I feel that I am," she spoke slowly, as if she was choosing every word with care, "extremely fortunate, I mean lucky, in finding two young people with such talent. Your brother Tom is to transform my gardens into something which has never been seen before. You, my dear – you are to work with me. We will learn and experiment together. We will uncover secrets and knowledge that no one has dared to dream – not for centuries. When you are not carrying out my special duties, I will have a tutor come to give you lessons.

"I know what it's like to be a clever girl. No one takes any notice of you. But I am taking notice of you. I will make sure you reach the height of your talents. We are of different ranks, you and I, but I feel we have something in common. You and Tom will want for nothing." She looked at me hard, waiting for me to answer in some way.

I swallowed. Her words felt as if they were coming from behind some veil, where their real meaning was hiding.

"Do you mean," I asked, slowly, "that you want me to go back to that hospital again? I mean, to dream about it. Or whatever it was I did."

Haggstone made a clicking sound with her fat tongue. "You are too direct, child!" she snapped.

But Lady Hexer waved her hand. I didn't know what to say so I gave a small shrug, staring at my blurred reflection in the glossy surface of the table.

"I will answer you honestly," Lady Hexer went on. "Yes, I want you to make your clever mind go back to that hospital. Do you understand what I mean? This house was built on the site of the old leper hospital. Although it was destroyed long ago, I think something of it is still here in some way, if we could only find it. When I was a child, I could sense its presence. But I didn't understand what I was seeing in my mind, not until I was much older and found out the history of my family. Even when I married, I refused to leave this house. When my dear Arthur passed away, I redesigned it as I always wished and reclaimed my family name. Now, I believe we have the right conditions and you are the right person to find out more about the past. I think you can actually see it!"

I could hear the excitement in her voice but I couldn't look at her face. I didn't want her to read my terror.

"Well? I know you have questions. Ask!"

I thought. There were so many, it was hard to know where to start. "Why do you want me to do this?" I began.

Lady Hexer thought for a long moment then took a deep breath. She spoke to me with her eyes closed, the lids and lashes trembling slightly, like butterflies on a flower.

"The hospital was run by an ancestor of mine, Edmond Huksor. I believe him to have been a wonderfully clever man – a genius. He wrote a book – of ... cures. Cures. This book was lost somewhere after the hospital was closed. What I want you to do is find out about his work and then fetch this knowledge back to me. I am trusting you with something I have longed for all my life – to bring this wonderful knowledge from the past, so that we can put it to use today. It is an honour, is it not?"

I nodded, carefully. It did sound like an important task – a noble one. But it still felt as if that unseen curtain was blocking out some piece of truth behind her words. I thought again.

"If I can do it – if I can find out what's in this old book – what will you do with it?"

"Why, I will use it to cure the terrible illnesses of the world! Leprosy, a terrible affliction that we think cannot be helped. Across the Empire, it is killing people and it is the most hideous way to die. But I believe that Doctor Huksor had begun to find a cure even for this, thanks to his experiments. If he could cure that dreaded condition, then surely he could cure almost anything! Typhoid! Smallpox! Cholera! Tuberculosis!"

I flinched at that last word. *Me Mam.* I tried to keep my mind on what Her Ladyship was saying.

"Imagine, if you and I were able to bring this healing power over the centuries and use it today. We would become legends! Don't you want that? We would surely be able to cure your own sad condition, too," she added, giving my patchy head a sorrowful look.

"I don't know," I said, truthfully. "Will Doctor Huksor let me see the book if I ask for it?"

"Let us think about that later," said Lady Hexer. "For now, I just want you to make visits, like you did the other day. I mean, in your head, of course. Find out everything you can. Will you do that? Your rewards will be great."

Haggstone coughed. "Lady Hexer," she muttered. "I am not sure–"

Her Ladyship held up her hand and Haggstone was silenced. "I chose Annie on the basis of your own predictions, Agatha. Now they are coming good, you seem to be unsure. But I think we should proceed. Immediately!"

"If I see all these things inside my head," I asked Lady Hexer, "just like a dream – then how do the people there see me?"

"What a clever question!" Lady Hexer breathed. "You are so intelligent. So quick!"

I waited.

"Why," smiled Lady Hexer. "Who can truly explain what happens in dreams?"

I didn't think this was much of an answer. I looked up at Her Ladyship and asked her one of the biggest questions that had been turning over and over inside me.

"If I keep going to this hospital," I said, trying to keep my nerve, "will I get ill too? Will I catch the disease?"

I thought her face showed a slight tremor, or it could have been a shadow, a change in the light. But she looked me in the eyes and said, with a smile: "Why, no! Of course not! How could you catch an illness from people who no longer fully exist? I know it is hard for you to understand, but you are making a journey of the mind, not a journey of the body."

I frowned. "But I feel like I am really there. The place feels real enough to touch, anyway. Why shouldn't the illness be real?"

Lady Hexer gave a small laugh. "No, I do not think you need concern yourself with that. I think you will be safe."

I glanced between Lady Hexer and Haggstone and thought I caught a look pass between them. It was like one of them had thrown a ball to the other one and I'd just missed seeing it go.

"Now then," continued Her Ladyship. "Shall we go on another, how shall we say, journey?"

I wanted to repeat the word "we" as a question, but didn't dare. I knew full well she meant just me.

She nodded at the fireplace with its sculpted tiles. Heavily, I got up and went towards the hearth, where the low fire crackled and gently spat. The designs were in light-ish colours, of mainly blues, greens and whites, so you had to look closely to see that the circles were actually coiled-up snakes. With my skin crawling, I held out my arm and placed my finger in the same coiled snake as before and traced its shape around and around.

It was bright day this time but still bitterly, bone-achingly cold. In this light, I could see that the walls were of a pale, newly-hewn stone. I could see no one, but I heard voices from further down the narrow passageway, and I followed them. I felt safer in the light and I hoped to find Meg. The thick walls were entirely plain. The first room I came to had a door of heavy wood, which was wide open. I peered around and saw a set of four beds, all with people lying on them. There was a terrible stench, reminding me of the room at the back of the church where Mam had lain before her funeral. A smell of death. The woman on the nearest bed turned slowly towards me and my hand flew to my mouth to stop myself from screaming. Her face was covered in livid sores and swellings. The skin was bulging and lurid, the lumps and crevices like a cauliflower painted red-purple and forced on top of her usual features. She faced my direction and her glazed eyes didn't seem to see me, yet she heard me. She raised an arm towards me, covered in lizard-skin, and I saw that her fingers were swollen and clumped together like fungus on the branch of a tree. For a moment I stared as if I couldn't move. I backed out of the door, cold but sweating. I'd never seen anything so horrible. I started to run, glancing back along the passageway as if the poor woman might somehow be chasing me. I flew round a corner and right into someone – a slight figure who I knocked to the ground as easily as a rag doll. It was Meg. I stopped and held out my hand to help her up, but she backed away from it and crossly dusted herself down.

"You ran away again," she scolded, when she was on her feet. She had to say it a few times before my ears got used to the melody of her words.

The memory of the woman on the bed returned and I felt my stomach lurch. I clapped my hand over my mouth, afraid I was about to be sick.

"Oh," said Meg. She looked sorry for shouting at me. She pulled her sleeve down to cover her fingers before placing her hand on my arm.

"I'm not dirty," I snapped as we walk.

"Unclean," Meg said, leading me towards a large door. Somehow, I heard that very clearly and it hurt.

We walked through the door and out into a small

cobbled courtyard patched with snow. Around it was a handful of small cottage-like buildings and what looked like a tiny chapel. I smelled frost mixed with animal dung and saw that the buildings backed onto a field where pigs and chickens were scattered about. We passed two or three people walking across the courtyard. One man sat on a bench, studying what looked like a prayer book, his long sleeves covering his entire hands. He had red marks on his face, but nothing like as bad as the woman on the bed. It struck me that all these people were dressed alike, in plain, russet-coloured tunics with hoods. Meg led me into one of the small buildings and into a kind of storeroom. A flat-faced woman sat at a table, sewing. She looked up at us.

"Meg," she nodded.

"Agnes, this is Annie. She's new. She needs clothes and a bed."

The woman raised her eyebrows at me. "Got your fee?"

Meg glanced sideways at me and said, "I gave it to the master. He knows Annie's family."

I said nothing, but felt myself blush at the lie. The woman gave another short nod, got up and dragged a heavy pile of the russet-coloured cloth from a low shelf. She pulled out a length of it and held it against me. I noticed she kept herself an arm's distance away.

Meg tried to explain that patients from the hospital had to wear this tunic and hood, so that the townspeople knew they were ill and could keep away from them.

I followed her into a second building. There were more rooms with beds in, but they were empty. Some of the patients could still get up and walk around during the day.

"They help with some of the work, because healthy people don't want to come here," Meg said. She pointed to a small wooden bed in the corner. "You can sleep here if you like."

Then she led me to a larger, square room full of people sitting at tables, eating some sort of mess from heavy bowls. Some of them looked up at me. I glanced around them, trying not to stare. There were men along one long table, women and some young children at another, all clad in their uniform and hoods. Some of them had trouble eating because their fingers were swollen and bunched up. Lots of food was being spilled. Some had swellings on their faces. My eyes fixed on a man whose skin was lined and folded so that he looked a bit like a lion, only not fierce, just sad. Others had clusters of smaller spots or patches of red, shiny skin. I turned away.

Meg looked at me crossly and snapped something like,"Get used to it." She pointed to the food but I shook my head.

"I couldn't eat here," I said, shuddering. "These people are so..."

"These people," Meg hissed, pointing at me, "are like you. Do you understand? Just like you. They're ill. That's what this sickness does to them. That's what it might do to you. It's a good job some of us will stay here and help them."

I shook my head again, furiously, screwing up my eyes. "No," I said. "I don't have this illness, Meg. These people are lepers, aren't they? I'm not. I've just lost some of my hair."

Meg glared at me. "If these patients weren't wearing their hoods, then you'd see that many of them have lost their hair too. It's part of the illness. That's what I keep telling you. You have to stay here, because you can't go round giving this sickness to everyone you meet. Do you understand?"

"I don't know how you can bear to look at them," I found myself saying, even though it made me feel bad to admit it.

"My father had this illness." Meg looked at the floor. "I stayed with him here till he died. He tried to pretend he wasn't ill, too, for a long time. Shall I tell you how I knew for certain he had the leprosy? I took him a meal while he was sitting dozing in his chair. I touched his hand to wake him up. He didn't feel it. That's what happens. You lose the feeling in your hands and feet. Then you cut them and burn them without realising what you're doing.

"I watched him while he turned from my father into someone I barely knew. In the end he looked like some creature from the depths of hell. But I stayed with him and put balm on his sores and fed him when his hands wouldn't work and when he couldn't tell if he was burning his mouth or not." Meg turned her eyes back to me. "Everyone should have someone who will do that for them."

I stared at her, my insides churning with shame. "I'm sorry," I mumbled.

Meg shrugged. "Not many people understand. You have to have lived with it. Watched someone die of it.

Everyone thought I would catch it from my father, but somehow I didn't. I think I was meant to stay here and take care of the other patients, because I don't mind it. Anyway, Doctor Huksor needs me."

I shook my head yet again, dumbly. I suddenly realised how well we'd understood each other, just for a few moments. But then I couldn't find the right words for a reply. She blinked a few times. I held out my hand but she didn't take it.

"You won't touch me," I said, pushing my hand towards her again.

It was Meg's turn to look shame-faced. "I shouldn't," she said. "In case you pass it on. I do all I can, but I try not to touch the patients on their skin. Not since my father. I couldn't help it with him. But I'm not taking a chance for anybody else."

I didn't argue. I took a deep breath and said, "Tell me some more about the doctor."

She brightened. "I'm Doctor Huksor's special helper. I'm the only one who knows all about his work. But I'm not allowed to tell. He's sailed to some far parts of the world with the trade ships and brought back things of which you would never dream, all to help his medicines. He's seen cities where the streets are made of water. He's been to places where the sun is so hot it's burned the skin of everyone who lives there, brown as a nut. I bet you can't believe that, but he swears it's true."

I thought about Lucy. "What were these places called?" I asked.

Meg couldn't remember. She chattered on like a whole flock of sparrows. "My father was a knight. He was a truly noble man, so fair and handsome. It was when he got the sickness that he had to come here. When he knew he would never go home again, he said that I mustn't mind, because some good would come of Doctor Huksor's work, one day."

She dropped her voice to a whisper.

"The patients here don't know it, but the doctor is testing the medicines on them. In time he will cure someone, I know it, and then we'll get rid of this sickness. I will have helped him do it!"

"What sort of medicines does he make?" I asked.

Meg shifted from one foot to another. "I shouldn't say. You'll be afraid. But you're not as clever as Doctor Huksor and neither am I, so we have to trust him." She looked at my hair. "I might ask him for something to make your hair grow," she said, importantly. "Would you like that?"

I thought for a moment. "All right. I mean, yes, please."

She looked delighted. "Promise you won't run away again, then," she said, getting up. "I'll see if I can find him now, if he's not busy."

Meg scuttled out of the room. I followed her at a distance, across the cobbled yard and into the first hospital building. I shadowed her along the narrow passageways until she disappeared through the dark archway. I started towards it but found myself stopped dead with fear, as if I were about to step off a cliff. I heard the whispering sound and, again, the moans from the sickrooms. I tried not to think about the woman on the bed and the way she lifted her arm towards me. I wanted to make myself step through the archway, but my feet didn't want to work again.

I looked up at the pale stone of the ceiling, took a deep breath and forced myself up the shallow steps. A new smell hit me, like damp, musky earth. Just around the corner, a small, lean man walked towards me, his hair black and cropped close to his head, his thin legs sticking out from his heavy cloak like gnarled sticks. But my eyes were drawn, right away, to the thing around his neck. A thick, brown-patterned snake-like creature. It was bigger than I've ever imagined real snakes to be, with a sturdy head and a flicking tongue. It curled around the man's shoulders like a hideous shawl, its coils constantly shifting. This thing, I realised after a moment or two, was more than just a snake. It had what looked like horns on its head and its scales glittered and changed colour as I watched. The man had one hand held up to his shoulder, to keep the thing steady. I was rooted to the stone step, like an animal caught by the beast's glinting eyes. It was looking right at me. A hot, sick feeling gushed through me and as I stared, the creature poked its head towards me and opened its mouth. Its forked tongue darted in and out like a lash. I caught a glimpse of small, white teeth. I opened my mouth to scream.

CHAPTER SIX

There was dizzying darkness, for a moment, and then I could see the fuzzy shape of the snake, fading from brown to a paler olive-green. I was trying to scream and scream, but nothing was coming out, just like in a bad dream. My eyes weren't working properly. Was the thing getting fatter? Was that reddish colour the inside of its terrible mouth? I groaned and strained to see properly. My arm hit out – and touched softness. I was lying on Lady Hexer's carpet. A velvety cushion, patterned with green leaves and deep-pink flowers, was under my head. When I tried to sit up this time, my brain whirled and I blacked out completely. I came round to a sharp scent being waved under my nose. Lady Hexer was clutching a tiny bottle of smelling salts.

"Are you all right?" she asked me, her voice sounding

as if it came from somewhere along a tunnel. I shook my head, breathing in gulps, my limbs all feeling like air.

She helped me onto the sofa. "Tell me everything! You were there for almost two hours! What did you see?"

As best I could, I told her all the details of my dream of the hospital, though my head still felt light and my thoughts were hard to collect. Lady Hexer turned to Haggstone, looking as if she'd won a victory. "I think we can agree this account is real," she said. "The child is not capable of inventing this sort of detail. We have already made a huge breakthrough! Your childish sensitivity means you can see things that happened in the past. This is more exciting than you can possibly know. Before we let the world in on our secret, we must show how it can be used to do good."

I didn't have to look at Haggstone to sense her frowning at me.

Lady Hexer peered at my face. "You are very pale. How are you feeling?"

I shook my head. I didn't want to tell her how sick I felt inside and how it all felt so wrong, because I couldn't find words that made sense. Eventually I blurted, "I was frightened! I was terrified! The snake-thing was so– so– and the people who were ill ... they looked..." I ran out of words and just hung my head, trying my utmost not to cry.

Lady Hexer smiled and took my hand. Her smooth fingers felt comforting. If I'd thought Lucy's hands were soft, then these were rose petals.

"It must have been very frightening indeed," she said. Her voice was velvet. "You have been so brave. So very brave. I am proud of you."

I swallowed and nodded. I couldn't help enjoying this praise.

Lady Hexer got up and went for the servants' bell. "I am going to fetch us some sweet tea, and then we will talk further. We must decide what to do next."

At the sound of a knock on the door, I turned, hoping to see Lucy. But it was Becky who brought in the tea tray. She looked no more pleased to see me than I was to see her.

"Shall Annie bring the tray back down, madam?" she asked, with frost in her voice.

Lady Hexer gave her a sharp look. "No, Becky. Annie is staying here with me for a while."

Becky waited for a moment. Then she burst out, "Ma'am, there is something I would like to ask you, please."

Lady Hexer gave her a short nod. She began pouring tea into a china cup that looked too thin to hold hot water.

Becky flushed. "Please, ma'am, it's a private matter."

Lady Hexer sighed, stood up and nodded for Becky to follow her out on to the landing. She left the door open just a crack. I listened, wondering if Becky was going to complain about me and my special treatment. But she didn't. Instead, she told Lady Hexer that her own younger sister was still looking for work and asked if there was anything for her here.

"I'm afraid there is nothing at the moment, Becky, but

I will bear your sister in mind if any of my younger girls move on," Lady Hexer said.

I breathed out. I didn't want another Becky around. One was bad enough. Then I peeped guiltily at Haggstone. I guessed she'd also been listening, just as closely as I had. Her eyes flickered from the door to me.

"You're a lucky girl," she said, in a low voice. "I hope you realise how lucky. It's not everyone who goes for a nap on their mistress's hearthrug and wakes up a heroine. But I haven't fallen in love with you yet. What Lady Hexer does is of importance to me. I'm watching you, miss." I didn't know what to say to that, but it scared me.

Hexer Hall
2nd January, 1899

When I first met Agatha Haggstone, I was so full of grief that I thought I would never be able to face the world again. First my child, then my kindly husband: these are losses no woman should have to bear so closely together. Attending the famous Miss Haggstone's session in Edinburgh was the first time I had left the Hall in almost a year. The report of her séance in the newspaper claimed all sorts of phenomena that once I would have dismissed as nonsense: that chairs and tables flew unaided through the air, that unearthly music was heard and that unseen hands passed around important messages from beyond the realms of death. It was this that interested me, of course. Who would not try anything, risk anything, pay anything for one more word from a loved one who has died?

My trusted Mrs McKinnon accompanied me, although I knew she did not approve. We sat at the back of the room, and I hoped not to be noticed. It was true that there were disembodied hands, unearthly wailings and objects that flung themselves around without human help. In the dark of the room it was impossible to see how such marvels were brought about. I was not there for entertainment, however, not like most of the audience. When Agatha stood up and stared directly at me, I trembled so hard I had to clutch Mrs McKinnon's hand.

"There is a message for you," she said, in a deep, hypnotic voice, as if someone else was making use of her tongue. "It is from the one who has passed over at a young age. You must grieve no longer. You must carry on with your good and important works."

I gripped Mrs McKinnon's hand more tightly, and she patted it to console me. I wanted to hear more, of course, but Agatha moved around, giving messages to others in the room. Afterwards, I told Mrs McKinnon I wanted to speak to the medium alone. She advised against it.

"But she knew," I said. "How could she know, not only that I had lost a child, but that I have a dream of important work to be done?"

"Why, madam," Mrs McKinnon said, "perhaps she knows who you are. Your sad loss is common

knowledge. You are wearing mourning clothes."

"But the good work? What would she mean by that?" How I wanted to find something – anything – to give me a purpose for living again.

"Many ladies of your standing undertake acts of charity," Mrs McKinnon said.

But I knew there was something more to it. When Agatha came out of the hotel where the séance was held, I approached and told her I wanted to spend more time with her, to hear more. She was reluctant at first.

"The spirits do not like to be pestered," she said. "They will not speak to order. And it is hard work for me," she added, mopping her brow with a handkerchief.

"I will reward you well for it," I said. "Come and stay at Hexer Hall, where you shall want for nothing while you contact my loved ones and bring me their messages."

After some persuasion, she consented. Once she arrived at the Hall, I found she knew so much about me and my sadnesses that I felt able to take her into my confidence entirely. With her help, I pieced together my family's history. Rumours of witchcraft and dark magic have followed us through the centuries, dating back to my early ancestors and their experiments in medicine. It became my most burning ambition to rewrite these stories, telling the truth about our attempts to heal. Not only that, I determined to rediscover those experiments and prove their efficacy.

When I recounted my experience as a girl, in which

*I was sure I had travelled to my family's past, it was
Agatha who told me that I needed to find another
sensitive child to journey as I had done. She helped me
to create the symbols around the Hall, for when the
right person came along. The excitement of the work
helped ease my grief, although Miss Haggstone's fees
were high and her predictions often hard to follow.
Perhaps a boy, perhaps a girl, then one who may be
either: where would I find such a child? At times, the
mission seemed hopeless.*

I spent the afternoon in Lady Hexer's room. She kept
talking excitedly about the "great discoveries" we were
to make together. She showed me a story book called *The
Time Machine* by a Mr Wells. It is about someone who can
travel through time. She has lent it to me but it is hard to
read. Lady Hexer laughed that we would write our own
story and it would beat the book into a cocked hat, because
it would be true. Again, she warned me not to tell anyone
else about what she calls "the experiment".

"Not even Tom?" I pleaded.

"I'm afraid not, my dear," she replied. "He is unlikely
to understand it. He may worry about it and want you
to stop, and then where would we be? Without your help
in finding the book, I can't even proceed with my new
garden." She gave a shrug. "That is Tom's special project,
of course."

I was not allowed to leave until almost four o'clock,
when it was dark outside. A sleeting rain rattled the long

windows of the drawing room. As I started down the stairs, I heard Haggstone's voice muttering and I caught the words "the girl". I crept back up to listen at the door.

"But people will become suspicious!" I heard Lady Hexer whisper. "The brother quite dotes on her. He may start asking difficult questions."

"This is your life's work, Lady Hexer!" came Haggstone's voice. "Take my advice. Keep her closer. Do not put all of your trust in her so soon."

The sounds dropped, too low for me to hear. I slunk down the back stairs to the kitchen. As I turned the heavy door handle, I heard Becky's thin slice of a voice. "All sitting around like three witches," she was saying, with a pretend laugh. "Fat witch, skinny witch and titchy witch."

I stepped into the kitchen and Lucy and Mrs McKinnon both turned.

"Annie, pet!" said Lucy. "We were wondering what on earth you were getting up to, up there all day with Her Ladyship and old Rag-face."

I glared at Becky. "Putting a curse on you," I snapped at her. "And your sister." Straight away I felt sorry about those last words. Becky narrowed her eyes at me but she said nothing.

"Now, now," said Mrs McKinnon. "I have all sorts of nice things for you to take home to Tom. There's plenty of food left over from the New Year's party, although, I'm afraid, none of the pudding he liked so much."

"You'll have to get the recipe, Lucy," said Becky, making Lucy squirm. "Tom won't love you if you can't cook. He will have high standards now. Though not as high as Little Lady Annie's."

Mrs McKinnon clicked her tongue. "What is the matter with everyone today? There's enough poison around for a barrel of snakes."

My skin prickled again. The kitchen was one of the few places around the Hall where I thought I was safe from paintings and carvings of serpents. But even here the monsters were all around me, their poison in the air.

The image of Huksor's dragon-like serpent creature would not leave my head. Every time I thought of the thing I felt sick. I even had dreams about it. Its horrid head was moving from side to side and fixing me with its mean eyes. I woke up sweating and crying out. I tried to tell Tom that I'd had a nightmare about a snake.

"Where on earth has that come from?" he asked, half-laughing and offering me his shirt sleeve to wipe away the tears. I barely slept for the rest of the night. I just clutched my thin pillow and shook for hours, it seemed.

As I walked across the grounds to the Hall early the next morning, I saw a coach being trundled out onto the cobbles. It was getting ready for a journey. The squat figure of Haggstone was bossing a servant as to where he should put her trunk. I tried to disappear into the dark of the morning and slip past without being seen. But she swung round as if she could smell me. She beckoned and I trudged over in her direction. Apart from anything else, it was shiveringly cold so I couldn't wait to get inside the Hall to the bright kitchen, or even the stiff, quiet warmth of Lady Hexer's rooms.

"Here, girl," the old woman grunted, making a rough gesture with her pudgy hands. I bobbed her my usual makeshift curtsey. Not that she deserved it.

"I have business in Edinburgh for a few days," she told me. She was speaking in her usual quiet rumble, so that only I could hear her. "But I want you to know that I'm having you watched. Oh, yes. Lady Hexer may fall for your fantastic stories, but I don't believe a word of it."

I was as angry as I was scared. "I wouldn't know how to make that stuff up," I said. "I just say what I see."

Haggstone gave her pig-like snort. "Everyone in the village has heard the legends about the old hospital. Oh, you're clever, I'll give you that, cleverer than you look. Patch-headed piece that you are. But I've got my eye on you – yes, even while I'm away. Not everyone's in thrall to you, don't think so for a minute."

"I don't know what you mean," I blurted out. "You told Lady Hexer to find someone like me! I'm just doing what I'm told!"

"I didn't want you, you stupid girl," hissed Haggstone. "I had someone else in mind. I still have. Lady Hexer got carried away with some romantic ideas about you and your long-haired brother. She couldn't be patient. But I will get back in charge of this whole thing. So don't get too comfortable, miss. You won't be here much longer."

I found myself going hot and red-cheeked, even

though I'd done nothing wrong. I stared miserably at the damp ground, my eyes on my shabby boots. I still didn't understand why this woman hated me so much.

I made my way upstairs to the silent, dead air of Lady Hexer's rooms. "Annie!" she cried, when I entered the drawing room, as if I was her long-lost daughter. "How are you feeling? How did you sleep? A good rest, I hope, like I told you?"

She patted the space at the table beside her and her delicate jet bracelet made a light, clattering noise. There was a sudden movement by the window and Becky emerged from behind the curtain, armed with a pile of dusting cloths and a tin of polish which gave off a faint smell of honey.

"Must you do this now, Becky?" asked Lady Hexer.

"I'm afraid so, madam," said Becky, pleasantly. "That bit of winter sun the other day has been showing up all the dust. I won't get in the way of your, er, studies." It didn't take much of a brain to see who Haggstone's spy was likely to be.

Lady Hexer and I looked at each other. There was a kind of understanding between us. We were not going to talk where Becky could listen.

"Very well, carry on," said Lady Hexer, quite firmly. "As a matter of fact, you won't get in our way. I was about to show young Annie something." She stood up and it struck me how very tall she was, how narrow. "Come with me," she said. I turned to look at Becky on my way out of the room. She looked furious. I enjoyed that. I couldn't resist sticking my tongue out at her, behind Lady Hexer's back, of course.

I followed Lady Hexer along the landing. It was silent apart from the odd creak of the floorboards under the carpets. She turned the handle into a small bedchamber. The first thing I noticed was the sweet, clean smell of lavender. A bunch of it was hanging above the narrow bed. The room was one of the prettiest I had ever seen. The paper on the walls had patterns of birds and flowers, in soft shades of silvery-grey. A kind of flimsy white lace fluttered over the windows like a hundred night-moths. The silky, padded bedspread matched the walls. There was a dressing table and, above it, an oval mirror. I stepped inside the room, noticing its chill, wondering what it was that Lady Hexer wanted to show me.

"Is this your room?" I asked her.

She smiled. "No, dear, not my room. But do you like it?"

"It's very pretty," I said. "Like a princess's room."

"I wondered if you would like this to be your room," Lady Hexer said, softly.

I didn't really understand. How could this be my room? I lived with Tom. Housemaids like me didn't have rooms like this, anyway, wherever they lived. Lucy and Becky slept in the attic.

Lady Hexer put her hands on my shoulders and steered me further in. I found myself standing in front of the mirror. I tried to look down. I hated looking at myself. The maid's cap barely covered the pinkish patches on my scalp. It was pinned at a silly angle, the only way Mrs

McKinnon could get it to stay on. Lady Hexer stood behind me. Her own reflection was so much more beautiful, but she was looking at me. Her hair was the glossiest black I'd ever seen, even on a horse after grooming. A thick, coiled ringlet trailed over one shoulder. I imagined how sleek it would feel in my fingers, like a ribbon. Her face looked as if it had been carefully carved, from white-polished wood. Her face never moved much; this was something I noticed about her. I couldn't imagine her throwing her head back to laugh like Lucy, or screaming wide-eyed like Becky when she saw a mouse. You had to watch her very carefully to see how she was feeling.

"What I am suggesting," Lady Hexer said, "is that you move into the Hall. At least while we are doing our experiments. I am greatly concerned for your health, for one thing, and I do not think that sleeping in that draughty old cottage can be good for you."

I opened my mouth to argue but she held up her hand. There was something about those long, pale fingers that made you know you should obey her, in spite of the way they seemed so thin and barely there.

"Yes, of course, I know that Tom does his best, but he is still a young boy. You need to be fit and strong if you are to do our special work. I can see how your mind's journeys back to the past use up your energy. This way, I can make sure that you are warm and dry and that you are eating properly."

"I don't–" I started, but she spoke over me, with that unbending note to her voice that I'd heard before. "Also.

There is another reason." She paused and gave a deep sigh. "This will probably sound rather strange."

I shrugged. "Nothing much sounds strange to me after the last few days," I said. Her eyes gave the flicker that meant I had amused her.

"I suppose so. What we are doing: it is quite momentous. I am sure you understand that. I think we are going to have to get to know each other very well. And we are going to have to learn to trust each other, trust each other utterly. I believe that if you were to live here with me then we could begin to form that friendship."

I stared into the mirror again. How odd we looked, this scrap-headed, plain, grubby girl and the stately figure standing over her like a winter tree. And the keen, almost hungry look on Her Ladyship's face. It was hard to turn her down. It was also hard to turn down the thought of sleeping in this beautiful bed with its cover like a dove's wing and the white, white sheets underneath. I was not very proud of this. But sleeping on my own, too, instead of top-to-toe with Tom. What a luxury! I'd miss the way he's always warm, but I wouldn't miss the stink of his feet. Outside the window I could see the grounds and, beyond them, the sea. It looked from here like a thin grey pencil line. All that sky. That would be my view. Mine, as if I was a great lady too.

She was watching me closely as I gazed around the room. I could tell she was finding it hard to wait for my reply.

After a few minutes, she spoke again. "What is it you want, most in all the world? Tell me."

I sighed. There was no point in answering that question. The thing I wanted was impossible.

"Is it for your hair to grow? To be beautiful? To be rich?"

I shook my head. I had to fight a thick lump forming in my throat.

Lady Hexer tightened her grip on my shoulders. "Tell me what it is, then," she whispered. "Trust me with that wish. What is it you want, more than anything at all?"

The faces in the mirror blurred. My voice came out like the peep of a bird. "Me Mam."

There was a silence, just for a second or two. "I'm sorry. I didn't quite understand what you said."

"*Me Mam. I want me Mam.*"

Silence again. For once, Lady Hexer didn't know what to say, and a small, nasty part of me was glad. I didn't want her to come out with some creamy dribble of words that sounded wonderful but didn't mean a thing, like pouring sauce onto an empty plate.

Then she gave a heavy sigh. "Oh dear. You have asked for probably the only thing I can't give you. Poor child. I'm so sorry."

I didn't reply.

"Shall I tell you my biggest secret? It may interest you. I always wanted a daughter. I wanted to be a mother – a mam." She couldn't say it properly, the word mam. It came out like she'd said it down her nose, and it sounded like "mem". She gave me a sad smile and added, "I had a child. Yes, I thought you may be surprised."

I stared at her face in the glass. Her eyes were bright

and I suddenly saw some tiny lines along her eyes and mouth, that I had never noticed before. It was as if just saying the words had made her grow a little older.

"But where is she?" I asked. "Your daughter. You don't even have a portrait of her."

"I cannot bear to have a picture of her. My daughter died. Her name was Bella. She was just two years old."

I didn't know what to say. What I do know is that when someone important dies, people often say very stupid things, such as that they are sorry, or that the dead person is in a better place, and that makes me angry. So I just nodded.

"There is not a day goes by when I do not think about Bella, even though I do not find it easy to speak of her. My longing for a daughter has never, ever gone away."

She left that hanging in the air between us for a moment.

A clock chimed faintly in the distance and I blinked.

"Lunch, I would say," Lady Hexer said, all brisk again. "Let's go to my drawing room and see what delights the kitchen can send up for us."

We sat at the long table together. Much more than the food, I enjoyed the taste of Becky's pained face as she served us. I knew she'd had to help make this lunch. It must have killed her to give it to me, on Lady Hexer's grand gilt-edged plates. She clattered the bowls and plates down, as slowly and noisily as she could get away with it. Then she moved over to the hearth and started fiddling with the grate.

Lady Hexer looked over at her. "That will do, Becky. I

am not going to eat my lunch with you cleaning around us. I insist that you go back downstairs and find some other duties there. I don't want to see you here again this afternoon."

Becky left, with a scalded face. I couldn't help a grin.

"Tom would be hurt," I said, then. Lady Hexer raised her brows.

I went on. "If I moved in here, Tom would be upset. He's worked so hard on the cottage. And he wants to look after me. He thinks it's his duty. I don't think I could tell him I was coming to live in here."

Lady Hexer nodded. "What if I were to explain things to him, that it was just for a short while, until you are back to full health?" she asked.

I thought this over for a moment. This didn't feel so bad.

"You liked that room, didn't you?" Lady Hexer added, leaning towards me like we were two girls sharing a little secret. "If there were just you to think about, you would have said yes, wouldn't you?"

I hung my head. "Probably."

"Well, then. Let's think of how we can make it possible," said Lady Hexer. She sounded pleased as Punch. "I feel sure that we can get Tom to see the sense of it. I shall speak to him myself. This afternoon."

Hexer Hall
3rd January, 1899

*Young Annie has brought a brightness into my life
and I must confess that it is more than I expected.
Certainly, she appears to be the child I was seeking, and
clever enough to bring me the knowledge I need. But
in some ways she is wise beyond her years. She told me
how she was often teased after her hair fell out and that
this was another reason why it was sometimes easier
to pretend to be a boy. People are so much fussier about
how girls look, she said, and I couldn't help agreeing
with her.*

*"You know, people will often find reasons to tease
and ridicule other people, whoever they are," I told her.
"You must learn not to mind them. I did."*

*She looked at me in surprise. "I can't imagine
anyone teasing you," she said. "You're so noble. And
beautiful."*

*"Ah, as I say, people will always find a reason," I
said. I found myself telling her something I had never
told anyone: how one time, when I was around her age,
I had taken myself off into Hexendale all on my own,
which was strictly forbidden, of course. It was a great
adventure to press my face against the shop windows
as if I were a grown-up, and I wished I had brought a
penny for some of the sweets in the glass jars. I was
looking at them and thinking that I might ask one of the
maids to bring me some of the coloured bon-bons some
time, when I noticed that behind my own reflection*

in the window was a little group of other children. I turned around and somehow I knew, by their faces, that they were not going to become my friends.

"I know who you are," one of the children said. A boy spat on the ground at my feet.

"How dare you?" I said, trying not to sound scared. "I shall tell my father and he will have you all whipped."

"Your mother's in the lunatic hospital," one girl said.

"That's not true," I said. "My mother is dead." I had to work very hard not to cry.

"She's in the madhouse. Everyone knows it. And you come from a family of witches."

A girl stepped forward and pulled at my hair. I squealed and pushed her away. Then I started to run, with the urchins all calling after me, "Witch! Witch!" as I clattered down the street in my silly rich girl's shoes.

I never told my father, of course, but I did ask my maid about it. She would tell me nothing about my mother. But she said there were old stories about the Hexer name.

"I doubt that half of them are true," she said to me. "But you know how these tales go. They say that the Hexers have always dabbled in witchcraft and even that, hundreds of years ago, Hexers were burned at the stake. But I expect it's all nonsense. Can you imagine your father having anything to do with all of that?"

I couldn't. But it explained a great deal: the way some older people looked down their noses at us in church or in the town, as if we had an unpleasant smell, the way my father would never speak of my mother.

Annie listened to all of this with her gravest expression. Then she said: "Being teased about your mother is much worse than being teased about yourself."

This is what I mean when I say she is wise beyond her years.

CHAPTER SEVEN

In the next few days I turned into a new hobby of Lady Hexer's. Of course, she told Tom that I should move into the Hall, only for the time being, till my health improved. He could hardly say no to her. The dove-grey and lavender princess room was mine. First, I had to be made to look more like a lady. I had to sit in a steaming tin bath and scrub the muck from my fingernails and feet. Mrs McKinnon was called up to take my measurements. She cluck-clucked a lot about how I was all skin and bone. She'd pass out if she saw Meg, I thought. Then she was sent out to the dressmaker in the village to order me some new clothes. I found all this rather daft. I couldn't see what it had to do with helping Lady Hexer find out about her ancestors or find cures for illnesses. In fact, we didn't talk about the hospital for a while, just a lot of dress fitting and shoe buying and fussing. Mrs McKinnon looked at me differently, too: not quite so kindly. It was as if a line had been suddenly drawn between us and she had to be careful how she spoke to me. As if I was someone important, not just one of her own staff. But I suppose I did look very different. I was given a long, soft, blue dress. It had a matching silk scarf which wrapped around my head, making me look like an exotic princess from *The Arabian Nights*. (This is another book Lady Hexer gave me.) I loved this. And what I wore underneath – well, I'm not sure if it's proper to mention it. But when I walked about, I rustled with secret snowy-white flounces and laces that only I knew were there! I felt like some exotic fluffy bird waggling my tail feathers. I used to laugh at silly dressy-uppy girls. But it only took a few frills and bows for me to think that old Annie was some other person altogether.

I'd never before had a room that was just my own. It's what Mam would have called a mixed blessing. The first night I spent in it, I couldn't wait to get into my own new bed with its stiff, snowy sheets. Except that when I got into it, I almost howled with the cold. It was like plunging into a bath of icy water. I shivered so hard I made the bed rattle. It didn't warm up all night. I slept so badly, I got up and stood at the window watching the white moon, wondering if I should brave walking across those eerie grounds to the cottage to find Tom. I imagined curling in beside his always-warm back, as he snored like a gruff old bear asleep for the winter, and making him jump by poking him with my cold feet.

When I woke up in the pale winter morning, I spotted, out of the corner of my eye, what I thought was a dark stain on the clean pillow. It was yet another clump of my hair. I scooped the baby-soft strands up with my fingers and ran to the window, pushing it open. Then I scattered the hair out into the chilly morning air. I went over to the mirror and stared. I looked just the same, almost. It was hard to tell which part of my poor scalp had given up more hair. I ran my fingers over it. It felt like some baby animal, like a new-born mouse, waiting for its fur to grow. I was annoyed with myself for caring how I looked. Secretly, I wished I had Lady Hexer's shiny tendrils to comb and adorn and curl around my finger.

I told Lady Hexer about the cold and the next night, when I got into bed, I found someone had placed a large, hot stone wrapped in a cloth in the bed. This warmed it up good and proper. I slept a lot better after that.

Lady Hexer said if I liked, I could go to church. Then she laughed when she saw my face. She leaned towards me and said in a half-whisper, "I don't enjoy it either. So dull. I only go because I feel I ought."

"Aunt Catherine used to make me go all the time," I told her. "But it was too late for prayers to help me, wasn't it? Mam was already dead."

Lady Hexer patted my hand. My pale, clean hand.

"Quite so," she said, softly. "In this house you are a young lady of independent thought." She did use long words, but I was starting to learn them.

"Does that mean I don't have to go to church?"

"Exactly that. As long as you have good reasons for what you do, I will respect your decisions."

In other words, I could do what I wanted. It was hard to get used to that idea, but it sounded fine to me.

Hexer Hall
4th January, 1899

As I sat in church this morning, my thoughts drifting as usual, I dreamed of a time in the near future when my status will be different. I pictured how the members of the congregation who look at me with such barely disguised mistrust will be forced to acknowledge my contribution to medical science.

Some of those here are the very people who, as children, teased and spat at me in the street. Even on my own wedding day they lined the pathway outside the church, and I could see in their eyes that they would still shout and curse at me, if manners allowed it. Their respect for my dear husband kept them silent. But when Arthur passed away, many of them dropped their pretence immediately. The wild stories and gossip began again not long afterwards, and they got worse when I brought Agatha Haggstone in to help me with my work.

Little Annie is another of life's misfits. Agatha says I must not become attached to her, and I try to bear this in mind. I have decided, however, to make her some financial provision, without her knowledge, to help her after our work is done. And then: oh, the triumph! Perhaps there will be a Lady Hexer College at a great university; perhaps a bursary in my name for clever young women. The likes of these people will try to stop it, of course; there are always those who let fear impede progress. I shall not allow it.

I also had a velvet-trimmed coat and hat, blue to match my favourite new dress and the warmest things I've ever worn. When Lady Hexer's coach rattled off into the grey January morning, I put on this outfit and went into the gardens looking for Tom. I hadn't seen him for two days. I had to wander through the gardens for ages, as usual. There was a cruel wind wrestling the bare trees. The sky was the colour of the sad old scarf I used to tie around my head. The earth had that old, dead smell, of rotting leaves or something, a bit like someone had weed. I made my way to the huge glasshouse. It was as big as a mansion and decorated with snow like a white-trimmed wedding cake. I found Tom inside, among those special plants that need to be kept warm. He was leaning on a wooden bench and frowning over the huge book that Lady Hexer had given him. He looked delighted to see me. But he shrank back when I tried to give him a hug. "Hey, you'll get that posh coat all covered with muck and clarts," he said, keeping me at arm's length.

"I don't care about that," I said, punching him on the shoulder. "Anyway, it's a dark colour, it won't show up."

He raised his eyebrows. "Well, Lady Annie, how are

103

you? And what have you done with my boggle-faced sister?"

I smiled, without really wanting to. "I'm bored. I've done nothing but try on clothes and I feel like I haven't seen you for ages."

"I can hardly just march up to Her Ladyship's grand rooms and demand to see you," he said, with a laugh. I jumped up and sat on the slatted bench, loosening my coat buttons.

"It's too warm in here," I grumbled.

"It's supposed to be. These plants are used to the sun." Tom pointed out the palms and the trailing vines and fruit trees. "Figs, peaches, apricots," he started listing. "Plums, nectarines. Even grapes."

I'd heard some of this before and there wasn't much to see on the branches at this time of year. They just looked like a load of old twigs to me. But it felt so safe to be with Tom that I didn't stop him. I like it when he gets all excited about bits of leaves and buds and sticks.

"What were you looking at?" I asked him.

His frown came back. "There are some plants appearing in the new garden that have got me baffled," he said, scratching at his thatch of hair. "For one thing, it's far too early for anything to be growing. You see how cold it is out there. Nothing much should be coming up in January, whatever's been planted in the past. And for another thing, I can't put a name to some of them. I was trying to see if they were in this book. I just came in here to look at the pages out of the wind."

"Show me," I begged. We went out into the chill and walked across to the new garden. I saw what he meant. There were clumps of shoots, complete with new green leaves, sprouting from the hard ground, which only days ago had been completely bare. Tom bent down and rubbed at some of the long, wrinkly leaves, picked one off and sniffed at it.

"Very, very unusual," he said. "I have no idea what this is."

I shivered in a way that had nothing to do with the wind. For some reason, I knew he shouldn't have torn off the leaf. "Careful," I said. "It might be poisonous or something."

Tom took no notice. "That" – he pointed out another clump of a duller green – "looks a bit like hellebore. You know, those Lenten Rose things. With the leaves that can make your skin itch. But I thought the ground was thoroughly dug over, so I don't know where it's come from. Look at that spiky thing. It's quite pretty but it shouldn't be here."

I wished I could help him. I took the first odd-looking leaf from him in my gloved hand and turned it over and over. It looked like an old green rag to me. Tom went on muttering about the spiky shoots that had found their way out of the frost-covered soil. But I was beginning to feel very dizzy, in a way that I recognised. I started backing away from the plot.

"I need to go inside," I said, panicking. I couldn't fall asleep and start dreaming of the hospital here, in front of Tom. It was supposed to be a secret. What would happen if Lady Hexer wasn't here to wake me up? Would I ever come round? I kept staggering backwards. I could feel a strong pulling feeling, dragging me back towards the mystery plants. Tom's voice, asking what was wrong, seemed like it was a long way in the distance.

I opened my eyes and looked straight into the glistening, dark eyes of Doctor Huksor.

I jumped and gave a cry. He stared at me with a mixture of interest and fear, as if I was a wild animal and he didn't know whether to trap me or kill me.

"Well, well, now," he murmured. His skin was a sallow colour with a yellowish tinge, his eyes tiny and black. "Look here. Our unearthly demon is back."

I was suddenly aware of Meg bobbing around behind him, her hands held at her mouth in shock.

Wild thoughts scampered through my mind like mice. If I was dreaming about the hospital, were Meg and Doctor Huksor dreaming about me? It didn't make sense. Meg stared at me as if I were a ghost. Which in some ways I was. That must be just how I looked to them. As far as Meg and Huksor could see, I'd disappeared in front of their eyes. Now I was back, like a spirit out of the air. I wasn't sure how much time had passed in the hospital since I was last here. Or dreamed I was here. If it was the same as my time, it had been days. Where was I all that time? Where were they?

Doctor Huksor held out his hand to me and I noticed it tremble. This wise doctor, who by Lady Hexer's account was a nobleman and a genius, was afraid of me. This made me want to laugh, just for a second. He touched me lightly on the sleeve, as if he thought I might crumble away into nothing again. Then, like a schoolboy carrying out a dare, he touched me again, harder, grabbing my sleeve and feeling the material, squeezing it through his none-too-clean fingers. His eyes went into slits.

"As real as you or I," he grunted. "Yet able to disappear into the air. What is this hobgoblin you've brought me, eh, Meg?"

Hobgoblin. The name made me want to smile again.

"That's what my brother calls me, too," I said.

"Brother? Is he here too?" Huksor asked, glancing around.

"No," I laughed. "Only me."

"And are you?" asked Huksor. "A hobgoblin? Or something worse?"

I smiled and shook my head. "Just a girl, sir. Just a girl who–" I thought quickly, "who wants to learn about your work."

This didn't flatter him in the way I'd hoped. His straggling eyebrows knitted together across his thin face.

"Why?" he asked. "Who has sent you?"

Now I wasn't sure how far to go. But I'd started. "A– a relative of yours, sir. My own employer. Perhaps we could share our knowledge. Your medicines and my, er, talents."

"And what are those talents, exactly?" Huksor glowered at me.

I swallowed. "Well, sir, as you see, I can disappear. That is just the start of my powers. I could show you more,

107

but in return I wish to know more about the marvellous medical work you are carrying out." I was amazed at how I could lie, straight-faced, and talk as if I was reading out of one of Lady Hexer's books. Huksor stared harder. He was torn between his interest as a man of learning and his sheer outrage at the nerve of this child.

"My work is very secret," he said, warily. "Meg is aware of some of it, but only as my helper. I am not yet ready to share my experiments with anyone. Especially not with a creature that just jumps out of nowhere. How do I know you won't steal my life's work and turn into nothing again?"

"You don't," I admitted. "But I can see I'm of interest to you. Perhaps you would let me help Meg? As an extra servant?"

Huksor thought. At this point I suddenly wondered, with a tremor, where the snake was just at that moment. I hoped I had not accidentally offered to look after Melusina, taking her for her daily exercise or buffing her hideous scales. The doctor made a *hmm*-ing sound and turned to Meg. I looked her in the eye for the first time. I was ashamed that she had tried to help me and I hadn't told her anything like the truth. The look on her face told me she was thinking the same thing.

"Master, I don't trust this girl," Meg said. "She has the sickness but she won't stay in the hospital. She's too quick at slipping away. Also–" she gave me a cross look, "you don't need another helper. I work hard for you. She would just get in the way."

Huksor looked surprised at Meg's outburst. "She has

the sickness?" he repeated. "How does it show itself?"

"Look under that headpiece," Meg said. Before I could stop him, Doctor Huksor snatched the velvet wrap from my head and saw my scalp.

"Ah," he said. He fingered the threads of my hair, making me wince. I hated anyone looking, never mind feeling it. The bald bits of leathery-pink scalp felt disgusting even to me.

"What else?" he asked me. "Do you have swellings? Any lumps and bumps? Can you feel heat and cold?"

"Yes, I feel heat and cold. For one thing, it's cold as clay in the rest of the hospital but it's sweltering hot in here. No, I don't have any lumps," I snapped. "I don't have this sickness. I just lost some hair. It's ugly, but I'm not ill. I'm not one of your patients."

The doctor turned towards Meg and they began mumbling together. It was hard enough to understand them at the best of times, never mind when they were speaking so quietly. Half the time with Meg I only recognised the odd few words, although the longer I spent with her, the more my ears grew used to this old-fashioned way of talking. It was a bit like the way your eyes get used to the dark and start to make out shapes after a while. I gave up trying to listen in and started looking around the tiny room. There were thick, mottled jars and pots everywhere, with scrawled labels that were too hard to read in the dim light. I noticed Huksor look sideways at me, then pick one of them up and place it behind some others. If he was trying to hide it, he didn't do a very good job. There were huge, heavily-bound books and piles of thick, yellow-brown paper covered in charts and drawings. Some of the drawings and scribblings were plants and flowers, I noticed. Tom would be interested, I thought, if only I could tell him. I was glad I couldn't see the foul serpent anywhere.

I unbuttoned my coat. I was starting to sweat, although there was only a small fire in the hearth. Most of the heat seemed to be coming from a larger fire in the dark room next to this one. I could just glimpse it through a doorway. All I could make out was the orange light it was giving off, dancing on the stone floor. The earthy smell coming from the next room was very strong. Wafts of steam sneaked around the door like a thief's fingers.

I leaned over to see further in, when Huksor suddenly said, "Very well then, creature. You can help Meg with her duties as long as you stay away from my writings and my medicines. In return, we will see if we can cure this baldness which is so unbecoming in a girl – if, as you say, it's not part of the leprosy. I take it you are a girl?"

I nodded, then snatched up the hat and pushed it firmly back on my head. Everyone seemed to want to cure my hair loss much more than I did. It's an odd thing. If you look different, everyone else feels funny about it.

"Don't do anything unless you're told to, either by me or Meg," Huksor added. "And don't touch my potions. You can start by helping her clean the glass tanks." He got up and walked out, saying he had a meeting with important men from the parish. I was left with Meg.

"I'm sorry," I said, quickly. "I couldn't help those times when I disappeared. I didn't mean to frighten you. But I did keep telling you I shouldn't be a patient here."

Meg still looked like she didn't trust me. "So what are you doing here? Why would you come to this place if you didn't have to? No one from the town even comes into the grounds. When the patients go to church, they have to stay outside and look through a hole in the wall. When they go into town to beg money, they have to ring a clapper to warn people not to come too close. Everyone's afraid of us. Why not you?"

I sighed. "It's hard to explain. I am afraid. But I do want to help and learn. You're the only friend I have here."

Meg said nothing.

"What are the glass tanks for?" I asked. Then I wished I hadn't.

Meg beckoned me into the steamy cell next to Huksor's room. There was, as I'd thought, a huge fire and over it was a large iron pot of water, giving off steam in warm huffs like dragon's breath. Now the heat was too much, so I took off my heavy coat altogether, wrinkling my nose at the strong musky smell. I noticed Meg looking at the coat with interest as I folded it and laid it on a wooden bench. Then I peered around to see that the room was full of large, thickened glass bowls containing greenery. I went up to one and pressed my face to it. I jumped back with a scream as something threw itself against the glass with a smack and gave out a vicious-sounding hiss. It was another serpent, a long black creature.

"Not more snakes?" I asked, weakly. "Or whatever they are."

A sick feeling came over me like a wave of warm water through my stomach. I couldn't move. I didn't want to go any nearer to any of the glass cages. I felt like the horrid beasts would see me moving and jump out at me. They were the worst creatures I'd ever seen.

Meg looked a bit pleased that I was the one who was scared for a change. Even more scared than she was of me. "Yes. Snakes. Serpents and dragons and all manner of creatures." She looked smug. "Twelve of them, at the moment. All different kinds. Oh! Do you want to see a real mermaid?"

"A mermaid?" That sounded a bit nicer. Only when Meg led me to one of the tanks I found out I was wrong. I expected to see a beautiful, fishtailed woman with long hair. What I saw instead, swimming around in a murky tank, was a small dark shape, half-fish, but with an evil monkey-like head that turned and snapped at us as we stared.

"These animals have come from all across the seas," said Meg. "Doctor Huksor has collected them. But they take a lot of looking after. That's why it's so warm in here. They die if it's cold. We have to clean some of their glass cages and then we feed them."

"Clean their ... what? But they could bite us and–" I couldn't believe it. Couldn't even stand the thought of going near their mouths. Those tongues, those fangs, the horns and claws and slime of them all.

Meg grinned. "I don't go near the very bad ones unless Doctor Huksor is with me. He can charm them and they go all floppy. But some of them will just let you lift them into another tank while you clean theirs out. Then we give them their dinner." She pointed to a barrel in the corner of the room.

"What do they eat?" I asked, with the sour taste of vomit at the back of my throat.

"Mice, mainly. Some rats. Just drop them in by their tails and try not to get bitten. By either the rats or the snakes, I mean."

"The rats and mice are still alive?" I asked, still feeling like retching.

"Some of them. That's how the serpents like them," Meg explained. Then, as I took a step or two backwards, she gave me a wicked grin. "Watch where you're going," she said. "I'd look behind you before you go any further."

I glanced over my shoulder and at first I couldn't see what she was talking about. Then I spotted a movement on the floor. It was something I'd thought, without really looking at it, was a rolled-up carpet or rug. It took my eyes a few seconds to realise what it was – the biggest snake you can possibly imagine. Or was it? In the dim light it seemed brownish and patterned very like Melusina. But this beast was many feet long and its body was thicker than Tom's. Evil-looking horns stuck out of its head and some of its yellow fangs stuck out of its mouth as if it was ready to eat anything in sight. I let out a moan and clapped my hand to my mouth.

"That," said Meg, "is Melusina's mother. We call her Bess. She's quite old and the biggest serpent you ever saw. Part-dragon, Doctor Huksor says. The master's had her for years. She had her baby just after he brought her to England."

"Baby?" I repeated, horror-struck. "Melusina is hardly what I would call a baby. Babies are supposed to be sweet and helpless." Sweat dripped off my face and my hands were so sticky I had to wipe them on my dress. I was still trying to stop myself being sick.

"There's no need to be so scared," said Meg. "Bess just lies around most of the time. She's fine as long as we don't let her get hungry. Speaking of which, I ought to get on with giving the serpents their dinner."

Dinner! It was a grand name for the creatures' meal. Limp dead mice and great big grey, wriggling rats. Even a stinking dead pigeon which Meg said had gone bad and couldn't be eaten otherwise. She wrapped a cloth around her hands and arms before getting on with the job. I wanted to help but I just couldn't make myself go near the creatures. Panic came over my body like a great wave from the sea. I was scared I might pass out with the sheer horror of it. The hissing and the movement of the beasts as they writhed in Meg's hands was one of the worst, most disgusting sights I've ever seen. I'm ashamed to admit I shook and cried like a baby. When I saw how their necks bulged with the shape of their food I thought I really might bring my breakfast up, right there on the floor. All I could do was sit down and cover my head with my arms. I pleaded with Meg to tell me when it was finished and they were all safely back in their tanks. I know she thought me stupid. I couldn't do anything else. I was also terrified she might bring one of the snakes close to me, so all the time I trembled and rocked back and forth on the floor, sobbing whenever something brushed past me.

After what seemed like an age Meg said she'd finished.

"A great help you're going to be," she grumbled. "Going on like that. Baby."

"Can we just get away from this room?" I begged. When I stood up my knees were knocking and my legs didn't want to carry me. Meg snorted but took pity on me and I followed her, still shaking, along the stone passageway and out into the cobbled, dung-smelling courtyard. I breathed out hard in the icy air, my body still sticky with sweat and fear. "I'll do anything, absolutely anything, except go near those monsters," I told Meg.

"But you're supposed to be helping me. That's one of my jobs," said Meg, stubbornly. "If I can do it, you can. Those serpents are important to Doctor Huksor's work."

"How?" I asked.

Meg shook her head. She was going to take a long time to trust me, I could see. Then I had a bright idea. "Meg, would you like to have my coat? You liked it, didn't you?"

I watched her face as she thought about it. I could see that she wanted to say yes. But then she shook her head again. "I can't."

"Why not?" I asked.

"Because if you have the leprosy I might catch it," she said.

115

I frowned. "I'm sure you can't catch it from a coat," I said. "Could you? Anyway, for goodness' sake, Meg. I don't have leprosy. Really."

Meg thought a bit longer. "It's a funny shape," she said.

"It's just a different fashion," I smiled. "In fact, you'll be in fashion a long time before anyone else. Even the finest ladies."

"I don't know what you're talking about," said Meg. "You use such stupid words. But I'll think about it. I like the soft stuff it's made from and it looks warm. I'll ask Doctor Huksor if I can have it without catching anything."

I sighed. Meg offered to get me some bread and cheese and now that my stomach had calmed down from the sight of the reptiles, I did feel hungry. I sat in the courtyard while she went to find the food. It was a small, busy place, still with patches of hardened snow here and there. The odd pig and goat wandered across the cobbles. There were one or two workers helping with the animals. I'd seen them before. They peered at me and muttered to each other. I suppose my clothes must have looked foreign to them and they must have wondered what I was doing there. I nodded back, trying to be friendly.

I noticed the whole place was encircled by stone walls and a heavy iron gate. I walked over to it and peered out onto white snowy fields. In the distance there was the sea. The same sea that I looked at from my new bedroom window, I thought. The sky – the same sky, too – was turning deep winter pink. Smoke puffed out from some of the buildings and greyed the air. Suddenly I thought I

116

could hear an animal whine. After a few moments, though, I realised it was some kind of musical instrument. A reedy pipe, playing a simple tune. I listened hard as Meg came running towards me, a dry-looking hunk of bread in her hands. Her eyes were bright.

"Can you hear it? Players! Oh, I love to hear music!"

The sounds grew louder. Pipes and a flutey whistle and drum. We saw a small group of brightly cloaked figures making their way towards the hospital. They stopped a short way from the gate. I watched Meg start to clap along with the tune, a short, bright refrain like a child's skipping song. The instruments sounded slightly off-key, but very merry. The tune seemed to get into my blood and I wanted to clap along too, tapping my feet on the frosty ground. One or two other patients in the courtyard wandered nearer to the gates.

"The players won't come inside," Meg said, though I'd already guessed that much. "But I hope they play a while." She leaned towards the gates and shouted, "Play a dance! A dance!"

I caught the eye of a young man with the flute-like instrument. He had dark hair and eyes and an infectious grin, making me think of a young fox. He took a step nearer and I thought he didn't look much older than me.

"A dance for the lady in blue!" he announced, with a sweeping bow. Meg and I both giggled. The players struck up another tune, which I thought I'd heard before somewhere. As Meg started to dance, hopping around from foot to foot, I realised it was a Christmas carol, but played faster and more cheerfully than I'd ever heard it. I started to dance too. I just couldn't help it.

There were more patients in the yard now, drawn out by the music. Some of them couldn't walk well but they stayed in the courtyard, swaying and grinning. I even noticed Doctor Huksor standing by a door, clad in a thick black fur-collared cloak and a round flat hat, wearing half a smile on his haggard face. No serpent. I suppose it was too cold for the horrid beast. The patients who could move around were limping gingerly, most not quite in time with the music. But Meg and I stole the show. We jumped and skipped around, getting hot and pink in the face. Some people formed a rough circle around us as we danced, laughing and clapping. The music got faster and faster. I held out my hands. After pausing for a beat, Meg grabbed them and we swung each other around and around, with all the others laughing at us. Then Meg slipped on an icy patch and I tried to stop her falling and we both skidded across the cobbles and landed in a heap, laughing like idiots. The musicians stopped to laugh too. As the patients clapped the players, the dark-haired young man held out his hand towards us.

"And applause for our wonderful dancers!" he shouted. "What grace! What elegance!"

Everyone laughed again. Meg made a terrible face at them. "Shut up and keep playing," she shouted, grinning.

"Meg," I hissed, going red. I turned to the band. "That was wonderful," I said. "Thank you."

The young man bowed again. "We played the town this

afternoon and made good money," he said. "It's a good act of charity to come here and play for you poor lost men and women."

"Oh," I said. Charity: that didn't feel so good, somehow. The young man saw my smile fade. "What is your name?" he asked me.

"Annie," I replied.

"Then this is a song for Annie," he declared and in a loud, clear voice he began to sing a ballad. I didn't catch all the words, of course, but it was a sad, pretty tune. Some kind of a love song. I smiled at him, twirling the end of the ribbon on my hat as I listened.

When the players came to the end of their songs, Doctor Huksor walked to the gates and thanked them, wishing them goodwill for the season. I watched them as they made their way across the smooth, white fields, their black shapes getting smaller and smaller against the red, fevered sky. I wondered about the Christmas carol and turned to Meg, frowning.

"What date is it?" I asked her.

"St Stephen's Day, of course," she said. "We saw the townsmen ride past this morning, hunting the wren."

"A little wren? How cruel," I said. "It's not even worth eating, is it?"

Meg gave me one of her looks, as if I was quite mad. "It's just a bird. It's for luck," she said, with a shrug.

"So is today before or after Christmas?" I asked Meg.

Now she looked at me with a shocked face. "Christmas was yesterday," she said. "Didn't you know? I don't know of many days, but I know that one."

"Where I'm from, Christmas was a few days ago," I told her.

Meg shook her head, not understanding. I couldn't blame her for that.

"The parish brought us extra meat and ale," Meg told me. "They really did their duty. We had quite a feast. You should've been here."

She broke off some of the forgotten bread and handed it to me as we made our way back into the hospital. It was the driest I'd ever tasted, but I didn't want to be rude.

"Will the players come back?" I found myself asking.

"They might," Meg answered. "Or else the mummers. Last year they did a play outside the gates. We had cakes."

She was in a chattier mood now, so I asked where the big snake-creature might be.

"In Doctor Huksor's study. It doesn't go outside in the winter," Meg told me. "It stays in the study at night too. Those rooms are kept warm all the time."

"Why does the doctor need the serpents?" I asked again. I knew I was making slow progress in finding out about Huksor's work.

"They're more than just snakes," said Meg. "They're magical creatures. He's trying out different kinds of cures. Sometimes he uses the serpents for his medicines. Their skin or hair or spit or that sort of thing."

"Has he cured anyone yet?" I asked, as we walked towards the archway.

"Not the worst cases," Meg admitted. "He's made a

medicine that can help with many things, though. Agnes's bad skin all went away, but then no one would give her work so she came back here anyway. And he will find a way to cure the leprosy, I know it. He is so clever. I don't think he'll make any more mistakes."

I glanced at her. "Mistakes?" I repeated. "What kind of–?"

But we could see Doctor Huksor slowly coming towards us, now with the wretched Melusina around his shoulders. I stopped talking and froze in my steps.

"It's all right, come on," said Meg, tugging my sleeve and sighing. But I found I couldn't go any nearer to the serpent.

Huksor came closer. "Ah," he said to me, with a leery grin. "Afraid of my Melusina, eh? That's a good thing. It might keep your nose out of my books and your fingers out of my pots. She guards them for me, you know."

I stood still as a tombstone. I couldn't bring myself to look at the serpent, but I was also too afraid to close my eyes, in case he pushed the creature at me.

"I just don't like snakes," I said, through gritted teeth, willing him to go away, go away, *go away*.

Huksor took a step nearer. I knew without really looking that he was lifting the beast's head and pointing it at me.

"Take a good look at this one, Melusina," he said, in the sort of soft tones that some people might use to train a puppy. "She's a trickster. She disappears into nothing and pops up again when you don't expect it. But you would spot her anywhere, wouldn't you, my pet? You could catch her as fast as you can catch a rat, eh?"

The huge, muscly serpent kept me in her black gaze. I could tell her coils were stronger than any man's arms. I tried to make myself stare her out, but I was too repulsed and I couldn't meet her eyes. Her forked tongue, thicker than my own wrist, flicked rapidly in and out of her mouth. Coiled around Doctor Huksor's other shoulder, her tail end moved slowly, like a bell rope, as if helping her think. I took a step or two backwards.

CHAPTER EIGHT

Melusina hovered before me. Her tail – or was it her tongue? – flicked back and forth. The scaly patterns of her skin seemed to fill my vision for a moment. Then I heard a voice. Was she actually talking to me? No. Oh Lord, the relief: it was Tom's voice I could hear. He was saying something about how I'd been fine one moment and then keeled over the next. There was Lucy, fussing and flapping. It took me a few minutes to realise I was back in our cottage, lying on the bed. I thought I heard Lucy tell Tom that it might be "something like your own funny turn".

I raised my head and Lucy's worried face lit up.

"There she is!" she exclaimed, her lovely voice all relief. "Oh, Annie! How you scared us!" She handed me a cup of water and I was glad of it. My mouth felt dry as sandstone.

"What happened, my hen?" Lucy asked, stroking my forehead. "Was it the cold? Are you hungry?"

I shook my head. I hated keeping this thing a secret. "I get these funny dreams sometimes," I said. I was bursting to say more.

Tom shifted about.

"We didn't want to get help from the Hall in case you got in trouble for coming to see me," he admitted. "I think you oughtn't to have come outside in this cold."

I frowned at him, looking for any signs of illness on his rosy face, but couldn't see anything different. "What was that about you being ill?" I asked.

I spotted Tom giving Lucy a look. Then he shrugged. "Nothing, nothing at all. The cold got to me the other day, that's all. Went to my head for a moment. But it's nothing to worry about. You know me, as fit and healthy as it's possible to be."

Lucy bit her lip. "But this cold is very bad indeed. The mercury's dropped further than anyone can remember around here. There've been people dying in the village, just from the chill. You should be more careful."

"I'm not an invalid," I told them, doing my best to give them a grin. "It wasn't the cold, it was ... oh, I don't know. But I'm getting used to this weather. I won't get into trouble. Nor will you."

I was sure of that, too. Lady Hexer would be pleased to hear everything I had learned. I was getting the feeling that she would indulge me in almost anything – at least as long as she needed me to do her fantastical duties.

There was a nasty surprise waiting for me, however, when I got back to the Hall, Lucy clutching my hand all the way. I tried to ask her about Tom and what had made him ill. But she kept twisting the talk in all sorts of other directions. Then I saw that Lady Hexer's carriage stood in the courtyard, the horse puffing out huge steamy breaths, and her footman heaving down a heavy old bag that I recognised. It belonged to Haggstone. "She must be back," I said, out loud.

"Old Miss Rag-a-Bones? Yes, she arrived around lunchtime," said Lucy. "With all sorts of bags and boxes that had to be taken up to her room. I think she's planning to stay a while."

I groaned.

Lucy looked surprised. "Is she so bad?" she asked. "I know she's a bit odd and a wee bit short-tempered, but—"

I sighed. "She doesn't like me, Lucy. I don't know why."

"Ach!" Lucy gave me a gentle poke in the ribs. "Who wouldn't like you?"

I put my head around the drawing room door nervously, expecting to see Haggstone glaring at me along the table. But only Lady Hexer was there. She looked up from her book. "Have you been for a walk? Isn't it rather too cold for that?"

"More than a walk, Lady Hexer," I said. I settled myself beside her and told her about my latest journey into the past. I made sure to talk about it as if it really happened – as if I'd travelled to the hospital rather than seen it in my head. I took note that she didn't argue with this.

125

"Lady Hexer," I said, taking a deep breath. "I don't think I imagine any of these things. When I think about the hospital, I can feel the cold and touch the walls. It's too real to be just in my mind."

Lady Hexer looked hard at me, directly in the eyes. It was difficult to look back at her without blinking, but I set my mind to do it.

"I really go there, don't I?" I went on. "You said we had to trust each other. Please tell me the truth."

"Well, I–" Her voice shook. "I didn't want to frighten you. But you are too clever to be fobbed off. Yes, incredible as it seems, I think you really go to the old hospital that has not been here for hundreds of years. I think you can travel through time."

I swallowed. It made my head reel, even though I'd guessed at it for a few days.

"Now. Tell me again all that you've done today," Lady Hexer breathed.

She was very excited about it all. Full of questions. She got me to draw a picture of the hospital and its grounds. I hummed the tune the players had made. She laughed when I told her I'd almost bartered my new coat.

"Good thinking!" she said, warmly. "I knew you were smart. A coat can be replaced, but this knowledge – it's priceless. Now, you must start trying to get close to those books of Doctor Huksor's. I need to know what he has written in there. His writings are the key to everything."

I winced. "The thing is, Lady Hexer – it's the snakes. Not just snakes, there are all sorts of magical creatures.

More like dragons, some of them. I'm more afraid of them than I can tell you. That doctor says the big serpent guards his books. I don't think I dare go near it."

"Hmph. Then perhaps we should find someone who will have a bit more nerve," said a low rumble of a voice. We both turned to see Haggstone standing in the doorway, her wide girth filling it.

I looked to Lady Hexer for support and she sighed.

"Agatha. Welcome back," she said, standing up. "Come and sit with us. We are getting closer to our prize, I feel. Annie is a natural time-traveller. Yes, she has worked out what's happening. She is also quite the detective. She will bring us back this book of cures soon, I know it."

She took my hand and pressed it.

"Perhaps he told you about the snakes to scare you, my dear. Perhaps they are not left guarding the books at all. Let's not worry about that now." She shook my fingers, gently. "Go and warm up those hands, child!"

I could feel Haggstone watching me as I stood with my back to her, holding my hands up to the fire. Lady Hexer was retelling my latest journey, in a voice that was musical with excitement, like a flute trilling up and down a scale. Haggstone didn't say much at first.

Then she said, "So the child claims to have been able to get to the past without the help of our magical symbols? This latest escapade happened out in the garden, she says?"

Lady Hexer paused, but only for one tick of the clock. "Why, Agatha, there are symbols throughout the gardens.

The topiary, for a start–"

"Indeed," said Haggstone. "But the girl says she was nowhere near those shapes. She says she was in the bare ground that has yet to be planted up with anything."

I turned towards them and saw Lady Hexer looking at me with a slight frown. "But that's right, isn't it?"

"Yes, that's right." I gave Haggstone as much of a glare as I dared. "I didn't want it to happen then. I was with Tom and he's not supposed to know."

"What did you touch?" Lady Hexer asked, urgently. "What could have been the key?"

I thought about it. "I didn't touch anything– oh! Wait a minute! There was the leaf."

Haggstone gave her pig-like grunt. "A leaf! Really!"

"No, listen," I said, ignoring the woman and looking directly at Lady Hexer. "Tom found a new plant that he couldn't name. He couldn't understand how it had got there in the first place. He picked a leaf and I took it from him. It was only a minute or so afterwards that I went ... back."

"Oh! We must look at this plant while there is still daylight. Can you face going back out in the cold?" Lady Hexer's face had a pale, excited glow. Haggstone said she wouldn't join us, but would settle back into her room. We put our coats, hats and gloves on and hurried down the wide staircase.

We marched briskly through the grounds until we reached the new garden plot. There wasn't much light left, but I was still able to find the clumps of greenery.

128

They seemed even thicker than they had this morning. I pointed, but I didn't want to pick one up. Lady Hexer looked around and breathed out as if she had just seen something like a miracle. "Why, I believe it is ... but surely not..."

"What is it?" I demanded. "Tell me. Is it something poisonous?"

"I believe it to be a mandrake plant," said Lady Hexer, bustling me back in the direction of the Hall. "They are unusual in this part of the world and rather difficult to grow. Yes, my dear, they are poisonous, but they are also highly magical. Tom is right to wonder where it has sprung from. I can only imagine it is a sign that we are making true and deep connections with the past."

"Tom touched it too," I told her.

Lady Hexer took no notice of this.

Back at the Hall, Lady Hexer took me into a room I hadn't visited before. There were so many rooms, I couldn't understand how she used them all. This one was a library. The door was rather stiff and, as we went inside, I was struck by how silent it was, as if a conversation had suddenly stopped. But of course there was no one in there, just shelves and shelves of books, stacked so high that it made me almost lose my balance as I looked up at them. I couldn't see how it would be possible to find the book you wanted among so many, but Lady Hexer had no trouble. Most of the books dated back to before she was born, she told me. They were very valuable. She placed a heavy volume on the table and it coughed up a cloud of dust as she set it down. The pages were stiff with age, and some of them had mouldy spots on them. They smelled sad and frail. I didn't want to touch them in case the pages crumbled into pieces. But Lady Hexer found the page she wanted and showed me a drawing of the plant we'd found in the garden. Next to the drawing were the words *Mandragora officinalis* and a whole screed in old-fashioned script that I struggled to read.

"One of the most magical plants in the world. And that's not all," Lady Hexer went on. "It was hard to tell in the poor light, but I believe I spotted something else."

She showed me another page and I recognised the clump of spiky blue-ish fronds.

"Viperine," she said, with a glint in her eye. "A kind of borage. Named after a snake, of course."

"Why do you think they're coming up?" I asked. "Tom says he hasn't planted anything there. He says it's too cold for anything to grow yet anyway."

Lady Hexer closed her eyes and gave a long sigh, like I might do after a spoonful of cream.

"I think it can only mean one thing. You went to the past and opened a door. You made a link. Now the past is coming to us, with these signs. Magical, healing plants are springing up from our bare earth. It surely means we are on the right track. Our medicines are coming to us, without us even trying. All we have to do now," she opened her eyes and looked at me fiercely, but happily, "is find the way to use them. That means the book! The time has come for you to bring me that book."

I was about to remind her of the snakes, especially the big one that looked more like a dragon. But then we became aware of a noise. There was shouting and the sound of running footsteps. Then a frantic knocking on the library door. Lady Hexer swung it open to find Lucy there, pale and out of breath. "Oh, ma'am, please come quick! It's Miss Haggstone, ma'am. She's– she's– well, you'd better come along and see. I didn't know what to do."

We all hurried back up the stairs and along the landing towards Haggstone's room. We could hear terrible sounds coming from it – banging and thumping, low groans and a second, shrill, grating voice, sounding like a much younger girl. Lady Hexer flung open the door. A wooden desk was rocking violently back and forward. No one was pushing it. The whole room was very dark, with just a tiny candle lit in the corner, in a red glass. We could just see the figure of Haggstone sitting in an armchair – but not sitting still. She was rolling around as if in great pain and making low moans. It made me think of a cow about to have a calf. It smelled to me as if someone had weed on the carpet, although I didn't think even horrid Haggstone would do that. There was another smell mixed with it, a sickly one, and on top of that the powerful, dizzying scent of whatever perfume Haggstone was burning in a bowl on the floor. But what was really shocking – what made Lady Hexer step back and made Lucy and me scream and clutch each other – was that there was some sort of white-ish, ghostly figure hovering above her. I couldn't make it out very well, but that made it even more terrifying. I'd already met ghosts, in a way, at the leper hospital. But they were just like ordinary people, as alive as I am. They hadn't been like this, this half-there, fluttering spectre, floating above Haggstone and wailing, high-pitched, somewhere between a girl and an animal. All my skin felt pricked and sweaty. Lucy clapped her hand over her mouth and turned away.

"Get some lamps," I whispered to her, "and find some help. Tom or one of the stable lads or someone." She hurried off.

Then the horrible ghost-like shape suddenly shrieked: "*Liar! Fraud! Deceiver!*"

I was shaking so hard I couldn't speak. I knew this frightful thing was talking about me. I knew it, somehow, even though I hadn't told any lies. Lady Hexer held out her arm to stop me going further into the room – not that I wanted to.

Part of the fluttering rag seemed to form a stiff arm. Its too-long finger pointed straight at me. I could feel its anger and hatred, as surely as if it had picked me up and shaken me. It went on: "*The wicked girl must leave this house! She is making a mockery of my life and my death!*"

Lady Hexer spoke in a voice that sounded in command, in spite of its tiny tremble. "What are you?" she demanded. "What do you want?"

The high-pitched voice cracked. "*Get – rid – of – the – girl! She is lying over and over again. I am the spirit of Jenny who died of the leprosy here many centuries ago. This girl is a fraud! She is a deceiver! She invents tales of a hospital and of the people who died with me, but she is a liar!"*

No one spoke and for a second or two the only sound was the banging of the wooden desk as it rocked back and forward as if it was alive. I was shaking as hard as if someone had hold of my shoulders and was pulling me back and forward. I couldn't even bear to look at the ghost girl. Then Lady Hexer said, her voice like an icicle: "I believe Annie to be telling the truth. You are a thing I can barely see. How do I know that you are to be trusted?"

The spectre let out an ear-splitting scream, making both Lady Hexer and me jump back. *"Your true messenger is still to come! Get rid of this deceiver!"* it yelled again. I was sobbing with terror.

Heavy footsteps pounded along the hallway towards us. I turned to see Mrs McKinnon, grim-faced, carrying a bright lamp. She was followed by two stocky lads from the stables. But just before Mrs McKinnon pushed past me into the bedroom, the tiny red light went out, everything went black as the grave, and the ghost-shape completely disappeared. Mrs McKinnon marched right in and held up the lamp, so that we could see Haggstone panting and sweating in the chair, as if she had just run a mile. The desk had stopped rocking. But as for the ghost girl – it was as if she'd never been there.

Haggstone looked around with wide open eyes. "What happened?" she asked. "I was sitting here asking for guidance from the spirits and then I must have passed out."

Mrs McKinnon sniffed in disgust and ordered the stable

lads to search the room. They looked behind Haggstone's chair and under her desk. She didn't get up, but leaned forwards and they shook out the cushion from her chair. They opened her wardrobe door and glanced in, but there was nothing more than a few of her smelly shawls hanging up. They picked up books and vases and turned them over. There was nothing unusual to see. In the lamplight, apart from the stench that hung around, it was like any ordinary room.

Lady Hexer stared hard at Haggstone for a moment. Then she said, in a flat sort of voice, "Agatha. I really think you ought to rest." She put a hand on my shoulder and pushed me out of the room and along the hallway.

I glanced up at her two or three times as we swept along the carpeted floor. But I couldn't read her face. I still had this feeling of shame, even though I knew I had done nothing wrong. Mrs McKinnon caught up with us. She just looked angry.

"Ma'am, what happened? Lucy came running down with the most terrible tale and she was too afraid to come back up again. That wretched Becky was nowhere to be found, so I came up myself. Are you quite well? And Annie? May I fetch you a drink?"

Lady Hexer stopped dead and I came to an unexpected halt too and stumbled. She didn't look at me but her face was almost as white as the ghost we'd just seen. "I will go to my room, Mrs McKinnon, and you may bring me a glass of brandy. Take Annie to the kitchen and give her some hot milk. Then I think she ought to spend the night in the cottage with her brother. I think she would prefer the company, after our ... ordeal."

I stared at her. Was I being sent away? I couldn't speak.

Mrs McKinnon held my hand as we went down to the kitchen. She sat me at the big table and patted my shoulder.

"Where's Lucy?" I asked.

"I've sent her to wash her face," said Mrs McKinnon, with a cough. "Whatever went on up there, she found it very upsetting."

She put some milk in a pan to warm and as she did so, the kitchen door opened and Becky came in. Mrs McKinnon rounded on her. "Where do you think you've been? I called and called for you. You were wanted upstairs."

"Oh," said Becky, round-eyed. "I was making up the fire in the drawing room and I got my pinny all covered in coal dust. I had to find a clean one." She looked at me then back at Mrs McKinnon, who was tut-tutting about the extra washing that would have to be done. "Why? What's happened?"

"Never you mind," snapped Mrs McKinnon as she put the cup of warm milk on the table in front of me. Then she left the room to take Lady Hexer's brandy upstairs. Becky sat down and smiled at me, but not in a nice way. She stuck her finger slowly and deliberately up her nostril, pulled it out and stuck it into my cup of milk. She stirred it around, still smiling at me, then took it out and licked it.

I was about to say something when Lucy came in, her face still a sickly colour. When she saw me, she cried, "Oh,

135

my pet!" and I stood up and hugged her tight. She sat at the table and, waving her hands and rolling her lovely brown eyes, Lucy recounted everything she'd seen.

"A ghost? I don't believe you," smirked Becky. "You're just trying to frighten me."

"She is not," I said, hot with fury. "Look at the state of her. How can you think it's a trick?"

Becky gave me that nasty smile again. "You haven't drunk your milk. Mrs McKinnon will be cross."

That was enough for me. I picked up the cup and threw the milk at her, right in her face, just as Mrs McKinnon came back into the kitchen. Both she and Lucy gaped at me.

"I will not have this behaviour in my kitchen!" Mrs McKinnon shouted. Becky leaped up, wiping her face with her hands. She started to yell about how I was completely mad and had just attacked her with a cup of burning hot milk.

Lucy tried to defend me. "Annie is very, very upset, Becky," she said, putting an arm around my shoulders. "And it wasn't hot. Only warm."

"I don't care!" interrupted Mrs McKinnon. "Becky, go and get cleaned up. Again. Lucy, take Annie back to the cottage. Lady Hexer says she is to stay there tonight. And," she glared at me, "I expect to see you a changed person by tomorrow." She handed me my hat and coat.

I was burning with rage. The hot tears I kept blinking back felt like scalding spurts from a pot about to over-boil. I wasn't just angry at Becky, but at all the events of the evening. I was angry with Haggstone for whatever had happened in her room. I still didn't know what to make of it. But I was even angrier with Lady Hexer. It felt like she hadn't believed me. She'd trusted some wailing bundle of dead rags over me. After all I'd put myself through – for her. As Lucy and I crunched over the frosty, black gardens towards the cottage, holding on to each other against the cold and so that we wouldn't slip, I made up my mind. I would tell Tom I didn't want to stay here any more. We would both be able to find work somewhere else. Surely, when he heard about tonight's horrors, he would agree with me.

But as we came nearer to the cottage, we could hear raised voices. One of them was Tom's. He was arguing with someone. Lucy and I glanced at each other. We both knew Tom almost never lost his temper. As we got nearer, we heard two of the other gardeners talking at once. They were saying something about evil plants covering the garden and men falling ill after touching them. Tom was saying it was nothing to do with him. But the others were shouting him down.

He turned as he saw us. "Annie! Lucy! What's happened? You haven't got this sickness too, have you? Come inside." He ushered us into the cottage and told the men they'd have to talk about it all in the morning. He slammed the door on them. One of them kicked it hard, but then they left.

We were all worn out. I sat down and started to cry again. Lucy tried to explain what had happened in the

Hall, but Tom seemed to find it hard to take in.

"Ghosts and banshees and all that silly stuff," he snorted. "It must have been some sort of trick."

"Tom," I tried to explain. "I'm telling you. I couldn't understand what I was seeing with my own two eyes. When Mrs McKinnon brought the lamp in, everything disappeared. The ghost got snuffed out. There was nothing to be found."

Lucy shuddered. "She must have been doing a séance," she said. "When you try to bring back the spirits of the dead. I heard about one in Edinburgh once. A lady saw her dead baby, floating around the room, and–"

"This is just rubbish," Tom cut across her, rather sharply for him. "All of these things are done with tricks. People see what they want to see."

"But Tom," I said. "None of us wanted to see anything like that. It was horrible. Like a nightmare."

"Well. I won't let any wailing witches or ghoulish ghosts in here," Tom said, with a weak grin. I knew he was trying to sound braver than he felt. "Let's try to get some sleep. Tomorrow I'm going to get rid of all these weeds and plants that're taking over the gardens. None of the other lads will touch them, they think they're poisonous or some such thing. More superstition and daftness, if you ask me. Although I still can't, for the life of me, think where they're coming from."

CHAPTER NINE

I didn't have a good night. Tom was restless and the fluttering ghost girl, with her terrible screams, came back to haunt my dreams. But I must have fallen into a heavier sleep in the early hours. When I woke up, although it wasn't quite light, Tom had gone out. I knew he'd gone to start work on the gardens. I hated thinking of him out there on his own in the cold, with no one to help him and everyone thinking he had done something wrong. I wonder if there are many worse feelings than people blaming you for something you haven't done. I thought perhaps I could spend my day helping Tom. I could pull up weeds as well as any gardener's boy.

I didn't want to dress up in Lady Hexer's fine clothes today. So I rooted under the bed and there were my old trousers and woollens, a little smellier and more ragged than I'd realised, but comfy once I had them on. Also, I decided, I could talk to Tom about getting away from here.

He wasn't too far away. He was working feverishly, trying to rip plants up from the ground. I couldn't believe my eyes when I saw how the greenery had sprouted in thick clumps over every visible patch of hard soil. This had happened in just a day, in what everyone said was one of the coldest weeks in living memory. But Tom wasn't doing very well. I could see that as he pulled the plants up, tiny tendrils were creeping up from the ground straight afterwards, like fingers. They seemed to be spreading thicker and faster than a man could pull them out, as if the earth was infected.

"Tom," I said, shivering, because my old clothes also weren't as warm as I'd remembered. "I don't think that is working."

Tom stood upright, his usually rosy face grey and sweating. He took some deep breaths.

"I think this is a waste of time. As fast as you pull up these plants, they take root again and go back to the earth."

He let out a sigh. "You're right. But I don't know what else to do. I have to put the garden right. Everyone thinks I've planted poisonous seeds."

"I want to help," I told him. "I think we need to go–"

But I didn't get any further. Tom's face brightened as he saw Lucy heading across the garden towards him. "Oh, my goodness," she said, staring around at the grounds. "So this is what everyone is talking about. All these weeds and things!"

Tom shrugged. "I don't even know if they are weeds," he began, but Lucy carried on.

"Although I don't see how they could have made Joe's wife and child sick."

I stared down at the hard, brown soil and poked at it with the end of my boot. If these plants are somehow linked to the old hospital, could they bring some kinds of sickness with them, I wondered. There was no point in trying to explain this to Tom or Lucy, but Lady Hexer might listen. If she still believed a word I said.

Lucy rubbed her eyes. She noticed me looking at her. "I didn't have a very good night. I share a room with Becky, you know, and she kept teasing me about the ghost. She thinks it's funny."

"I hate her," I said, clenching my hands into fists.

Lucy shook her head. "She was only fooling about. She's no idea how scared we were. She even made a silly fake ghost out of her white pinnies and waved it at me in the dark. I jumped out of my skin! I thought the ghostie-thing had followed me into my room."

I remembered something from the night before. "Was one of the pinnies covered in coal dust?" I asked.

Lucy frowned. "No, they were both very clean. Becky's a bit fussy about how she looks. She has a special old pinny she keeps just for cleaning out the grates."

I thought about this.

Hexer Hall
6th January, 1899 (Twelfth Day)

*After the disturbing events of last night, I am in a state
of great turmoil. I do not know who to believe, what is
true and what is invented, or why. I know I was hasty
in sending young Annie away for the night and I fear
she may have been very hurt. I cannot bring myself to
believe the child is false. I sent her to her brother more
for her own comfort and safety than anything else. Yet I
can hardly ignore what I saw; what we all saw. I know
Agatha Haggstone has her tricks, and I am sorry if she
resorted to these rather than talking to me more frankly.
But then she has constantly expressed her doubts,
and I also know she has an unmatched reputation for
communicating with the spirits. I do not know if I
would ever have recovered from my own losses without
her counsel.*

*I know Annie is a very clever child. Indeed, her
rebellious streak reminds me of myself as a girl. Agatha
has spotted how I have allowed myself to become quite
fond of her. She is not your Bella, she reminded me,
rather cruelly I thought. Nevertheless, I thought that
perhaps, when my need for Annie is done, I may pay
for her to go to a good school. But then what if she is
making up stories? What if she is even shrewder than
I imagined? Agatha seems to think so. I have worked*

with Agatha for years, preparing the Hall with all the right magical symbols for my purpose, and of course I have grown to put my total trust in her – so perhaps I should listen to her judgements, rather than my own more sentimental feelings.

Now a new element has come into play. This morning, Agatha came into the drawing room, followed by the maid Becky and another small girl. This girl, it turns out, is Becky's younger sister who has come to pay a visit. But, according to Agatha, it is this girl who may be my true envoy. She claims to fulfil everything in the prediction, including the lines about being neither a boy nor a girl. I especially asked about this part, as Annie, with her cropped hair and her boy's clothes, seemed to fit the part so well. Becky told me, with her usual perfect curtsey, that when Jeannie was a young child she couldn't say her name for a long time and called herself Jon. The whole family used this name and so people often thought the child was a boy, not a girl. But it is not Annie – Iannua. The opener of doors.

I looked at this tiny, trembling waif, with her wispy blonde hair, who was chewing her lower lip and blushing at being the centre of so much attention.

"Do you believe she will be able to...?" I asked Agatha. I couldn't finish the sentence as I wasn't sure how much Becky or her sister knew of our experiments.

"Indeed. She already has," Agatha told me. "Jeannie, tell Her Ladyship what happened to you on the staircase this morning."

Jeannie went pinker than ever. "I – went – to – an – old – hospital," she said. She has a voice as thin and flat as the plucking of a violin string. "I – saw – a – doctor. He – was – carrying – a – big – book."

I questioned her but she couldn't give me much detail, in spite of much prompting from Agatha and Becky.

"She is ever so shy, ma'am," Becky explained, and Agatha followed with: "It was a very brief experiment. We did not want to overwhelm the child on this first attempt. But it was successful, nevertheless. I feel this girl is the one you should proceed with. She is more trustworthy than the bald brat."

"Agatha." I must have said this rather sharply, for she raised her brows in response. I still feel desperately sorry for Annie's condition and I'm considering asking my own doctor to look at her hair.

But now I don't know which way to go. This fair-headed child does not ring true to me. Yet Annie seemed as true as the day – and she may be a liar. Inside myself, I am very fearful. I feel that everyone around me is speaking with forked tongues.

Lucy was staring at me, those round brown eyes even wider than usual. I almost felt guilty about what I was saying. Lucy is one of those kind-hearted people who thinks the best about everyone. I felt as if I was somehow dirtying her with my charges against Becky. But I had a fury racing through my blood like a poison. I could almost taste it, like

I'd eaten raw meat. Like I'd swallowed a dagger.

"I'm telling you, Lucy. Becky was working with the Haggstone woman. She was waving some old sheet around and pretending it was a ghost. That's why Mrs McKinnon couldn't find her. She claimed she was changing her pinny but she couldn't have been. It's all to get rid of me."

"But why would they want to do that?" asked Lucy, bewildered.

I shook my head. "I can't answer that," I said, still hot and red with temper. "But I know it's true. Haggstone has always wanted rid of me and Becky was her ideal helper. We need to let Lady Hexer know the whole thing was some sort of trick."

"I don't know what to think," Lucy said. "I don't want that ghost to be real. But I can't imagine Becky would be so wicked. Anyway, why didn't the men find her in Miss Haggstone's room? There was nothing that would point to a trick. I can't see how she would do it."

I thought about this for a few moments. "If I could get into her room..." I said, with Lucy shaking her head at me and saying, "Oh no, no, no."

"Just listen," I said. "If I could get into Haggstone's room and have a good look around, I'm sure I could find her out. Lucy, are there any times of the day when she's away from her room for a while?"

"Lunchtime, I suppose," Lucy admitted, without really wanting to. "She has a very good appetite and always gets through three courses. With second helpings, sometimes. But, no, really, you mustn't think of it. If she was to find you!

You would both be sent away, for sure. You and Tom." She looked wistfully over to Tom, who was still furiously hacking and dragging at the greenery, barely noticing us any more.

I had to do it. I knew it was a terrible risk. If I was discovered – well, so be it. I headed back to the cottage where I changed into my maid's dress and made my best attempt at putting on the cap. Lady Hexer hadn't forbidden me from going back to work, after all. This seemed to be the best way of being able to wander around the house without having to answer any questions. When I told Tom I was going to work in the kitchen, he barely seemed to hear me. I put a hand on his sweating shoulder for a moment but he shook it away and continued pulling up plants.

I made my way across the gardens. The air was so thick with cold, I couldn't even smell the sea. I kept my breaths small so I didn't take too much of this bitter cold inside my body. The spiral-shaped hedges were still white with frost and looked more like twisted bones than shrubs. The sky was grey-white as an old bandage, covering whatever ailing sun there may have been up there. I couldn't see a single patch of real brightness.

There was a door that led straight onto the back stairs without going through the kitchen. I could smell the lunch cooking. It gave me a sharp hunger pain deep in my stomach. I could hear the bustle and clatter from behind the kitchen door. I heard one of the Hall's clocks strike noon. I'd timed it just right. I crept up the stairs and along the quiet, chilly hallway. I listened at Haggstone's bedroom door for a moment, then carefully turned the handle. The door was locked! I cursed under my breath and slipped back down the stairs into the busy kitchen. Mrs McKinnon – red in the face, because the kitchen was so warm and steamy – looked surprised to see me, but not angry. In fact, when I told her I thought I ought to earn my keep today, she seemed quite pleased and said I was a good girl. She set me to stirring a vat of creamy sauce meant for a fruit pie, while she took a tureen of soup up the stairs. Lucy and I were alone.

"Lucy," I hissed. "Haggstone's door is locked. Who would have a key?"

Lucy's eyes popped. "Oh, no. This is getting worse. You mustn't think of going into her room if it's locked. It will truly look as if you are – I don't know – stealing or something. Forget this idea. Please."

"Do you have a key?" I demanded. She shook her head determinedly.

"Becky, then," I suggested. I knew Becky cleaned the bedrooms, as a rule. Lucy said nothing.

"Where does she keep them?" I asked. "Does she keep her keys with her?"

"I mustn't say," said Lucy, looking tearful. "You'll only get yourself into deep trouble. I can't help you do that."

I glared around the room. I felt like a mad, angry animal and I wouldn't be stopped. I spotted a set of large hooks on the side of a wooden dresser. A bunch of keys hung from it. I turned back to Lucy and knew, just from the look on her face, they were the ones I needed. It was lucky Lucy was such an open book, I thought.

147

I didn't have as much time left as I'd hoped, so I ran over to the keys and snatched them all before Lucy could stop me.

"Tell Mrs McKinnon that I felt unwell," I said, pulling my arm away from Lucy as she tried to hold me back.

Back up the servants' stairs and along the hallway. All was still quiet. It took me a few tries, but I found a key that turned in Haggstone's lock and I went inside, closing the door quietly behind me and locking it from the inside.

The sickly smell from last night still hung around, just faintly. I stared around the room. It was much grander than the room Lady Hexer had given me. It gave me an uneasy feeling. I think it was a mixture of fears: what if that ghost had been real? What if it jumped out at me? I'd be in such trouble if I was caught. Not much of the grey daylight came in through the windows, which had heavy, embroidered drapes in deep green and gold. There was a large, carved wardrobe in a dark wood, the writing desk and of course Haggstone's chair. In the corner was an ornate vase with some dried flowers in it, the penny-shaped ones.

Honesty plants, I thought. About the only kind of honesty I would find around that old fraud.

The problem was, I wasn't sure what I was looking for. Like the men last night, I turned over papers and ornaments, pointlessly, finding nothing. I opened the wardrobe – it made a terrible creak – and put my hands inside, feeling around. I couldn't find anything other than Haggstone's old shawls and a couple of dresses. I took a deep breath, trying to think straight in spite of the way

I was trembling. What had happened that couldn't be explained – and how could I find a way of explaining it?

The desk, for one thing. It had rocked backwards and forwards, as if someone was pushing it, but all on its own. I bent down and inspected it closely. That's when I found some fine black wires, thin as silk threads, tied around the legs. I let out a "ha!" before I could stop myself. I gathered them up. They were strong and wouldn't be snapped, so I had to lift the desk legs one by one and slip the wires off, into the pocket of my pinny.

Then there was the terrible wailing ghost girl and the way she had disappeared into nothing. I was sure, if I looked hard enough, I would find some raggy old sheets that had helped play the part of old Jenny. If I could find out how Becky had helped with the trick, all the better. I spotted a large carpet bag and was about to open it when I heard a rustling outside the door. Someone put a key in the lock and it began turning with a click that shot fear straight through me. I darted for the wardrobe and jumped inside, pulling its door almost closed just as the bedroom door opened. Then I sat in the dark, shivering, as Haggstone's heavy tread made its way across the carpet. If she'd spotted my movement, she'd be on me like a cat on a baby bird.

She was definitely heading for the wardrobe. I was aware of her shadow just outside it. But then she pushed the wardrobe door fully shut, with a smart clack. Oh Lord, I thought, I'm not sure if I can get out again, now that it's properly closed. Then I heard her chair creak gently as she lowered her great backside onto it and sighed. Full of Lady Hexer's food, I thought, calling her a rude name in my head that I won't repeat. But I will not pretend I was feeling brave at this point. I could barely breathe for fear. What if she decided to have a nap? I'd be stuck inside the wardrobe for hours. I'd be missed shortly and so would all the keys. I heard Haggstone give another satisfied grunt and creakily settle further into the chair. She *is* going to sleep, I thought, with a silent groan. I'm stuck.

Then there was a tap on the bedroom door. Haggstone coughed and said crossly, "Come in."

I heard Becky's voice. "Ma'am, I thought you ought to know. Some of the keys have gone missing from the kitchen. The key for this room was among them. Mrs McKinnon is looking for them now, but I can't help thinking that the patch-head has got them. She might be planning to come in here and, well, look around."

"Really?" Haggstone sounded interested. "The bold child. Well, if she comes in here she'll be very sorry. I'll have her in the courts for thieving. That'll get rid of her altogether. How's your young sister?"

"Jeannie's still very afraid, Miss Haggstone. I've told her that all she needs to do is play some pretending games and say what you tell her. But perhaps you could teach her some more? She finds all this stuff about the old hospital very hard. She's only seven, ma'am."

I listened to this with my mouth open, my breathing as shallow and silent as I could make it. What was this? Becky's sister was taking my place, just as Becky had always wanted. And Haggstone was feeding her the stories about the hospital. For a moment, I forgot how angry I was with Lady Hexer. In fact, I almost felt sorry for her. She was being conned by this smelly old trickster. And spiteful Becky was in on the plan. I struggled to stay still and silent, the heavy keys ready to clink and give me away at my slightest twitch.

"Yes, yes, girl, we will go through the story again in the morning," Haggstone rumbled on. "She needs to remember to keep talking about the book. Lady Hexer is desperate to get her hands on an old book of medicines. If she thinks your sister will get it for her, then Her Ladyship will keep going along with it all.

"We need each other, Becky. You want to have your sister stay here with you. And I want to stay here too. Lady Hexer's generosity has become very important to me. Vital, you might say. I have given up all my other card readings and psychic work for her. I can't afford to lose my place with her."

"Why do you imagine Lady Hexer is so taken with the Cotterill girl, Miss Haggstone?"

Haggstone gave a throaty sigh. "I played some part in that. I read some of the history of Lady Hexer's family and found the long-forgotten prediction that they would become great healers, thanks to a special child. I passed it all off as my own, but I didn't expect that little brat to turn up and fit the picture quite so perfectly."

I heard her make a slurping sound and a cup clinked gently.

"So is there really a book of cures? I thought it was all a trick," Becky said.

"Why, it was, at the beginning. I rather gambled on leading Lady Hexer by the nose – and the purse – for some years to come. No one is more surprised than I am, to see it all coming true."

She paused. "A word of this to anyone, mind you, and you will be dismissed, I will make sure of it. Let's stay on the same side and we will both be secure. What have you done with the gown?"

"It's safely under my bed, for the moment, ma'am," Becky answered. "There's to be a bonfire this afternoon, to burn the holly and ivy now that it's Twelfth Day. I'll wrap the cloth up in some rags and drop it on there. No one will think anything about it."

"Good," said Haggstone. "You're a smart one." She took another loud gulp of her drink.

"Well, Miss Haggstone. Now that you know to be on your guard..."

"Yes, girl, thank you for that."

There was a pause. Then I heard Haggstone clink a coin onto the desk and add, grumpily, "There you are. As if I haven't given you enough already, for all your useful gossip."

"Thank you, ma'am," Becky replied, more brightly. I heard her leave. Then – oh, thank heavens! – the chair creaked again and it sounded as if Haggstone was getting up. I waited for the click of her key in the lock. Then I breathed out hard – there wasn't much air in this wardrobe – and moved my stiff legs from their painful, crouching position. I leaned on the side of the wardrobe with my hand, which was damp with sweat, but it slipped along the inside of the wood. I almost fell – and part of the wardrobe back folded inwards. With a gasp, I examined it. A slender girl, such as myself, or indeed Becky, could easily slip in or out of the wardrobe this secret way and hide behind it. That, I knew, was how the ghost girl had disappeared so quickly. The men had looked inside the wardrobe. But not behind it.

I hurtled down the back stairs, clutching the bundle of keys tightly to stop their jangling, and almost ran right into Lucy.

"There you are! I've been so worried," she gasped. "Mrs McKinnon is having a fit about the missing keys. Give them to me and I'll slip them down behind the dresser and make out they just got knocked down. Run off back home, pet, before anyone spots you in here."

Quickly, I handed her the keys and she put them in her apron.

"Lucy, I need to go to your room now," I told her. "Don't ask why. Just tell me where it is."

Lucy pointed further up the back staircase. "Right at the very top, at the end of the passageway," she said. "But... "

I waved at her and ran up the chilly back stone steps that led to the very top of the house. The stairs seemed to keep going for ever. I pushed open the uneven door to the maids' tiny quarters. There were just two small beds and a wooden shelf with a washing bowl and water jug. The floorboards were almost bare, apart from a rag-rug. Under each bed was a bag. I pulled one out and rifled through it quickly, before deciding the few things in there probably belonged to Lucy. But then I put my hand in the bag under the second bed and pulled out a dirty, yellow-white cloth. It had the same stink as Haggstone's room.

Something fell out of the cloth and clattered to the floor, making me jump. It was a kind of plaster mask, very badly made, with black holes for eyes, a bulbous nose and a gash of a mouth. I stared at it. This must have been under the cloth, forming the fake ghost's face. It was quite a scary-looking object, though, so I bundled it back into the cloth and ran back down the stairs. I had my proof and I couldn't wait to show it off.

Chapter Ten

I panted along the hallway and burst through the doors of Lady Hexer's drawing room. She turned with a jump as I ran in and she did not look pleased.

"Lady Hexer!" I gasped. "Lady Hexer! I'm sorry to run in like this but it's important. I've found it out. That ghost girl was a fake. Miss Haggstone set up the whole thing and Becky helped her." Lady Hexer stood up as I waved the shroud-like cloth and the mask as if they were trophies.

I don't know exactly what I expected her to say. I hadn't really thought too far ahead. But I did expect she'd be pleased. Pleased that I was not a liar. Pleased, for goodness' sake, that there was no real ghost girl haunting her house. Pleased that I had shown her how clever I was, like she'd always said. "Quite the detective," she'd called me once. But she didn't look at all pleased. If anything, she looked absolutely furious.

"How *dare* you," she shouted at me. "How dare you come running into my room as if you belonged here? How dare you raise your voice to me and make accusations about my trusted friends and staff?"

"But–" I began.

"Don't interrupt me! You are making the situation much worse for yourself. I shouldn't even listen to you. Miss Haggstone warned me you would try to talk your way back in here. But I will give you one chance – a chance to explain yourself – and then you will go. I am in no mood for this today."

Lady Hexer glared at me. Her eyes, when she was angry, held a terrifying light. It came to me, suddenly, that she didn't want to hear bad things about Haggstone. Haggstone had been her friend for a long time and knew all her secrets. If Haggstone was a fraud, Lady Hexer didn't really want to believe it. If she was caught out trying to trick Lady Hexer over the séance, what else might she have lied about? I stared at my feet for a moment. Then I thought, I'd gone so far already I might as well say what I had come to say. Even if I knew it wouldn't be welcome.

I started by telling her about Becky and the pinny and how I'd realised that she must have been involved. Lady Hexer sighed and raised her eyes. Somehow, as it came out, it sounded like a silly quarrel between two young maids. Then I told her how I had been into Haggstone's room. She looked horrified.

"You stole keys and entered a room without–" she began.

"I hid in the wardrobe," I cut in. "I heard Miss Haggstone and Becky say they were going to teach Jeannie what to say, in order to fool you. Jeannie is only saying what Miss Haggstone tells her to say. I heard Becky say she'd hidden the cloth from the séance under her bed. She plans to burn it on the bonfire this afternoon." I held out the black threads and the smelly cloth and the mask. "Then I found out that the wardrobe has a secret panel and..."

"I think I have heard enough," said Lady Hexer, with a sigh. "You must think I am very gullible–"

"I don't even know what that means," I blurted out.

"I mean, you may think I am easy to fool," Lady Hexer went on. "Perhaps I have been. I like you. I thought we understood each other. But Becky has worked for me for several years and I have trusted Miss Haggstone with my most important secrets. I simply do not know who or what to believe."

"But what about all this?" I asked, helplessly holding out my prizes.

Lady Hexer shook her head. "You say you found these things in Miss Haggstone's and Becky's rooms. But Miss Haggstone will say, of course, that you're lying. You could have got these objects anywhere. And it is a child's trick to slide the back panel of a wardrobe. I did it myself as a girl, many a time. I can no longer take what anyone says on trust."

I felt my face burning. How is it that people can make you feel ashamed of something you haven't done?

"What about all the plants in the garden?" I asked. "You said you thought they were growing because we'd made a link with the past."

"I know your brother is capable of doing wonders with plants. Perhaps he is helping you," Lady Hexer said, although she sounded less sure about that.

"Very well," I said, "you don't want me to go back to the hospital any more. You don't want me to find the book of cures. Even though I know exactly where it is."

Lady Hexer paused for a long moment. Then she said, "But I am also promised that young Jeannie can get it for me."

"All right, then," I said, a sudden bright idea dropping into my head. "Why don't you see which one of us brings the book back first? I bet I can get it before Jeannie does." Because Jeannie is a fibber and she can no more travel back in time than she can fly up to the moon, I thought. Now I can prove myself.

Lady Hexer thought this over. After a minute or two, she said, "Now then. I still don't know whether to trust you or not. But I don't know whether to trust Jeannie either and I rather like your challenge. I will give you one week. Seven days. No more. If you haven't brought me that book by then, I will ask you to leave. Tom, too, I am afraid. The trouble in the garden is causing a lot of unrest among my staff."

It was decided that I would move back into the Hall while this last part of the experiment took place. Lady Hexer knew I needed looking after while I was back in the old hospital, because my body looked as if it was in a deep sleep or a faint. She promised no harm would come to me during these times. She also told Haggstone and Becky about the plan, after calling them both to the drawing room. It was almost worth all the trouble just to see Becky's face when she saw the old cloth and the mask. But Lady Hexer didn't say anything about them, other than to ask Becky to put them on the bonfire outside.

I could tell Haggstone was angrier than ever. When she heard that her new girl had just one week to bring back the book of cures, she was stumped for words. This was another moment I enjoyed more than a big slice of sponge cake. But of course, she couldn't really argue about it. As for the looks I had from Haggstone and Becky – well. Let's just say it's a good job you can't be wounded by the way someone glares at you.

The last thing I did today was go to tell Tom that I was going back to the Hall. I went with Lucy and we took him some supper from the kitchen. He was sitting at our table, his face grey and dirt-lined. He was so tired he could barely speak to us. My news cheered him up a little, though.

"So Lady Hexer isn't angry with you any more? That's wonderful. She hasn't realised what a bad goblin you really are," he said with a faint smile. "I thought we might be sent away and..." then he gave a long sigh that tore at my heart, "I couldn't bear it. Not to lose this job. Our home. And..." he glanced at Lucy, but didn't finish his sentence.

Lucy gave him a smile that was full of comfort. She was just a young girl but I could easily imagine her as a mother, all softness, cuddling and stroking a lapful of babies, soothing them with the music of her voice. She was worried for Tom, I knew, and I loved her for that. She told me, after I pressed her, that he'd had one or two short blackouts and woken up sweating and telling crazy stories. For a moment I wondered ... but then I thought that was daft. It was my own wishful thinking, my own longing for someone I could really trust to share my magical journeys.

I went back to my room at Hexer Hall, where just a day or two ago I'd thought myself so grand. Lady Hexer came in to see me, for a few moments. She had something for me, a small square shape wrapped in a white cloth. When I opened it, I saw she'd brought me one of the snake-patterned tiles from the drawing-room hearth.

"I have had this one taken out for you. If you have been telling the truth, this is your key to my past," Lady Hexer told me. She spoke in a clipped, formal way, her words snipping at me like shears. As if she couldn't bear to be friendly with me again, in case I let her down. "You can stay in this room for seven days and nights. No one will come into the room except for me. I will bring in your meals and make sure you are well. In that time, if you are able, you will go back to my ancestor's hospital and retrieve the book.

"If you get it, you will be rewarded. Whatever you ask for, I will give it to you, and I do keep my promises. If you fail, however, you will leave here and never return. Tom will go with you. Now – this is very important. You will tell no one what happened here. If you do, I will personally see to it that you are sent to a lunatic asylum and you will never come out. Tom will never find work again. Do you understand?"

"Of course," I replied, as sulkily as I dared. "But none of that will happen, because I'm telling the truth. What will you do to Becky and Jeannie if I bring you what you want and they turn out to be the liars?"

"That's my business," Her Ladyship snapped, turning away from me with a swish of her skirts and firmly closing the bedroom door behind her.

I felt very alone and suddenly I started to worry that I'd boasted too much. What if, for some reason, I couldn't get back to the leper hospital? Even if I did, what if I couldn't get near the book? That doctor trusted me less than his own snakes. Even Meg, my only friend there, was none too sure about me. As for those hideous serpent-creatures, whatever they were, I couldn't even picture them in my mind without feeling sick to my stomach. But I was going to have to brave them somehow. For my good name. For Tom. For Lucy.

I had the bright idea that I would eat the supper left for me and get a good night's sleep before I tackled what would be one of the hardest journeys I've ever made. But instead I found I had no appetite for food and I hardly slept. In the icy black of the early morning, I decided to dress and try to get back to the hospital there and then. No sense in putting it off any longer. I put on my favourite blue dress with its warm velvet trim and the soft blue headscarf. Then I sat on the bed and with cold, shaking fingers I unwrapped the snake tile from its cloth cover and began tracing my finger around its coils.

I ended up not far from my usual spot in the stone corridor, looking directly at the archway that led to Huksor's study. Agnes shuffled past, carrying a pile of the rough bed sheets in her pudgy arms. She jumped when she saw me.

"Where did you come from?" she asked, sounding cross. "You gave me a fright, creeping up like that."

"I'm sorry," I said, and gave her a half-smile.

She leaned down and looked into my face. "I don't know," she said. "No one can tell me anything about you. No one knows of your family or where you're from. Not even Meg, and you're great friends, or so it seems."

"I'm from a long way away," I said, and hoped I sounded truthful.

Agnes walked away, clicking her tongue and shaking her head.

It was darker than usual and I could see through one of the slit-like windows that it was snowing heavily outside. I peeked through the narrow gap, blinking at the cold draught that jabbed my eyes and made me blink. In the courtyard Huksor was ordering a servant of some kind to load two large, long-ish, cloth bundles onto a wooden cart. The snow made it difficult to see properly. I watched as the man did as he was told and trundled the cart away towards the gates. Huksor turned back towards the hospital door.

The archway itself looked even more scary than usual. It felt like I was about to walk into an open mouth. I heard hoarse groaning somewhere behind me – the very sick patients, I knew. Something, I don't know what, made me walk towards the sounds. I turned into the small room where I'd first seen the poor woman on the bare bed, with her blemished face and her deformed hands, reaching out for help. The room smelled bad – like the sourest breath you can imagine. There were two women in the room this time, both lying on their beds, both moaning, but softly, as if it hurt them to do it. One was barely awake. The other turned towards me as I came in.

I walked up to the bed and looked down at her. She was hard to look at, but, thinking about what Meg had said, that the patients needed people to care about them, I made myself do it. "Hello," I said, as gently as I could. "Is there anything I can get for you?"

Her face was covered in red-blue swellings. Her hands and feet were blown up and fat. She seemed to find it too hard to breathe through her nose, which was covered in sores, and she could only manage short gasps through her mouth. Her voice, when it came, was thin and rough, like a tuneless pipe. "Please," she rasped out. "Please. No more snake. Not the snake."

My skin prickled and I glanced around the room. I couldn't see the beast anywhere, thankfully. I frowned at her. "What happened with the snake?"

She moaned again and shook her head. Her hood fell back against the bed, revealing an almost bald scalp covered in shrivelled skin. She had no eyebrows or lashes either, I noticed. Her scaled skin reminded me of a fairy tale I'd once read with pictures of an evil wood sprite, its limbs made out of tree bark. The illness had turned her into something that hardly looked human. In spite of this, I had an urge to stroke her. I'm sure no one has touched her kindly for a long time, I thought.

"Tell me what happened with the snake?" I asked again.

"I– I– could not– I couldn't eat it," she groaned. "Doctor Huksor said it would cure me, but I couldn't eat it. It made me more sick. Please, no more snake," she moaned again, more to herself than to me.

"You had to eat snake?" The thought made me gag.

I spotted a drinking pot on the floor nearby. I handed it to her but she wasn't able to drink, instead spilling most of it down her chin.

I could see there wasn't much I could do for her. I turned to leave the room. The second patient gave a rasping whisper that was too quiet to hear. I turned back. "Pardon me?"

"The cures are making her worse," she whispered. I walked over to her bed to hear her better. She had some of the same disfigurements as the first woman and in her eyes – which were red, crusted and swollen – I could see absolute terror.

"The cures," she breathed, her voice barely more than the rustle of dead leaves. "She is my sister. We came here to be cured. Our families have paid out all their money to the doctor, but she is worse and worse."

I had to hand her the water cup before she was able to speak again, but she too had trouble getting the water past her swollen lips.

"Snake meat. Snake hearts still beating. Snake ... I'm not sure, milk? Other cures. Herbs from foreign lands and flesh from unknowable animals. We have tried them all. Doctor Huksor says they will make us better, but we are both getting worse."

Her sore eyes brimmed over and I swallowed hard. I almost always cry when someone else does, I can't help it.

"My sister is plagued by terrible nightmares and visions. I am afraid she will soon die, little girl. And I will follow her to the grave." Now she began to sob, painfully.

"I am so sorry. I don't know what to do. Is there anything I can get you?"

She shook her head and waved me away with her arm. Hopeless and helpless, I went back to the narrow window to suck in some cold, fresh air. Then I made myself walk through the dark archway and turn into the doctor's study, which, to my relief, was warm from the big fire roaring in his hearth. I guessed he would be back there by now, and I was right.

Huksor looked up when he saw me and raised his woolly brows. "Ah," he said. "The return of our ghost girl."

"I'm not a ghost girl," I said, thinking of Haggstone and her silly fluttering sheets. "You're more dead than I am, truth be told."

He placed a rough finger on my hand and laughed.

165

"Cold as the grave," he said. "Go and stand by that fire, you cheeky imp. Let's see if you warm up."

I noticed him watching me carefully as I stood in front of the sputtering flames. "You won't be able to see through me, if that's what you think."

He laughed again. "Able to know my thoughts too. What a singular child you are."

"Listen to me," I said. "I know you think I'm just a young girl who couldn't possibly know anything. But let me tell you how I can appear and disappear. I come from the future. From hundreds of years in the future. I've come back here because I need your help."

He narrowed his eyes at me. "Why should I believe that lunatic's tale?"

"Because it's true," I shrugged. "Look at my clothes. Have you ever seen anything like them? Listen to the way I talk. It's English, but nothing like your kind of language."

He sat up. "It's true I have to work to understand you, even though I speak many languages. What time do you say you come from?" he asked, slowly.

"I come from the year 1899," I told him. His bushy brows rose higher.

"Where this hospital is now, there is a great big house in my time. It belongs to a Lady Hexer. She knows about you and your work and she wants to carry it on. She needs–"

Huksor held up his hand. "Slow your speech. Remember your words sound other-worldly to me. I want to ask more questions about this future time. Tell me about life in Scotland in 1899."

"England," I told him. "Near to Scotland, but still England."

"Ah, well," he looked almost pleased. "You have come from the wrong place. This is most definitely part of Scotland."

I scoured my brain, trying to remember the scraps of history I'd been taught.

"Oh," I said. "This part of the country belongs to England now. I think it has done for a few hundred years. I'm not sure, though. I've never had much schooling in history."

"England?" Huksor spluttered. He used a word to describe the English which for decency's sake I won't repeat.

"Never mind that," I went on. "We live very differently to you. The food's better, for one thing."

"And girls learn as much as boys," he muttered, as if that was almost as bad as his village being taken over by the English.

"Some do," I said. "Not all of them. But many girls and boys do go to school."

"Is it quite usual," Huksor asked, stroking his chin, "for people to be able to go back and forwards through the years, in the same way they might travel on a boat or a horse and cart?"

I hesitated. "Well, no. That's very unusual. Magical, in fact. Not everyone can do it. But I can."

When I said this last part, something warm bloomed inside me and I felt a sudden sense of pride in this special gift of mine.

"But," I'd thought through this part in my head, because I hoped it might get me into his favour. "But the one science that hasn't moved on very much is medicine. There are still lots of terrible diseases in the world and no one knows how to cure them. That's why Lady Hexer, who is part of your family– I mean, who will be part of your family, wants me to speak to you. She sent me here. She needs your cures so she can pass them on to doctors now, I mean, then– I mean, in 1899."

"Ah," said Huksor, leaning back in his chair. "Now that's the bit that makes me wonder about you. You tell a very good story, girl. But you're not the only one who'd like to get their hands on my work. You could be anyone's spy. I'm not about to hand over my findings to you."

"I understand that. At least just tell me a bit about it," I said, "and I could tell Lady Hexer when I go back. You would be doing great work for people in years to come."

Doctor Huksor looked at me, flint in his eyes. "I'll tell you what," he said, at last. "You stay here for a few days and let me watch you carefully. No disappearing this time. Let me ask you questions as I think of them, about the future that you say you're from. If you convince me that your wild story is true, then perhaps I will think about sharing some of my secrets with you."

His eyes darted briefly over to a heavy wooden desk, where a huge book sat next to a pot of ink and a pen made of a bird's feather. So that was the book of cures, I guessed. Next to it was something shaped like a pot, but covered in a cloth. And curled fast around the book, apparently asleep – how had I not spotted the creature before? – was Melusina, the serpent. I swallowed.

At that moment the study door opened and Meg burst in.

"The players are back!" she squeaked. "I can hear them coming!" She caught sight of me. "Oh," she said. I could tell she wasn't sure whether to be pleased to see me or not.

Huksor stood up. "Annie is to stay with us now," he announced. "No more flying off into nowhere, eh? So now I have two young helpers again."

Meg gave me a small smile. I know she thought I was pushing into her special place. But she also liked me, I hoped. There were no other young girls for her to talk to.

"May we go and listen to the musicians, sir?" she asked the doctor. He nodded, keen, I guessed, to hide his book away before I came back. As I followed Meg, I glanced back and saw him make straight for the covered pot. I wondered what was so special about that.

Out we went into the empty courtyard. Meg was right. I could hear the sounds of the drums and pipes, faint but getting louder. The whirling snow made it impossible to see the players.

Meg clapped her hands. "Twice in a few days, and in this foul weather too! They almost never come to us. Usually it's only at special times."

"So today isn't anything special?" I asked her, shivering hard. "Not a feast day or anything?"

Meg shook her head, watching as the band of musicians gathered outside the gates. I was pleased to see the handsome young piper lad from last time. His mouth turned up in a sideways grin. "The blue lady," he said, with a very dashing low bow.

"Never mind the blue lady," yelled Meg. "Play a dance! Let's get warmed up!"

So they blew and bashed their way through more merry tunes. None of the patients braved the snow, but I guessed they could hear the music from inside and I hoped it gave them a tiny moment of happiness. Meg and I had great fun again, although it was a slippery job to try to dance on the snowy cobbles and the players kept breaking off to laugh. We got warmer though and my face got pinker each time I caught the piper lad's eye.

After a while, Doctor Huksor came out and offered the players some coins, holding them out through the gates. They shook their heads and muttered about charity again. But the dark-haired young man beckoned me over to the gates.

"Miss Annie," he said. "I have thought of you many times since I saw you last. Tell me – why are you here in this place? Do you suffer from this dreaded disease?"

"No," I said. "Certainly not. I'm helping the doctor here."

He looked puzzled. "But aren't you afraid that you might catch the leprosy?"

I shook my head. "Someone has to take care of them," I said, glad that Meg didn't hear me pinching her words. I noticed her watching. She picked her way across the slushy cobbles towards us.

"Now, what's this?" she asked, an impish look on her face. "Don't come too close, mister. We're all diseased, remember."

"Not me," I burst out.

"Yes, definitely you," said Meg, shaking her head at me.

The young man looked from me to Meg and back again. I could see he didn't know what to think.

"You sound like a noble young lady," he said, with a slight bow of the head. "I thought, with your way of speaking, that you could be from over the sea. Tell me, Miss Annie, do you read letters?"

"Of course I do," I replied.

"I thought so," said the young man, with a smile. "Then this is the right gift for you."

He pulled out a small roll of yellowish parchment from a pocket and handed it to me, through the gate.

"For you," he said, with a nod of his head. The group turned away and continued playing as they faded like spirits into the heavy snow.

"So what's that?" demanded Meg, trying to take the paper from me.

"I don't know," I said, pulling it out of her reach.

"Is it a love letter?" She poked me and grinned.

"Don't be so silly," I said, cross with myself for blushing again. I unfurled it and found it was written out like a poem. It was very hard to read the writing – even harder than trying to work out what people were saying in this old language. But it was something, I thought, picking out some of the letters, about a lady in blue. Still hot in the face, I rolled it up again and slipped it into the pocket of my dress, batting down Meg's attempts to take it from me.

As we made our way back, the cart I'd seen earlier came rattling back into the courtyard. It was empty.

"I saw that go out earlier," I told Meg. "There were long bundles of cloth on it. Do you know what they were?"

Meg looked away and frowned. "Well, what do you think?" she said.

"I don't know, that's why I'm asking," I grumped back at her. She could be so annoying at times. Meg stopped and sighed.

"Two patients died last night," she said, looking down at the ground. The snow had soaked her thin boots.

"You mean, they were bodies?"

Meg shrugged. "It's a leper hospital. People die. We can't keep the bodies here to rot."

"So where do they go?" I asked. "To church, to get buried?"

Meg paused then said, "Not exactly."

"Go on," I urged her.

"They take the bodies down to the sea," she said. "It's the easiest way to get rid of them."

"They throw the dead bodies into the sea?" I repeated. "But that's horrible."

"It's only when there are a few too many deaths," Meg says. "Doctor Huksor doesn't want the monks coming around and asking questions. We say prayers for them but we don't send them all to get buried in the churchyards.

Doctor Huksor says we have to keep some of the deaths a secret. Or they might say he is not doing his work as he should. They might close the hospital down."

What a terrible way to end your days, I thought to myself, as we headed back towards the doctor's study. Thrown out to sea like a bundle of old rubbish. I wanted to ask: is that where your father ended up, Meg? But some questions are better left unasked.

Huksor was in a good temper. He kept firing questions at me, all about life in the year 1899. Which king is on the throne, he wanted to know. He laughed in disbelief when I told him it is a queen. Who is the lord of the lands hereabouts? A lady, I told him, grinning at his face. He found it only just easier to swallow when I told him again that Lady Hexer was one of his own later family.

"It seems to me," he said, half-laughing, half-annoyed, "that you ladies have taken over the position of men."

"Well, hardly," I said. "It seems to me there's quite a lot we're not allowed to do." This was an idea that would never have entered my head before I'd come to Hexer Hall. But it was the sort of thing Lady Hexer often said and she'd read an awful lot of books.

Doctor Huksor pretended to cuff me around the head. He let Meg and me sit in his warm study and share his supper. I thought how dull the chunks of bread and salty meat seemed, after the meals at Hexer Hall, with their sauces and cakes and puddings.

He told me how Meg's father had been a brave and well-respected knight before he caught his illness.

"I promised him I would let young Meg stay here until she grew old enough to marry. It was a sad day when he finally died. But he left me his money, to help me carry on my work. This disease is running throughout the land like a wild animal and no one dares try to fight it. My work is more important than you can imagine."

"So why do you keep it secret?" I asked, placing my hand on Meg's knee as she wiped away a tear. "Why don't you let other people – other doctors – help you?"

Huksor finished a mouthful of bread. "My work is very new. I try out experiments that others daren't. If some of those high up in the parish knew about parts of my work – well, I may be stopped. Worse, I may be condemned for witchcraft. I need to be sure of success before the world gets to know about it."

I noticed that once or twice his gaze slid towards the jars and pots on his desk. Then it slipped quickly back again, as if he didn't want me to notice. I paused for a moment because I didn't want to get Huksor angry, but I knew I had to ask.

"Is it working?" I said, very carefully. "Have you made anyone recover yet?"

The doctor's head snapped up and he glared at me. "What are you suggesting?"

"Nothing." I held up my hands.

Huksor rounded on Meg. "What have you been telling her?" he growled, leaning towards her.

She shrank back. "Nothing, nothing," she cried. "I haven't told her anything, sir."

He sat back down. "There have been one or two ... unfortunate mistakes." His voice was gruff and guarded. "But, the deaths – well. The unfortunates would have died anyway. The people in here are sick in a way that means they can't get better. Why shouldn't I try out my cures on them? They may work, given time. If not – what harm? These people are already doomed."

There was a moment of silence as we thought about this. Then there was a dry slithering sound, so quiet it was almost impossible to hear. Melusina made her way down from the table and across the stone floor. I gave a yelp and jumped. I pulled my knees and skirt up on the chair away from the ground, sitting as far back as I could. It didn't seem to matter how many times I came across the beast, I never felt anything less than sheer terror. She slid up to Huksor's lap, curled up and sat there like a kitten. Huksor gave a horrible smile when he saw my face.

"This is your weakness, isn't it, Miss Clever-talk? Melusina makes you too afraid to move. No doubt her mother, the noble Bess, does the same. I'll remember that. Wherever my secrets are kept, remember this: Melusina will be there too. If you try to steal my work, then Melusina will find you, I promise you that. She will follow you wherever you go. Yes, even back to the year 1899, if that is truly where you are from."

"Forward," I couldn't help answering back.

Huksor glared at me again. "What?"

"I think it must be forward to 1899, not back."

He gave a snort. Then he wound the great snake around

175

his shoulders and strode out of the room – to check on some of the patients, Meg said.

"You shouldn't get him angry," she told me, now we were alone. "He frightens me when he is like that."

"Well, he shouldn't," I said. "You're just a young girl and he's supposed to be your better. He oughtn't to bully you."

"It's because he thinks I've been telling you things I shouldn't," she said. "It's not fair."

"Even so," I said. "He shouldn't shout at you and scare you. You should leave."

She shrugged. "I've told you. No one else will want me, not when I've been around lepers for so long. Who would take care of me, out there?"

"Meg," I said. "I spoke to some of the patients. They don't like being used to try cures out, not horrible things like eating snake meat. They're scared of Doctor Huksor. It's not fair, because they're too ill to stand up for themselves. Is that why the two patients died? Because of these mad medicines?"

"No!" Meg insisted. "They died of the disease. They just– p'raps–" She stopped and bit her lip.

"What, Meg?" I asked her, urgently. "Tell me. I won't say anything."

"I was going to say," Meg went on, "that maybe their deaths came quicker than they ought to have done. But that's probably a blessing. They were in awful pain."

I stared into the fire, where the flames danced crazily to the snapping sound of the wood.

The evening dragged on. It was Meg's turn to ask me lots of questions. She was disappointed to find I was just a maid and that I didn't have a big house of my own. She fingered my dress with a look of longing.

"Is this how servants dress in your time?" she asked.

"No," I smiled. "If only that were true. Lots of us are very poor – no money for fine clothes, I'm afraid. I only have this dress because I'm doing this special job for Lady Hexer. I think once I've given her what she wants, I'll be back wearing my old rags again, like Cinderella after the ball."

"Like who?" said Meg. I tried telling her the fairy tale, but she said it was stupid.

It got very late. Meg said we ought to get some sleep, because we'd be up early in the morning to work. Because it was so cold, she said, we could sleep in the room next to the study, which was always kept warm with its huge fire.

"The monsters' room?" I said. "No thanks, I'll stay in here. It's bad enough knowing all those horrid beasts are just next door."

But Meg said we weren't allowed to sleep in the study itself. The doctor's most important items were there. Faced with a choice of bitter cold or a room full of serpents and all those other freakish creatures, it wasn't hard for me to decide. I took a candle and made my way alone along the pitch-black passageway. I peeked into the stinking room where the women lay, but from the sound of their breathing they seemed to be resting. I surprised myself when I managed to find Meg's tiny cell. I wrapped myself in her itchy blanket and tried to get some sleep. I couldn't relax, of course. Every sound – the crying and moaning, the wind sighing through draughty gaps in the stones – made me sit up, alert. In the end, I decided to make my way back to the study and, if Huksor wasn't there, I would take my chance to get hold of that book. Or look inside that mysterious pot.

The candle was out and I had no means of lighting it again. So I made my way back in the grey-blackness just by feeling, placing my cold hands on the even icier stone walls, rough as the ground under my fingers, making them numb. I inched my way along the passage and through the arch. The door was heavy wood, with an iron handle. Slowly I twisted this round and peered into the study. No candles were lit, but there was enough of a fire still left to cast some warm light around the room. Its corners were still in dark shadow. I couldn't see Huksor or his horrid pet, so I crept inside and glanced around. I was wrong: the doctor hadn't hidden his book. I saw it large as life on his desk. I opened it up at no particular page. The paper – was it paper? – felt thick and soft, almost like skin, and pages were folded in half. Some sheets were sewn together while others were loose. Carefully, I pulled out one sheet. On it were drawings and sketches – of some kind of animals, I guessed – and close-set writing in a fancy script. It was too dark to read any of the words, although I squinted hard and held it close to the firelight.

As I tried to make out the scrawled words on the page and enjoyed the feeling of the fire tingling through my fingers, I suddenly felt a prickling across my skin, as if someone was watching me. I turned quickly and tried to take in the shadowy room, looking for movement, but couldn't see anything. Then I felt it: a heavy, smooth weight rippling across my feet. I froze as sure as if I'd been turned to stone. Melusina was sliding across my boots. I was too sickened to move a muscle or make a sound. I went death-cold as I watched her long, scaled body slip heavily along, without pausing, as if my feet were just a bump in the ground. I didn't even breathe. The wretched creature seemed to go on forever – how long was it, for heaven's sake? At last her tail end slithered off me and I watched, shaking from top to toe, as she made its way onto a chair nearby, coiling herself up like a lady drawing up her skirts. Then she raised her ugly head and looked directly at me. The firelight made an amber glint in her unblinking eyes. Her head swung, gently, from side to side, but her eyes stayed fixed on mine. Still, I didn't dare move. I thought if I did, the serpent might strike at me. I stayed, fixed by her swaying body, for what seemed like an age. And then came a voice.

"O-ho! What have we here? Miss Clever is trying to steal my writing, eh?"

Chapter Eleven

Huksor stood in the study doorway, his face too shadowed to make out. He walked further into the room.

"Just as I thought," he said, staring at the piece of parchment in my hand. "Just as I guessed you would. Well done, Melusina. You guard my work better than any dog."

"No," I began, struggling even to speak because my throat felt stopped up. "No. I wasn't stealing, truly. I came in here because I was too cold to sleep and I was just– just looking–"

Huksor jumped towards me as if he was going to hit me. He placed a hairy hand just below my throat, his nails as long and filthy as those of an unclipped hound.

"I knew you planned to steal something," he muttered. "I knew it. But I also knew Melusina would do her duty."

I swallowed drily, feeling the threat in his fingers

around my neck. "I'm nosey, sir, that's all," I whispered. "My brother calls me Little Nebby-nose. I can't help poking into things, but I'm not a thief. You must believe me. I want to work with you."

"I can't see any reason," Huksor growled, "why I shouldn't kill you now. First of all, you're not natural and second of all, whatever you are, you are trying to steal my work. I've told you what could happen if this knowledge gets out before my cures are ready. You place me in danger, girl. I ought to get rid of you."

"Don't do that," I blurted out, quickly, trying to think on my feet. "Think what I could do for you. What would you like from my time?" I pulled some coins out of my pocket but I realised they were no use here. I tried to think of some modern invention that would impress him, but panic seized up my mind.

"I could kill you in a single moment," Huksor went on. His fierce, fire-lit eyes were terrifying as the very devil. "I have a dozen useful creatures in there that would be happy to despatch you. Quickly, or slowly – your choice, eh? I have a collection of deadly vipers who would give you a nip for nothing. Melusina and I could watch as your skin swells and your breathing slows and your heart gives out. No one would imagine it was anything other than the leprosy carrying you off."

I didn't move a muscle, other than the trembling, which I couldn't help. His fingers were just tight enough to make it hard for me to breathe. I wanted to swallow but couldn't.

The doctor carried on, still with a mad grin on his face.

"Do you want to know what Melusina would do to you, if you annoyed her? She might bite you and that would certainly be very painful. But it wouldn't kill you. No, Melusina prefers to wrap herself around her prey and squeeze it to death. I don't suppose you'd be so brave and full of yourself as you turned blue, gasping for your last breath, eh?

"Meg tells me you were interested in my mermaid. Not what you were expecting, I'm sure. If I let her at you, she'd go straight for your throat, with those sharp teeth of hers.

"Or I could show you a special prize. My black serpent from the Far East. You could see how interesting he is when he tries to defend himself. He twists into such pretty shapes. If he thinks he needs to attack you, then he will. I would be happy to watch you go quite mad as his poison courses through your blood. That's before you find you can't breathe and your whole body stiffens up. It would be quite a show. Quite a lesson for anyone else who thinks they may steal my work, eh?"

At this point he tightened his grip on my throat and I thought – either he's going to strangle me or else he's going to set one of his evil reptiles on me. Whatever happened, I thought I might be about to die.

Then the most unexpected and wonderful thing happened. A familiar voice shouted, "Annie!"

It was Tom's voice! Huksor whipped around and for just one instant – like the wavering flash of sheet lightning – I saw my Tom standing, white-faced and staring at us. Then, in the same wild moment, he disappeared again.

But Huksor dropped his hand and stared open-mouthed at the space where we'd both just seen my brother. "Tom!" I sobbed, barely able to take it in. "Tom! Where are you?"

Huksor whirled back round towards me. "What dark magic is this?" he roared. "What spirit did you conjure up for help?"

I shook my head. I couldn't speak.

The doctor stumbled towards a jug on one of his benches and poured dark-red wine into a cup. He threw it into his mouth, gulped it down quickly, then turned back to glare at me.

"What happened?" he demanded again.

I took some deep breaths and forced back my tears of relief. I gulped, my throat aching from Huksor's strong fingers. Then I thought as fast as I could.

"That was my spirit protector," I blurted out, hoping that the doctor was frightened enough to believe me. "He will always come to save me when I'm in danger. He wreaks a terrible revenge on anyone who hurts me. It's a good job you let me go."

Huksor sat down, heavily, and poured himself more wine. He stared at me rigidly, a red rim forming around the dry skin on his lips. I stood up straight and met his eyes. I knew I mustn't show him how scared I really was. You can use people's fears – that's what Haggstone did with her trick séance. That's why Doctor Huksor threatened me with his beasts. But *he* was afraid of what he didn't understand. And he didn't understand me.

At the same moment, we both turned to see Meg

standing in the doorway between the study and the snake room. I had no idea how long she'd been there or how much she'd seen. Huksor, pouring his third drink of wine, looked almost pleased.

"Ah, Meg," he said. "Take your slippery friend back to your room to get some sleep. It's almost dawn and we have work to do tomorrow." As I left the study, he made for that pot on his desk and slid it into his cloak.

Meg said nothing as we walked out into the icy passageway. She stared straight ahead and was quiet. I realised I was still clutching the page from Huksor's book. He's forgotten about it, I thought, with a tiny smile, and tucked it into a side pocket in my skirt. Then Meg glanced at me, sideways, and to my surprise she suddenly and firmly linked my arm in hers. She marched me along, speeding up my steps.

"I saw that," she said, under her breath. "All of it. I thought he was going to kill you. He might've done, you know."

"I know," I replied, as we pushed back the rough cloth that covered the entrance to Meg's cubby-hole. "So did you see–?"

"The boy," nodded Meg, as we huddled down into the smelly hide blanket. "The boy with the long hair. What was he, some sort of angel?"

"Not likely," I snorted. "That was my brother, Tom. But I've no idea how he got here. Or why. I'm as shocked as you and Huksor."

"But he saved your life, I'm sure," said Meg. "Doctor

Huksor was furious with you. You stole some of his book. I know you still have that page, by the way."

"Are you going to remind him?" I asked.

"Not me," said Meg. "But you're heading for trouble. He will kill you if he wants to."

I tried to make out Meg's face, but the tiny room was still too dark.

"Meg," I asked. "Has he killed anyone before? On purpose, I mean?"

Meg hugged her knees to her skinny body and shivered.

"There was a man," she told me in a whisper. "He was a monk. One of the ones who helped found the hospital. He was a pompous old man, to be sure. But he was worried about the cures. He accused Doctor Huksor of witchcraft."

"And?" I urged her. "What happened?"

Meg shivered again and I put an arm around her shoulder.

"Doctor Huksor knows each and every creature in that room. He brought them back himself from countries far across the sea. He bred them and they don't harm him. But he has a particular viper that's very poisonous. He picked it out and said he wanted to show it to the monk. Then he threw it right into his lap. I was there, I saw it all. The snake got angry and bit the man on the leg. He got ill in just a few minutes."

"Did no one ask questions?"

"Yes," Meg said. "The other monks came looking for him. Doctor Huksor showed him their friend in the hospital. His skin had swollen up and he could hardly breathe. The doctor told them he had the leprosy and they believed him. They couldn't get out of here fast enough. The monk died the same day. You must never tell anyone, though."

I nodded. It was horrible, but it didn't surprise me.

"Meg," I said. "I feel as if I've caused trouble for you. You should leave this place."

She looked at me, with a frown. "Where else would I go? If I stay here, I might be able to help people like my father. He believed in Doctor Huksor, that he'd get it right one day, even if he made mistakes along the way. He said that was how people found things out, by trying and sometimes making mistakes. I think he would have wanted me to stay here."

I decided it was best not to argue with this.

"Do you think Huksor *will* get it right?" I asked her. "You told me you did, when we first met."

Meg sighed hard. "He's such a clever man. It's not my place to tell him what's right and what's wrong. He's made a salve that does many good things, but it costs more than gold – and it's not finished. But perhaps one day, who knows? He might find the cure after all."

"Hmm," I said. So that was what was in his precious little pot.

We cuddled up and I closed my eyes, aching to get some sleep. But then Meg chirped up again. "Anyway, lady-in-blue. Was that a love letter from John the player?"

"Is that his name?" I asked, heavy-eyed. "John?" He was very handsome, I thought, and he had a smile that looked full of fun. Then I pinched myself. Really, he'd been dead for hundreds of years.

We must have managed to snatch some sleep, because before I knew it the room was a tiny bit lighter, although still just as cold. Meg stretched and yawned.

"Let's find some food to start the day," she said, pulling me to my feet. I was stiff and all my limbs ached; my feet and fingers hung on me like dead, bloodless limbs.

Now I was awake, Tom sprang back into my mind. What Lucy told me made sense now: Tom was time-travelling too, only for a minute or two at a time and without knowing what he was doing. Poor Tom, I thought. If I'd done it all on my own, without Lady Hexer's advice, I'd have been afraid to talk about it too. People would think I was crazy. I ached to get back to speak to him. But, I suddenly wondered, how would I get back this time? In my other journeys to the hospital, it was Lady Hexer, watching over me and calling me back, that seemed to pull me from the past to the present day. After that time in the garden, Tom and Lucy repeated my name and, without knowing it, they willed me to come back to them. In the year 1899, I knew my body was lying alone on a bed, locked in a bedroom in Hexer Hall. Part of me was centuries away and all alone. Lady Hexer might have lost faith in me and Tom couldn't reach me. Who would call me back this time?

*Yesterday was Twelfth Day. The staff were busy
clearing out all traces of Christmas greenery from the
Hall, to ensure that no spirits can lurk in there to bring
us bad luck in the coming months. It is all superstition
and nonsense, of course. It is astonishing how these
ancient beliefs can last for so many hundreds of years.
Like bad reputations.*

*As I look out over the grounds – still frozen solid –
and watch the smoke curling up from today's bonfire, I
begin to wonder how much nonsense I have taken into
my own head recently. I imagined myself capable of
great magic. I dreamed of being a bringer of knowledge,
a healer of sickness – a mistress of Time itself. But now
I fear it may all have been a great confidence trick. I do
not entirely blame Agatha Haggstone, although I think
I have wasted a great deal of time and money on her
grand illusions. I blame myself for being so arrogant
and utterly, utterly foolish.*

*Yesterday afternoon I was treated to a ridiculous
performance by Agatha and her new protégée, Becky's
young sister, a tiny, frightened young girl who is
clearly acting under instruction. The child pretended
to fall into a trance on my hearth. I watched as she
struggled to stop herself from opening her eyes and
peeping out at me. After a few minutes Agatha called
her name and she sat up with a broad smile, all gums
where her front teeth have fallen out. Then she parroted*

out some phrases about meeting a doctor who promised he would give her his book of cures. When I pressed her for details she was unable to give any – what the doctor looked like, a description of the hospital, anything at all other than the lines she'd clearly been taught to say. I sent her off to have tea in the kitchen with her sister. Then I confronted Agatha with my suspicions, that I was being taken for a fool. She acted as if she was hugely insulted, of course, and warned me that I should take her predictions and advice seriously.

It is true that when she first cast my horoscope, she impressed me with her knowledge and all she seemed to know of my hopes. But I find I no longer believe everything she says. She may have a modicum of psychic ability, but she uses a great deal of artifice. I am almost certain that the incident with the ghost was, as Annie claimed, a piece of clever theatre. I will have to think of a way to ask her to leave, with dignity, while making sure she does not ruin my reputation further by telling everyone what has been going on. Annie, I am yet to be wholly convinced you are my opener of doors; but you have opened my eyes.

The faint, pleasant scent of wood smoke is creeping like incense through my windows. There is a sharper undertone to this scent – something which smells dangerous and exotic. The men have tried to throw some of the new wild plants onto the fire. They blame young Tom for bringing the growths to the gardens. Indeed, it is all very hard to fathom: in spite of the

*cruel weather, which is killing the old and young
of the village, these plants are somehow thriving,
creeping throughout the grounds, gripping and choking
everything in their way. I would speak to young Tom
about it, but Lucy tells me he is ill with a fever and shut
away in his cottage. Besides, he may ask me awkward
questions about his sister.*

*Late last night, a further disturbing thing happened.
I had trouble sleeping and was overcome by a strong
urge to check on Annie in her room. Perhaps I wanted
to make sure that she was well, or else to reassure
myself that that she too is not tricking me. Whatever
my reasons, I found myself almost propelled along the
landing to her bedroom, where I found the door slightly
ajar. I dashed in to find Becky and Agatha leaning
over the girl, who was unconscious on top of the bed.
The light was not good, but I thought I saw Agatha
pressing down on Annie's sleeping face. Naturally, they
both jumped back as soon as I entered the room, so it is
impossible to say for sure. But it is just, terrifyingly,
possible that Annie was about to be killed. I was in
shock. I demanded to know what they were doing in the
room. They had a story ready, however. Agatha claims
she was walking along the landing when she thought
she heard Annie crying. Becky let her in, she claimed,
and they found the child having some sort of nightmare.
Agatha says she was moving the girl's pillows to
make her more comfortable. I ordered them both away.
Becky's face was as red as if she'd been slapped and she*

could not meet my eye. Agatha was as enigmatic as ever. I could neither prove nor disprove their version of events, but I have made sure I now have all copies of the key to Annie's room.

And even more remarkable: when the pair had gone, I felt Annie's forehead, which was damp with sweat. But she seemed to be breathing regularly. I pulled the eiderdown over her to keep her warm – and under her limp arm I found a folded piece of paper. No, not paper – some kind of old parchment, thick and brown with age. It looked like a page from a larger volume. On it were writings and drawings. I slid it out and took it with me. I need to study it with great care, when I can be sure of being absolutely private, but the writing seems archaic and the drawings remind me of one of the older family herbals from my library. Even Annie cannot be such a forger. It surely has to be genuine.

What are you, child? Are you the clever time-traveller I believed you to be, or are you an ingenious confidence trickster, smarter than your upbringing should have allowed? And what bond between us brought me to your bedside last night where – I do fear – I may have saved your life?

The unexpected thing is that I rather miss my talks with you. You have a spark that makes me smile, intelligence beyond your years and a sadness in your eyes that touches me in some deep, forgotten place inside.

CHAPTER TWELVE

Meg was unable to tell me the day. She only knew the feast days because of the church services. All I knew was that it must still be January and it was deepest winter outside. I'd been in the wretched place of sickness and death for longer than ever before. I'd lost track of whether it was two or three days and nights. I now knew my way well around the passages of the hospital and around the courtyard. My blue dress was tucked away in Meg's cell and I wore the russet-coloured tunic with a hood that all the lepers wore. It was made of stiff, rough, woollen material that itched my skin, but it was thick enough to keep out some of the cold. Under the hood, I liked to keep my silky scarf wound around my head. A secret bit of softness, only known to me. And it stopped me from scratching my scalp.

I knew the names of the workers and they would stop

and chat to me. Many of them were patients who wanted to make themselves useful. Even Agnes would nod and say good day, although I knew she could tell there was something different about me. I didn't care for her. She was too fond of the barley ale and I often found her asleep and drooling in a corner in the late afternoon.

Meg kept me busy helping with all her jobs and I was glad to do it. I learned how to milk the cows where the hens and geese laid their eggs. I was glad Meg didn't ask me to help her with the serpents again.

I found Doctor Huksor's herbal garden, too. It was covered in snow, of course, but I could see that it was laid out in the same way that Tom planned for the grounds of Hexer Hall, with low hedges and stakes for plants. I wished I could show him. I wondered if he knew he was following a design that had been marked out so many hundreds of years earlier.

I also now knew the names of most of the patients. I grew to realise they weren't horrible monsters because of the way they looked, any more than I was. They liked a kind word the same as anyone. One bitter night the sad lady along the corridor died and her sister followed her a few hours later, just as she'd known would happen. How terrible to know you are going to die and no one can help you. I saw their bodies being wrapped up in blankets and laid on the cart. I hoped they never knew they'd be thrown out to the icy sea for the fish to eat.

I was torn over what to do next. I desperately wanted to get back to Tom. I hadn't seen another glimpse of him yet. But I guessed that, in our real time, he would believe he was having terrible nightmares or wild imaginings. I was the only one who could tell him he wasn't going mad. He would also be worrying about me. But I had to get this wretched book of medicines. If I went back without it, Lady Hexer would always think I was a liar and a trickster. Tom would be sent away from his Lucy and neither of us would have a job or a home. The horrid Haggstone would keep digging her grasping claws into Lady Hexer's mind as well as her money. I knew I shouldn't care about Lady Hexer. She didn't truly care about me, only what she thought I could do for her. But I still didn't want to see her duped and diddled by that scheming old toad. So I couldn't go back until I'd done what I promised. It was just turning out so much harder than I thought.

Every time Huksor went out, he left his creepy guard Melusina in the study and I was too afraid to go past her. Meg told me that he couldn't take her very far at the moment because, like the other beasts, she really belonged in a hot country and the cold might kill her off. So I knew she would always be there. Then there were all the other monsters from his vile collection. They could have been lurking anywhere in his study, too.

After turning this over and over in my mind, I finally came up with a plan. Really it was only half a plan, to get myself into the study on my own. But I had to give it a try. Time was running out.

Meg had been plaguing me to show her the note from John, the young player. So as we sat in the courtyard watching a food cart arrive from town, I offered to read it to her. I hoped she would be able to tell me what some of the words meant, because although I was getting better at hearing Meg, John's writing may as well have been from another world. Meg, of course, only knew one or two words she'd picked up from her time with Doctor Huksor. So I picked out what words I could and said them out loud to her. I was squinting at his writing and struggling to get my tongue around the words. It said something about my eyes matching my blue ribbons – I think – and my having a sad smile. A bit soft-headed for me. But Meg clasped her hands together and put them next to her heart.

"He's fond of you! How sweet! He must have paid a scribe to write it out. That will have cost some money."

"Fond of me? I'm not thirteen yet," I pointed out.

She gave me her favourite sideways look, like she thought I was a complete fool. "I had a cousin who was married at fourteen. And young John himself is no more than fifteen, I'm sure. I think his father is a baker in the town. Quite wealthy. John's had a bit of schooling, just like you. You should answer him."

"Ah," I said, sadly. "But I'm too ashamed. What about my hair?"

"Hmm," Meg agreed. "It's not very pretty. You should've let Doctor Huksor try to cure it when he offered."

I pretended to think for a moment. "I'd be so happy if my hair grew back. But I'm afraid of asking Doctor Huksor. He was furious when he thought I was stealing his papers."

Meg put her head on one side. "You can't blame him for that."

I waited a moment. "Meg," I said, as if I'd just thought of it. "Would you come with me and ask if he'll try to cure me? He listens to you."

Meg frowned. "I could," she said. "But he might say no. And, the cures ... they may not be to your liking."

I swallowed. "Would they involve snakes?"

"I don't know," Meg admitted. "But even so, he might ask you to eat or drink something that doesn't suit you. You make such a fuss."

I took no notice of this. My thinking was that it might be a way to get back into the doctor's study for a good length of time and I could work out my next move from there.

We had some cleaning up to do. I tried to make some of the patients more comfortable, but it wasn't easy. Once all our work was done and the late afternoon grew dusky, we made our way back to Huksor's study. Meg knocked on his door, going in before me.

After a few moments, she beckoned me in. I saw the serpent curled up beside the fire.

Doctor Huksor looked at me through eyes full of mistrust, his arms folded across his chest. "So, Miss. There is a suitor outside the gates, Meg tells me. And suddenly you care about how you look."

I nodded, trying to look like a girl in love. The very idea made my face go warm and red. Huksor took this to mean he was right and roared with laughter.

"Ah, well," he said, winking at me. "I would hate to stand in the way of Cupid and his arrow. Let's talk about what we can do."

I pulled back my hood and he fingered the spongy skin on my scalp. I stopped myself from squirming away. He checked again that I had no other symptoms of leprosy, and then hummed and hah-ed to himself.

"There is a medicine for this," he told me. "It may be unpleasant. But worth it, I imagine, if it means you can look pretty for your young piper-boy."

"Does it," I asked, breathing hard, "involve snakes? Because, if so, I don't think I can face it."

He gave me his twisted grin. "Not snakes, this time. Are you afraid of any other animals?"

I thought for a minute. "None that come to mind. Unless you have a tiger hidden in the room somewhere."

Doctor Huksor laughed. "Certainly not. I think we will be able to try out our cures, then. Come back before the end of the evening and I will have prepared something for you."

I hesitated. "The thing is, doctor, I am so afraid of your creatures. Do you think, when I come back for my treatment, that Melusina could be in the other room? Where I come from – in my time – it is thought that being very afraid of something can stop you from getting better. It makes the heart beat too fast for, er, a proper recovery." I'd made this bit up, of course, but Huksor nodded wisely and said it made some sense.

It was quite late in the evening when I went back to

the study. Meg came with me and she carried the heavy Melusina into the stinky, steamy room where the other beasts were kept. She's braver than me, I thought, admiring the way she handled the serpent. I couldn't touch that serpent to save my life. Doctor Huksor was waiting and on his desk were two bowls. I smelled some kind of meat in one and Huksor handed it to me.

"What is it?" I wrinkled my nose.

He sighed. "Just eat it, girl. It's not poison."

I hesitated again and sniffed at the bowl. I couldn't tell what was in it. Huksor gave a snort of annoyance and grabbed a piece of the meat with his fingers. He stuffed it into his mouth and chewed.

"Not poison," he repeated. "See?"

I picked up a piece of the fleshy stuff and put it in my mouth, ready to gag. In fact, it didn't taste too bad, though it was very salty. I managed to finish the small amount in the bowl.

The next part was worse. Huksor put on a thick leather glove and picked up a sliver of something wrapped in a cloth.

"You won't like this bit," he warned me. "But you have to put up with it if you want that hair to grow back."

He pushed back my hood, and rubbed my scalp with whatever was in his gloved hand. I screamed in pain. It was like being pricked with a million pins and needles. "What *is* that?" Tears were pouring from my eyes.

"I'll tell you in a minute," Huksor grunted.

Then he picked up the other bowl, which had some sort

of thick, pale matter in it that looked like lard. I pulled a face.

"This isn't to eat," he told me. "This is an ointment."

Roughly, he rubbed the warm, thick grease into my scalp and then wrapped my stinging head in a muslin bandage. "Keep it on," he said. I was sure I could feel my scalp bleeding from the hundreds of tiny prick wounds.

"Are you going to tell me what you've used on me?" I asked again, blinking back tears.

He wiped his fingers. "Hedgehog, of course. Flesh, spines and fat."

"Oh," I said. No wonder it hurt. I tried not to think about what I had just eaten, although my stomach gave a lurch. I squeezed back the tears. My head still burned with pain. "How will that help?"

"It's common sense, girl. The hedgehog is all spiky quills. I use its elements to produce the same in you. Your hair will spring up too. This one works – I've seen it cure before."

Then he did exactly what I hoped he'd do. He went into the steamy reptile room next door and started talking to Meg. I took my chance and pulled the heavy wooden door shut behind him, dragging the thick iron bolt across. I heard him roar and hammer on the door with his fists. I also heard Meg shouting, "Annie! No! Don't be so stupid!"

I ran across to the desk, where Huksor's big book sat open. One side was propped up at an angle against some kind of mottled jar. I started pulling the huge book towards me. Then the jar toppled over – and that's when I saw it. A slim black-and-red patterned snake slid out of the jar as smoothly as blood from a wound. It hissed at me and raised its body like a forbidding finger. Its tiny tongue flickered so fast it blurred. For a moment or two I completely froze. Then – as the serpent was about to strike at me – I threw the heavy volume at it with as much force as I could manage. I didn't know if I hit it or not, but I ran to the bolted door and heaved it open, before running back out and along the stone passageway, panting and sweating.

For once, I was glad it was dark. I blundered along, the blood pounding through my head and chest. I was just ahead of Meg and the doctor because they'd taken a moment or two to realise they were free. But I heard Huksor shouting and gaining on me. I blindly felt right and left for somewhere to hide.

And then I saw him again. Tom. He was standing near the entrance to a hospital room, his face death-white and terrified.

"Annie!" he shouted and held out his arms. I ran into them and hugged him hard.

"Annie!" he said again, his breath heavy. "I'm having some terrible nightmare. But at least it's better now that you're in it!"

"It's not a dream," I told him. I pinched him hard on the arm to prove it. He winced and looked over my shoulder. I turned to see Meg and Doctor Huksor, standing still as stone and staring at us.

"What new trick is this?" Huksor bellowed, almost as afraid as he was furious. "What are you, sir?"

Tom just stood there looking baffled, with his mouth open.

Then, to my surprise, Meg blurted out, "It's only Annie's brother. He's not harmful. She told me so."

I stood in front of Tom. "He'll take me away with him if you try to harm me," I said, as boldly as I could manage. "And," I went on, thinking on my feet, "when I get out, I'll tell everyone about your witchcraft. All the priests and parish big-wigs will get to know. They'll close down your hospital and they'll put you in prison. Both of you," I added, meanly, to Meg, even though I knew that wasn't very fair.

Tom held my shoulders with a tight grip. I turned my face to him.

"I'll explain all this soon," I murmured. "But for now, just know that you're not dreaming and you're not going mad. It'll be all right, Tom."

Tom still looked as if he had no idea what's going on, which, of course, he hadn't. He dropped his grip on my shoulders for a moment and – of all the bad luck! – he suddenly faded away like a rainbow, into the dark.

I cursed. If he'd still been holding on to me, I'm sure I would've gone back with him. Now I was stuck. I looked wildly around but it was too late to run. Huksor marched forward and grabbed me firmly by the wrist.

"It looks as if you're not going anywhere." He pulled me roughly along the passageway with him, back to the study. Now it was my turn to be very afraid.

"Did you catch the snake?" I asked, in a bit of a whimper. "It's not still slithering around in here, is it?"

He pushed me onto a wooden chair and leaned down. His face was right next to mine.

"Perhaps I did," he snarled. "But perhaps I did not. It may be about to drop on your head from the shelf. It could be about to crawl under your skirt and up your leg. Who knows, eh? You'll just have to stay very, very still and hope you don't make it angry."

This was too much to bear.

"I'm sorry," I pleaded. I could hardly get the words out because my teeth were chattering so hard. "I don't know what came over me. I promise I won't–"

Huksor held up a hand. "I don't want to hear anything you have to say. You asked me for help and then you tried to steal my work. Again. You will stay here for the night while I decide what to do with you. Meg will keep an eye on you. Melusina will help."

He gave Meg a long speech about how untrustworthy I was and how she had to be on her guard all night. No sleep allowed. Then he stomped out, taking his flask of wine with him. I heard a bolt slide firmly across the study door. He was very angry but, I was sure, he'd lost his nerve as far as hurting me went. Perhaps he thought I might conjure up an army of big brothers to sort him out. Oh, if only I could!

Meg glared at me. "I haven't had any food for ages," she grumbled, "and now I have to sit with *her*." She nodded at Melusina, who was coiled up in front of the fire again. "And I have to look at your fool of a face all night."

"Think yourself lucky," I said. "I had to eat hedgehog."

She didn't smile. "There's nothing so wrong with that. I don't know what fine foods servants eat where you come from. You go on as if you're a princess or something."

"No, I don't," I snapped. "Anyway, it's not so nice when you have their prickles rubbed all over your head." I touched my scalp, which was tender and sticky through the bandage.

Meg winced for a second, but she wasn't about to make peace. "You acted like you were my friend. I trusted you. You asked me for help. And all you wanted was to try to steal the book again."

"I'm sorry," I said and I meant it. "I am your friend. At least, I want to be. I didn't plan to lie to you. But it's so important that I show Lady Hexer the book. It might be a matter of life and death. In fact," I wondered if this would work, "if I could just borrow it, then I could bring it back before Doctor Huksor even noticed?"

Meg made a snorting noise. "You must think I am stupid." She wriggled closer to the fire, carefully, so as not to disturb the big snake. It was going to be a very long night.

Hexer Hall
8th January, 1899

> *The cold weather has not relented. It seems to be following a pattern. First, the snow comes down, in fat flakes, thick and fast. Then the temperature drops and it all freezes hard. If the mercury rises a degree or two,*

then the snow falls again. It means that outside there is layer upon layer of thick ice, almost impossible to walk across. The window panes are so whitened with frost that it is difficult to see out and everything seems unnaturally still. It is harder and harder to heat up the Hall, even though there are fires in almost every room. I have never known anything like it.

I have spoken at length to Mrs McKinnon. The situation is very worrying. It seems some kind of sickness is creeping through the staff and many of them are most seriously ill. This includes young Tom and several of the labourers. This sickness may have come from the village, she says, and it may be because of the dreadful weather. But of course many still think there is some connection to the exotic plants which continue to strangle the grounds. I have never before seen a plant strong enough to force its way up through ice and snow, so I understand why so many people find them fearful. I do not have enough staff at the moment to cut them back, so every part of the grounds is now covered in these thick tendrils, bright green and firm, even though they're topped with ice as thick as marzipan.

Mrs McKinnon confirmed she has seen Becky having many secret conversations with Agatha. Mrs McKinnon believes Becky is a hard worker – I know this, of course – but that she has ideas above her station and longs to better herself and her family. This ambition may have led her to try to place her sister into my household. That, I think, I can forgive. But Mrs

*McKinnon, it appears, has never trusted Agatha. It is
her belief that Agatha Haggstone may not even be her
real name and that she has changed it several times
to avoid charges of fraud, connected with her medium
practice in Edinburgh. I only wish Mrs McKinnon had
felt she could come to me earlier with this suspicion – at
least before I took the wretched woman so far into my
confidence. It is now risky to upset her too much, and
let her tongue wag about me.*

*Now to more happenings that I cannot fully explain
but must record. I have to confess that I couldn't resist
stealing into Annie's room again this evening, just to
check that she was well. I am disturbed by what I found
there. She still lies sleeping on the bed, but I noticed
a stain on the pillow. Her scalp has been bleeding
badly and is somehow covered in tiny sores like pin
pricks. I wondered if Becky or Agatha could have been
in the room to harm her, but I am certain I now have
all the keys. I asked Mrs McKinnon to fetch me a jar
of Taylor's Healing Ointment and I rubbed it gently
over her scalp. I am not sure how useful this stuff is, of
course, but it is all I have to hand. It felt both sad and
sweet for me, after all this time, to be ministering to
a child, but somehow I knew it was the right thing to
do, whether Annie is aware of it or not. The poor child
whimpers and fidgets in her sleep and I wonder what is
going on in her world. It crossed my mind that I ought
to try to call her back immediately – that perhaps this
lengthy period of time-travelling is taking too much of*

*a toll on her. But then I thought: a few more days and
she may bring me the prize I've always wanted. And
then, surely, I could make it up to her. Yes, just a few
more days.*

I sat and stared into the fire as the night wore on. Meg
kept her back to me, like a sulky cat. I tried talking to her
but she took no notice. I even tried humming the tune the
musicians played.

"Remember when we danced out in the snow, Meg?" I
said. But she just made a snorting sound. I gave up.

I thought hard about Tom. It seemed so odd that I'd
seen him here only twice, but both times when I was in the
worst danger. Did he somehow know I was threatened? Is
that what pulled him here? But how could he know where
he was going? What symbols brought him into the past?
Or – and this is what I thought was the most likely – was it
me, somehow willing him to come? Did my need for him
drag him back over time to be with me? I didn't like that
idea, because it meant I was putting him in the same sort
of danger as I was myself. And he hadn't agreed to it. But
it might explain how he wasn't able to stay for more than
a few moments. Just long enough to save my life.

*Hexer Hall
8th January, 1899
Later*

I have studied the parchment I found in Annie's room.

Of course she cannot have made this up herself. I am ashamed of myself for ever thinking such a terrible wrong about the child. This document is written in a mixture of languages, as if to deliberately confuse the reader and to keep the knowledge secret. It has taken me the best part of two hours to make sense of this small fragment. But it is more exciting than I could have expected. It talks of the preparation called theriac, which Doctor Huksor will only use on his more wealthy patients because of its expensive ingredients – notably, the flesh of vipers, but a total of sixty-four other ingredients. He was able to bring some of this theriac back from his journeys on the merchant ships over the seas to Venice. After his supplies ran out, however, he created his own version. For this very purpose, he brought back his own reptiles and a true menagerie of creatures and has bred them in careful conditions in his hospital, but all in secret, for the drug and the very snakes themselves are associated with dark magic.

He is not the first to work with these cures. Theriac is used by our physicians even today. But Huksor combines them with his own form of magic. He talks of harnessing energies and natural powers to add great strength to the medicines. And of course he is able to test them directly on his patients.

The important note is this: the principle seems to be the same for any illness. The poison cleanses the body of the sickness so that it can be repaired, and the extra magic worked by this great doctor boosts the power

of the cures. I just need to know the right ingredients
and combinations and I too will be able to work these
wonders on the diseases of our time. Oh, Annie! Hurry
back and bring me more of this!

I boiled when I looked at Huksor's book, still sitting on
the desk like a fat old king on a wooden throne. If I made
a move towards it, Meg would be on me like a spring. No
doubt that wretched snake would do its part too. But there
it was, the only reason I was here, just a few feet away
from me.

Something else frightened me, though. What if I was
able to bring that book back to Hexer Hall in my year of
1899? It was full of Doctor Huksor's ideas about curing
people, and in spite of what Lady Hexer believed, weren't
they quite crazy? Worse, weren't they dangerous? I
thought about the poor sisters who were sent half-mad
before they died. The doctor didn't cure them. And what
of the other patients? Not one of them told me they were
getting any better. So many patients die, half of the bodies
are thrown out to sea so that the parish doesn't notice. All
I could see around me were people in terrible pain, people
turned into monsters by sickness. Lady Hexer thought
this dead relative of hers was a forgotten genius. Poking
around under my bandage, I stroked my sore, greasy scalp
and looked at the smears of blood left on my fingers. I
wondered if Doctor Huksor was forgotten because he was
a failure.

Time: even the very air is easier to pin down, I thought.

I have bent time and travelled through it. But it still carries on. It's behind me and ahead of me, wherever I am. People say Time will tell. And it has told. Time did not save the memory or the work of this doctor. If he cured people of terrible diseases, Time would have kept his work. There was a reason why this book was lost. I realised I shouldn't be the one to bring this book of spells and poison back to modern days. I might be doing something very, very wrong.

Hexer Hall
9th January, 1899

I barely slept and the night hours have ticked by interminably slowly. In the very early hours I crept back into Annie's room, in the faint hope that she would be back with me and fully conscious. But she still lay on the bed in whatever trance envelops her. I started to have unexpected thoughts, such as whether she was eating properly back in the past and whether those wounds on her head mean that someone is hurting her. For a long moment I was tempted to call her back, just to give her a meal and check she is quite safe. But I must take hold of my emotions. I am not the girl's mother. I must not allow myself to care more for her well-being than for the reason I brought her here in the first place, which was only as an expendable messenger to bring me something I need.

I got so sick of pacing the carpet that I pulled on my

cloak and crept downstairs. There has been so much
snow that the moon was not visible and the stars were
also clouded. Only the snow lightened the grounds.
The night was chilled and gloomy as a churchyard.
I wandered, without really planning it, to the site of
my new gardens and all along the way I saw these
unnatural plants and growths that make everyone so
afraid. I can understand it. They seem to give off a faint
odour of sickness and death. Have they come straight
from the past? Have they fought their way through
centuries? Has Annie's visit prompted something to
live again and, if so, is it good or evil?

I swear I saw a tendril grow longer even as I
watched it. A trick of the dark, of course, but I scared
myself enough to hurry back indoors.

CHAPTER THIRTEEN

The darkness faded to the dull grey of another snowy day. I heard the bolt creak and Huksor came into the room. He looked as if he hadn't slept well either. The rings under his eyes were almost as black as his hair and his chin was as grizzly as an old goat. Meg was dozing and she jumped to her feet when the door opened. The doctor looked relieved to find me – and his book – still here.

"Sleep well?" he asked, as if he really hoped I hadn't.

"All is good, sir," Meg said. "May I get something to eat? I had nothing last night."

"Off you go." Huksor waved his hand and Meg rushed out of the door. I heard her feet pattering along the stone passageway.

"Still here, then," the doctor said, sitting in front of me. "Not able to magic yourself away somewhere?"

I shook my head.

"I've been thinking hard about you," Huksor went on. "You give me quite a problem. You came here and asked for help. I was kind enough to treat your deformity without so much as a fee. Now I believe you only wanted to trick me, nothing more.

"I would send you away. But as you pointed out yesterday, you could cause me a great deal of trouble. The monks who fund the hospital are very nervous about any mention of witchcraft. They're already suspicious about some of my methods. It would just take one silly girl jabbering about snakes and the like, and I could be finished. What do they do with witches where you come from?"

I shrugged. "They don't really believe in them, much. They're just in stories."

Huksor scratched his chin. "Well, here they burn them. I don't intend to die in shame and agony because of a nuisance of a girl like you."

"All right," I said. I was worn out by now and couldn't think of anything clever to say or do. "I promise not to tell anyone about your work. No one at all."

"Ah. But I can't trust you. That much I do know. So what would you do if you were me?"

I looked up at him. "Can't we still work together? I'm cleverer than Meg, I can read and write. Perhaps I could help you."

Huksor gave a nasty laugh and shook his head. "You don't give up easily. But no. The safest thing for me to do is to get rid of you, so that mouth is shut for ever. You're dangerous."

"Get rid of me?" I asked, my skin suddenly crawling. "What do you mean?"

The study door opened and Meg came in. Huksor shot me a look that warned me to be quiet.

"I think you know what I'm saying," he muttered. Then he turned cheerily to Meg. "Ah. Food."

She'd brought oatcakes, ham and ale. My stomach gurgled hungrily. I thought about the breakfasts at Hexer Hall: bacon, eggs, cold meats, buttered toast with those wonderful preserves and hot tea.

"May Annie eat?" Meg asked Huksor.

To my relief, he nodded and I almost snatched at the food. The crumbs around Meg's mouth told me she'd already helped herself.

"Enjoy it," Huksor said. "But don't let her go anywhere," he added to Meg. He glanced back at me. "Remember my pet is still around. Don't touch that book." He gave me a last evil glare and stamped out of the room.

I looked at Meg. "Thank you for the food. I'm starving."

She didn't answer. I finished a mouthful and swallowed. "He's going to kill me, Meg."

"He says things like that when he's in a temper. You make him so angry."

I leaned forward and put my hand on her knee. I felt how thin and bony it was under the thick cloth of her skirt. "Just before you came back, he told me he was going to get rid of me for good. Do you think I deserve to die?"

Meg got up and picked up some bits of wood from a pile on the hearth. She threw them onto the fire and poked at it with an iron rod, making the bits of flames sputter and spit.

"Meg," I said, more urgently. "I have caused trouble, trying to get Doctor Huksor's book. But only for a good reason. Please don't say you think I should be murdered as a punishment."

"Of course I don't," she muttered. "But you keep making things up. I never know what to believe with you. You tell stories about the future and I've never heard anything so daft in my life. But really you just want to steal something."

"Listen," I pleaded with her. "You find my story hard to believe. If I'm honest, so do I. I know it sounds completely crazy. But here I am, Meg, with my funny clothes and my odd way of talking. I couldn't make up all that I've told you about the time I've come from. I'm telling it because it's true.

"I'm not trying to steal the doctor's book because I'm a bad person. I'm doing it for someone else, who has a lot of power, over me and also over my brother. Please let me explain it all to you."

We sat for a long while as I told her my whole story from the beginning. At first, she sat with her arms folded in front of her and her mouth set in a firm line. But some parts interested her so much that she couldn't help asking questions. She was wide-eyed when I described my bedroom at Hexer Hall and the beautiful clothes Lady

Hexer bought for me. I had to give her every last detail. I told her how my bed was specially warmed, what the fastenings on my coat were made of, what luxuries we ate at mealtimes. Other details touched her, such as when I told her how much I missed Mam. How I wanted to stay with Tom and how we would be homeless and penniless if he lost his job.

"But," I finished up, "now I'm not just worried that I won't get the doctor's works back to Lady Hexer. I'm worried what will happen if I do. Those cures don't work, Meg – some of them hurt people, instead of making them better. Doctor Huksor doesn't want to admit it, but I can see it. I really don't know what to do."

Meg stared down at her grubby hands.

"Look what he did to me," I said. "All right, eating the hedgehog meat doesn't sound so bad, to you anyway. But look at this." I shook back my hood. Carefully, wincing at the soreness, I unwound the sticky cloth from my head and showed Meg the mess of blood, scabs and ointment.

"Oh," she breathed and put out a hand as if to touch it. "I thought he would use his special–" Then she changed her mind and put her hand on my lap. I grasped her fingers.

"What if Doctor Huksor gets rid of me, as he put it?" I went on. "What will happen then? It won't help the patients here. They'll keep on dying. Tom will never see me again. He'll never know what happened to his sister. He'll be broken-hearted. Lady Hexer will just try to find someone else who can go back in time. She'll keep trying to get her hands on those writings. Some new child will be put in danger. It won't stop."

Meg bit her lip. There was a long silence.

"What are you going to do?" she asked. Her voice sounded wet with misery.

"I've been thinking and thinking," I told her. "Some of the pages in Doctor Huksor's book are loose. I think I could take some of them without him noticing, at least not for a long while. I just need to find a way to get back. One problem is that I don't know how to make myself get back on my own. But if I could, with just some of those pages, I might be able to make Lady Hexer see that they're not proper cures at all. The thing is, I have to do it quickly, before Doctor Huksor tries to ... you know, get rid of me."

There was another pause, but I could almost hear Meg's mind working. Then she said, "One time when you disappeared, you were in my room. You just stepped out and you were gone."

I thought about this. "Yes. Every time I've gone back I've been out in that passageway. Every time I've come back here, that's where I've found myself. So that's part of it."

I stood up and made for the desk. I glanced under the table. "Meg, is that snake still crawling around?" I asked, my gaze darting about.

"The one from last night?" Meg half-smiled. "Don't worry about that one, you idiot. It's probably the least dangerous one we've got."

"It looked pretty mean to me," I said. "I'm sure it was going to bite me."

"Well, it would if it had to," Meg explained. "But those ones are very nervous. We have a cure for bites. Yes, a proper cure that works," she said, seeing my face. "Horehound and camomile and ... something else. I'd have to ask. But anyway," she grinned, "I put it back in its glass last night."

"Right then." I turned some of the heavy pages of the book. Most of them were loose and folded. I slid four or five thick pieces of paper out from different parts of the book. I lifted my tunic and, with a wink to Meg, I tucked them into my underwear. She raised her eyebrows but said nothing.

"Come with me," I said. "If we get caught, say I needed to use the pot." We made our way along to Meg's cubbyhole.

"There's one more thing," I said. I unrolled the note from John, the player. On the back, I scribbled, trying my best to write in a way that would be understood: *Dear John. Thank you for your nice words but I am going away and will not be coming back. If you can, get Meg away from here. Then stay away from this place forever. This doctor is doing terrible magic. Everyone around him is in danger. I will not forget you or your music. Your lady in blue, Annie.*

I looked at it for a moment, wondering what magic had helped me find the words in this old language. Then I handed it to Meg.

"If the players come back," I told her, "give this to John for me."

"What does it say?" asked Meg.

"Just goodbye." Then I thought hard for a moment, trying to picture myself getting back to Hexer Hall.

"I don't know if this will work," I said. "But let's give it a try. I'll stand in your room, like I did before. You push me out through the doorway. Let's see if it, I don't know, makes something happen."

So we stood, looking at each other for a moment, feeling a bit silly. Then Meg leaned forward, awkwardly, and put her arms around me. I hugged her, not too hard because she was so thin I felt I might bruise her.

"If you get away," she whispered to me, "don't come back. It will be too dangerous for you. If you get away, stay away."

"Don't worry," I said. "I've no plans to come back. Goodbye, Meg."

Suddenly Meg gave me a firm push, out through the cloth which covered the way in to her sleeping quarters. It gave me a fright and I stumbled backwards.

Hexer Hall
9th January, 1899
Later

An awkward situation arose this morning. The maid Lucy brought up a tray of tea and after she set it on the table, she hovered around, clearly rather anxious. I thanked her and said she may go. But then she blurted out that Tom was still confined to the gardener's cottage, very unwell. She asked if she could take Annie to visit her brother, as she was sure it would make him feel better.

218

I tried to say a firm no.

"Why, Lucy, if Tom is ill then the last thing we should do is send young Annie anywhere near him," I told her. "She may well fall prey to whatever infection he has. He seems a robust young man. I'm sure he will recover soon, and then, by all means, you may take Annie to see him."

Lucy stood, twisting her apron in her fingers, looking close to tears.

"But, ma'am, he is having these bad dreams. He says he finds himself in some cold, dark, stone building and Annie is there, trying to get away from some evil-looking old man."

I stared at the girl, speechless.

"I've tried to comfort him and say they are just dreams, that Annie is quite safe, here in the Hall with you. But when he asks if I have seen Annie, I have to tell him I have not seen her at all, not for a few days. Nor has Becky or Mrs McKinnon. He's most anxious to see her just for a few moments, madam. Just to prove to himself that his dreams are, well, just dreams."

I was so taken aback that I didn't quite know what to do, but I held my nerve.

"Lucy, you cannot be suggesting Annie is not safe?" I said. "It should be quite enough for you to know she is in my care. It should be more than enough for that young man too. Annie will visit her brother when I decide she is strong enough and not before. Now go away and please stop pestering me *when I am having my morning tea."*

The girl ran out of the room. I stared down at my cup. What could this mean – that Annie's brother has followed her to the past? How could that happen? But she is Iannua, and she has opened the door to the past. How long could I keep explaining why Annie had not come out of her room for such a time; why no one is being allowed in to see her? Agatha knows the truth, of course, but I hope to come to a generous financial arrangement with her and I trust she will pack her bags as soon as Annie completes her mission. Becky is sworn to secrecy and she wants to keep her job. The fewer people who know about this experiment, the better. I can't have Lucy gossiping all across Hexendale.

Then I rather panicked. I should have been kinder to the girl. Lucy is a soft-hearted creature and was probably weeping in the kitchen, with all my staff around her patting her shoulders. I decided I would have to bring Annie back from the past, just to prove that she is alive and well. In a way, this is not too much of a hardship as her safety has been preying on my mind.

So I went into her room. There she was, apparently sleeping, but fitfully, as if in a very bad nightmare. I took the snake-patterned tile from her grip and called her name. I had to do it several times but suddenly – and this I cannot for the life of me explain – she seemed to land down on the bed as if she'd fallen from the air. Yet she had never left her sleeping position. I blinked and questioned my own eyes – perhaps anxiety had made them play that particular trick on me. A moment after this illusion, the girl sat up rigidly and gasped.

"Oh!" she said to me, wide-eyed. "Did you call me back, Lady Hexer?"

"I did," I said, gently, placing a hand across her forehead, which was still clammy with a cool sweat. She stared around the room for a minute or two, collecting herself. Then, asking me to excuse her, she turned away, hitched up her skirts and produced – I don't like to think where from! – a small sheaf of documents, with a similar aged appearance to the last one I'd found. She apologised again for the immodest display, but I shook my head. I was so relieved to find her well.

I persuaded her to wash her face and hands, and wrap a scarf around her head, then come with me to the drawing room, where I would order her some food and drink. She wanted nothing more than hot tea. And as we waited, I asked about the scratches on her scalp. She launched into a long story of incredible detail about visiting the hospital, about speaking to Doctor Huksor, about his serpents and about the rather painful cure that he inflicted upon her. It all fits together perfectly.

But one aspect of her story troubles me somewhat. She is convinced that the doctor is not curing his patients – worse, that he is harming them with his experiments. She said she has brought me the pages from the book for two reasons: to prove that she is telling the truth and also to show me how misguided

*the medicines are. She pleaded with me to believe this
and to give up my quest.*

*I tried to suggest that she has no medical knowledge
(or indeed the barest of any education) and is therefore
in no position to question the doctor's work. Just
bring me the complete volume, I told her, and I will
promise to study it responsibly. But I cannot carry
out any meaningful work on a mere handful of pages,
fascinating as they are.*

*"You must go back and complete your mission, my
dear," I told her. "I have only brought you here today to
visit your brother, who is feeling unwell. Lucy tells me
he would like to see you."*

*It was Mrs McKinnon who brought us our meal.
She told me that Lucy was "indisposed" and that now
Becky too has fallen prey to the mystery sickness that
is affecting so many of the staff, and is confined to her
quarters. Mrs McKinnon seemed very pleased to see
Annie though, and she did not question my story that
she has been unwell, but is now recovering.*

*I told Annie she would be allowed to visit her
brother on the strict condition that she returns within
an hour and resumes her quest to find me the book.*

I wanted to slap Lady Hexer. At last, she believed that I
truly went back in time. But she would not listen to my
worries about Huksor and his cures. I showed her what
he did to my head. I told her the terrible story of the two
sisters who died. I told her about the evil serpents he

kept and she didn't so much as flinch. I even told her that Huksor threatened to kill me. She said I was ... she used a very long word that I can't quite remember, but it meant I was over-doing my story just to frighten her and get out of going back. I was so angry I wanted to scream. But that would not have helped.

Lady Hexer made sure she came with me through the grounds to the cottage. I couldn't believe my eyes. All the grounds were covered in thick, choking plants, smothering every single patch of earth. This greenery was also covered in frost, so I couldn't understand how it could grow. It had crawled up every statue and wall and across every pathway. It climbed up the walls of the Hall. Mrs McKinnon said every day they have to pull more and more of it away from the kitchen door, just to get in and out. Our own home is almost lost underneath all this growth.

Inside, Tom was not in bed as I'd expected, but sitting at the table, Lucy at his side. He looked very poorly and I could tell Lucy had been crying. He was so pale his skin was a sickly green-grey. His hair was even wilder than usual and he'd become much thinner in only a few days. He was overjoyed to see me, but it was hard to have Lady Hexer hovering over us and listening to our talk. I longed to speak to him about the hospital. I wanted to say how he'd come to my rescue, but when he mentioned his "dreams", as he put it, Lady Hexer's eyes bored into me like needles.

I held his hand and squeezed it. "Now you can see that

I am quite safe. Your dreams are nothing more than part of your sickness." I promised I would come to see him again soon. Lady Hexer told Lucy she could collect some food from the kitchen to bring back to Tom. After just a few moments, she was placing a hand on my shoulder and ushering me out of the door.

We tottered back across the slippery grounds. For a change Lady Hexer didn't look very noble. Part of me hoped she would fall down on her bossy backside. But of course she didn't and she even grabbed me and stopped me from falling over. We had a bit of a laugh about it, until I remembered that I was angry with her. Back inside, I had tea and cakes beside her fire. She was feeding me up before sending me off to risk my life.

"I should have been able to tell Tom what was happening," I blurted out.

"I understand," Lady Hexer sighed. "But you will be able to tell him everything one day soon, when we possess the secrets to curing illness and when we are in no danger of being the subject of spiteful gossip. Then I shall reward you well. You and Tom will be wealthy and secure."

"What if," I said, taking a deep breath, because part of me didn't even want to think this thought, never mind ask the question, "What if I get killed? I'm certain that doctor would do it, given half a chance. What if I get bitten by a snake? Or squeezed to death by that great big brutish Melusina? Or what if I catch the leprosy? What will you do if I don't come back?"

Lady Hexer's white face flinched a little, although you

had to be watching closely to see it. She promised I'd be safe.

"How do you know?" I demanded, in a way that I would never have dared speak to her just a few days ago. But I felt I had the right to ask.

"Think about it sensibly. If you were killed hundreds of years ago, then you couldn't be here talking to me now, could you? You would never have been born. But you were. You are here. So you are sure to survive whatever happens when you are in the past."

I thought about this hard but, to be honest, it made my head hurt. I couldn't make any sense of it. "But going back in time is impossible," I pointed out. "The whole thing is impossible. So who's to say it will all work out the way you think? Who's to say it will all make sense like that?"

Lady Hexer frowned. She once said she liked the way I asked questions. But she didn't like being asked things when she didn't have the answer ready to roll off her smooth tongue. Instead she looked at the clock and said, "Talking of time: it's pressing on. I think you ought to go back to your room and complete your task."

I didn't move. "I'm not sure if I want to," I said, surprising even myself.

Lady Hexer looked as if I'd thrown my tea in her face.

"I beg your pardon?" she said. It wasn't because she hadn't heard me, but because she was daring me to say it again.

I swallowed. "I don't think I want to go back," I repeated. "It's all too frightening. I'm scared I might get hurt or killed. I keep getting my friend Meg into trouble because she helps me out and I'm afraid I won't come back, whatever you say about it."

"Perhaps you were never telling me the truth," Lady Hexer suggested slyly. "Perhaps you know you cannot bring me what I want, after all."

I glared down at my hands. "Think that, if you want," I muttered. "Send me away if you like. But I don't want to go back to that hospital."

The clock tutted gently. I could hear Lady Hexer's breathing. Then she said: "But you wouldn't want to see Tom sent away? Without a job? Or a reference? We had an agreement. You came up with the promise that you would bring me back that book."

I looked up and tried to read her face. "It's nothing to do with Tom," I said. "He's worked hard for you. Keep him here. I'll go back to my aunt's or find a new position."

Lady Hexer shook her head. "That wouldn't be possible. There would be too many questions if you left without Tom. I insist that you finish the job. Or else I will bring ruin on you. And Tom. And Lucy. Everyone you care about. Do you understand?"

My face felt like firelight and inside I boiled. It was as if she'd opened me up like a surgeon and found all my weakest parts.

CHAPTER FOURTEEN

I waited in Meg's room until it began to get dark. That horrid Huksor had kept her busy today. Then the cloth was pulled back and Meg came in, clutching her candle and yawning. She jumped hard when I spoke. As I'd guessed, she started telling me off.

"I can't believe you're so stupid! Doctor Huksor lost his temper with me when he found you gone. I had to make up a story about how you'd just disappeared into thin air while I sat with you in the study. You know he'd be happy to kill you. Why in the name of–"

"Because I had to come back," I cut in. "I had no choice. If I don't get the book, I've told you: Tom and I will be begging on the streets."

"You said the book was dangerous," Meg pointed out. "You said you were going to tell your lady."

"I did," I sighed. "At least, I tried. But she's determined, Meg. She wouldn't listen. I have to do this. It's the only way. Please tell me how to get that book."

Meg shook her head sadly. "All right. He mustn't know I'm helping you, though."

I promised.

Meg told me that the next morning there was to be a visit from some of the monks who founded the hospital and the wealthy townspeople who helped pay for it. Doctor Huksor wouldn't take them anywhere near his study because the terrible creatures he kept were a secret. Instead, these visitors would be saying prayers in the chapel. Huksor would have to be there with them and it would take some time. That would be a good chance, she said, for me to get in and snatch the book. She told me something else too. The brown pot Huksor watched so carefully had his best and most magical potion in it. This was the potion, Meg said, that worked better than anything else. She'd seen it take away bad skin sores and the doctor thought it would cure even the leprosy, when he found the right patient to test it on. But it needed such costly parts to make it up – snake venom, rare herbs – that he only made a tiny amount at a time. That is what I should take, she said. That would be the best prize of all.

She looked unhappy. "I feel very bad telling you this," she went on. "I believed in Doctor Huksor. I still think he is trying his hardest to make the patients well. But someone else died last night and, well, I think he may have been poisoned. He wasn't ready to die. It happened suddenly,

228

a few hours after he'd had one of the medicines. It was horrible to watch. He was in agony."

She pulled her thin rug around her shoulders and hugged herself. I put my arm around her and we huddled together. Eventually she fell asleep with her head in my lap. I noticed that at the back of her head there was a patch of skin where her mousy hair had come out. I stroked it gently. But I guessed Meg hadn't even noticed and I wasn't going to tell her.

It took a long time for dawn to arrive. But when the faint greyness crept into the tiny room, Meg blinked herself awake and ran off to find us something to eat. It was the same fare as last time: oatcakes and a chunk of chewy meat that tasted more of salt than anything else, and sour ale to drink. But we were hungry. As we ate, Meg promised that as soon as Huksor went to the chapel, she would call me along. She'd even check the room for serpents, she promised, and place Melusina in the side room out of the way. I told her how grateful I was.

It felt like hours before I began to hear sounds of movement from the passageway. Meg came scurrying back.

"The visitors are here. Doctor Huksor is in the chapel, and so are all the patients who can walk. They're just about to start their service. Now's your chance. I'll have to go to the chapel too. Please be quick. And good fortune."

So I slipped along to the study as fast as I could. Now that I knew the place well, I could scuttle like a spider, just like Meg, darting round corners without hesitating. I glanced around the room. It looked like Meg had kept her promise to get rid of Melusina. There was the book, sitting half-open on the desk. This time, I was careful to check for any other nasty creatures hidden as a trap, but I couldn't see any. My heart was pounding so hard and fast I thought it might burst out of my body. I knew this was my last chance to get the book. If I got caught today I wouldn't live to tell the tale, I was sure of it.

I put my arms around the great tome and heaved it off the desk. It was heavy and awkward and I grunted with the effort. Thick leaves of paper slipped out of it and flapped onto the desk and floor. I cursed and put the book down on the floor for a minute so I could pick up the loose leaves. I was scrabbling in the dust under the desk when I heard footsteps and the creak of the wooden door. Panic turned me into stone. For a wild moment I wondered if I could just stay still and Huksor – for now I saw his soft black boots – might not notice I was there. I heard him shuffling around in a pile of smaller books and muttering:,"There it is," as he picked one out.

There was a short, terrible moment of silence. Then he let out a huge shout and ran to the desk, giving it a furious push and almost tipping it over on top of me. Something told him to look on the floor and there was the book – with me, crouching like a cornered rat, next to it. Another roar, so loud it would have terrified a lion. He leaned over and lunged at me. I tried to swerve away but he grabbed my ear and pulled me up. I yelped in pain. I tried, uselessly, to prise his fingers off me and I tried to

230

scream. But he used his other hand to grab my throat and push me down over the desk.

"I have had more than enough of this!" he spat in my face, still gripping my throat. I was choking. My eyes were bulging. I could hardly breathe.

"This, you wretch, is your last attempt to steal my work. Indeed, it's your last at everything. I'm about to go to a service in the chapel. But when I get back it's you who should say your prayers."

Now he grabbed my arm, squeezing it painfully, and pulled me into the hot, steamy serpent room.

He breathed hard as he pushed me down to sit on the bench. "You will not get away again. Sit!"

I sat, wanting to be still but shaking madly. Just being in the same room as all the snakes and nightmare creatures was punishment enough as far as I was concerned. The musky stink was sickening. Still with his livid eyes on me, Huksor went into the corner where the massive Bess lay. Suddenly gentle, he stroked her huge horned head and lifted it up. She raised herself as if it was a great effort.

"This way, my Bess," he crooned softly. The great serpent slid further towards me. With a lurch, vomit rose painfully up into my throat. I tried to swallow and force it back down.

"Now then," he said to Bess, still in a quiet, sing-song tone as if he was nursing a baby, "don't take your eyes off this wretch of a thief. I want her still here when I get back. Then I will give her to you and all your friends as a plaything."

Bess lowered her marked head again. Her eyes, like chips of polished jewels, stayed on me. The fat, forked tongue flicked in and out of her mouth, which was as cracked and lipless as an old crone's. Her hideous daughter Melusina crawled across her huge body and coiled at my feet, laying her head down like a puppy. As Huksor expected, I couldn't move. I was trapped in my own worst nightmare. My skin was crawling as if a thousand insects were running across it. I felt I could easily go mad with fear.

Huksor's eyes were like a beast's. "I have to go to this service now, or too many questions will be asked. But I'll be back within the hour to deal with you. If you try to move, Bess will hold you in place. Very tightly, I promise you."

He made to leave the room. Then he turned back with a dark, lopsided grin. "I only came back for a prayer book," he said, with a short laugh. "Perhaps God is on my side after all. Or the devil himself."

So there I was. The room was still overbearingly warm and sticky. I was shaking so hard I made the wooden bench judder. My teeth chattered out of control and I bit my own tongue. I tasted blood. I tried to clamp my jaws tight to stop it, because the serpent seemed to be interested in the noise, or it could have been the movement. Sweat ran down my face like tears. All right, there were tears too. I had never, ever, been this scared. I thought, this is it. I am going to die. Lady Hexer's promises were all air, and Tom would never know where I went. For a moment, I felt fury with Meg, for failing to warn me Huksor was coming back. But when I thought about it, I realised there was no way she could have got to me first. I knew she would be worrying about me. But not as much as I was afraid for myself and my own life.

Hexer Hall
9th January, 1899
Later

> *I am surrounded by sickness. Almost all my maids and many of the workmen have succumbed to this fever which confines them to bed. I am very thankful for Mrs McKinnon's strong constitution – she seems quite determined not to be brought down by this mysterious infection. Lucy too is unaffected and she has moved into Mrs McKinnon's quarters to keep her away from Becky, who is stricken with this unnamed malady. The girl's young sister, who I was rather hard on, I admit, is also suffering. It was Agatha who told me this: she said the little girl was taken ill in her presence and it was she who put her to bed.*
>
> *Mrs McKinnon is urging me to send a messenger to the next village to see if there are workers available to help us out. In particular, she wants to get a team of strong men to cut down the choking plants from around the grounds and the walls of the Hall. It does look disturbing, I have to agree.*
>
> *Annie, however, appears to have done as I asked and returned to the hospital. I locked her in her room but*

returned after less than an hour to find her lying in her
trance, perspiring and trembling violently. I still have
the odd unwelcome thought that perhaps I should put
a stop to it. I do not, after all, want the child to come to
harm. But this behaviour may mean that she is close to
bringing the book, so I will not interrupt.

I sat, hugging my knees and trying not to move. I never took my eyes off the reptiles. For the most part, they didn't move much and I was glad of it. I wished I could think straight about these serpents. I wished I could be brave like Meg and stay calm about them. But the very way they writhed their long bodies about and the way they lifted themselves up without arms and legs, as if they were on an invisible string, made me sick. As to some of the other creatures in the cases, ones I couldn't even name, I had to put them out of my mind. I felt as if my own stomach was full of wriggling, knotted snakes, making my insides shift and churn. The beasts, however, seemed quite sleepy, as I watched them.

Sometimes, out of the corner of my eye, I saw shapes moving in the thick glass jars and tanks around the walls. But I didn't let myself look properly. In these, I knew, were some of the most dangerous of Huksor's collection. Somehow, I felt that if I looked at them directly, they would notice me and all would be lost.

The heat and steam in the room became almost overpowering. The dungy smell didn't help. All the time, sweat trickled down my neck, back and chest. My palms were wet and slippery. I tried not to think about what Huksor would do when he came back. I hoped that the monks in the chapel were saying something about forgiveness and mercy, something that might make him have a change of heart. What were those words in the Bible about suffering little children? I never took much notice of sermons. Perhaps they'd say that one and Huksor would listen. But I knew it was a faint chance.

Suddenly – making me jump and Melusina raise her ugly head – I heard a wailing scream and the doctor's voice shouting. His heavy footsteps stamped their way towards the study and the childish keening got louder. I tried to work out who it was. It didn't sound like Meg and none of the younger patients came anywhere near this part of the hospital. The door was flung open with a loud bang. The glasses and jars rattled. All the creatures were now awake, hissing, spitting and agitated. My heart raced so fast I thought it would surely burst. Huksor was dragging a kicking, wriggling girl along by her ear. He shoved her roughly onto the wooden bench next to me. I could hardly believe my eyes. It was silly Jeannie, Becky's sister. The one I'd accused of being a fraud: here she was, covered in her own tears and snot, yelling like a mad thing. She was so intent on her weeping, she hadn't even noticed Melusina and Bess. The younger serpent reared and shifted its head from side to side, as if it was trying to work out what this screaming creature was. Even Bess arched up her heavy, shovel-shaped head. I grabbed the silly girl by the shoulders and shook her.

"Shut up," I warned, through gritted teeth. "Be quiet, you idiot."

Jeannie opened her mouth to yell again. Then she recognised me and her eyes went wide. But she started to cry again and in despair I clapped my fingers over her wet mouth. "Shut *up*," I told her again.

Huksor watched it all with his arms folded.

"I knew it," he said. "I was walking towards my study when this shrieking spectre appeared right in front of my feet, making me trip over. I knew at once she must have something to do with you. I was right, as usual. Another in your band of thieves, eh?"

I loosened my grip on Jeannie's mouth but she immediately started to yell again, so I clamped my hand firmly back in place.

"Look," I hissed at her, nodding my head towards the beasts on the floor. "Look at those creatures, Jeannie." Her eyes popped and she made another attempt at a scream, but thanks to my strong fingers it just came out as a frantic *hhmmnnn* sound. She tried to wriggle away but I kept an arm tight around her shoulder.

"Stay still, Jeannie," I urged. "We don't want to get those serpents angry. Just calm down."

Huksor grunted. "My visitors are not yet gone. Stay here and keep quiet. Any more yelling and screaming and you will be all the more sorry when I get back." He turned and left.

I gave Jeannie a hard look. "If I let you go, you have to promise to stay still and quiet," I said. "Otherwise those beasts will probably attack us. Do you promise?"

With huge, watery eyes, Jeannie nodded and with relief I took away my hand and wiped her spit on my tunic.

"What are they?" she whispered in her tiny voice.

"That man – he's a doctor in charge of this hospital. Those foul nightmares are his pet serpents, or dragons or something. I don't really know what they are. But I know they're dangerous, Jeannie. We mustn't get them angry."

"The hospital?" squeaked Jeannie, lisping because her two front teeth were missing. "Am I really in the old hospital? That's where Miss Haggstone wanted me to go. But I thought it was just pretend. She didn't say there'd be snakes."

"You're here all right," I said, with a sigh. "But you'll soon wish you were somewhere else. How did you do it, Jeannie? I thought you were making everything up."

"I was." The child hung her head. "I was just saying what they told me to. Becky said I made a rotten job of it. She was so cross with me. Her Ladyship never believed me. But today Miss Haggstone told me to try once more. She made me put my fingers round all the snake shapes around the fireplace and I felt all funny and cold. Then that horrible man came and fell over me."

She looked down at Melusina and Bess and shuddered.

"They're scary," she said. "Will they eat me?"

I hadn't thought of that. "I don't think so," I told her, though I was only saying what I hoped might make her feel better. "I think they just eat rats and mice and things like that. But they can bite. Meg – she's my friend here –

she says these two big ones aren't poisonous." I pointed around. "But some of these ones in the jars are really dangerous. You mustn't go near them."

Jeannie nodded. "Have you got the book then?" she asked me. "The one they keep going on about, with the magic spells in it."

I shook my head. "I don't have it yet. I will try to get it, if we can get out of this room. But I don't think it's magic, not really. I think it's a lot of rubbish."

Jeannie looked miserable. "So you'll get all the money, then," she said.

"What money?" I frowned.

Jeannie wiped her runny nose on her arm. "Miss Haggstone promised that me and Becky would get a big reward if we brought her the book. She said if you got there first, you'd get all the money. She said you'd spend it on fancy wigs for your baldy head."

"Did she really?" I said, huffily.

"Sorry," Jeannie added.

"I don't know about any reward money," I said, swallowing my anger. "All I know is, if I don't bring Lady Hexer that book, she might send Tom and me away without any work."

Jeannie thought for a moment or two. "I want to go back, anyway," she said, quietly. "My Becky's not very well. I'm scared."

I put my arm around her shoulder. She seemed very small indeed. "We will go back, then," I promised her. "With or without that book. I just have to work out how to do it."

The door began to creak and open very slowly. I turned, wondering why I hadn't heard Huksor approach. But it was Meg who put her pale face around the door. She slipped inside and ran up to me, giving me a light hug.

"I'm so sorry," she said, her eyes tearful. "I couldn't get back in time to warn you. I was hoping you wouldn't be caught. But I could tell by the doctor's face when he came back to the chapel. Who–"

I quickly explained that Jeannie also worked for Lady Hexer and that she'd ended up here with me. "Jeannie's only seven, Meg. She's very frightened. Her sister's back in our real time and she's sick. We both need to get away, somehow. Can you help us? Please?"

Meg sat with us and stared down at Melusina and Bess.

"We have a bit of time," she told us. "Doctor Huksor is busy with that group of monks and people from the parish. They're asking a lot of questions."

"What kind of questions?"

Meg shifted on the bench. "One of the bodies washed up on the beach the other day. The men hadn't bothered to take off the patient's tunic like they're supposed to, so everyone knew where he'd come from. The monks wanted to know all about it."

"Did they find out?" I wanted to know. The more trouble Huksor was in, the better.

"In a way. The doctor said that patient had run away from the hospital. I'm not sure if they believed him. But they can't prove he's lying. They're worried about how many patients are dying. This hospital gets a lot of food and money from the people in the town and they want to know where it's all going.

"Also," she grinned at me. "I don't know what you said in your note to master John. But he and his father turned up to attend the service this morning. They asked to see around the hospital. Doctor Huksor is still trying to talk them out of it but they won't go away."

"Good," I said. "I hope they keep on asking lots of questions. I hope that doctor is having a very hard time answering them."

I gripped Meg's hand. It was so frail I thought it might turn to dust. "Now, Meg. Can you help us get out? I don't know how to get past those frights down there."

Meg sat up straight. She reminded me of a chicken hearing a fox creeping up. "He's coming back, I can hear him," she hissed. "Stay there. I'll think of something."

She slipped back into the study. Moments later I heard Huksor come in. He sat down with a deep sigh and started muttering about the fools from the church meddling with his work. Meg fussed around him and poured him something into a cup. His wine, I supposed. Just a minute later, I heard her offer to go and fetch him some more. Melusina slid off the great bulk of her mother's body and around the door to see her horrid master. One less snake to worry about for now, I thought. I gave Jeannie a wink and a cuddle, as if I had a plan and it was all going well.

*No changes to speak of. No relenting in the weather
and no one's health has improved. I had a talk with
Haggstone this morning and she became quite
hysterical. She admitted that she had been trying to get
Becky's sister to travel back to the hospital when she
became ill. She fears the leprosy illness may somehow
have been brought back – by Annie, in Haggstone's
opinion – to the present day. I do not want to believe
this. It may yet turn out to be a fever caused by the
terrible weather. She also said that it is our interfering
with the past which has encouraged these strangling
plants to appear all over the grounds and up the walls
of the Hall.*

*"It's as if they're trying to choke us," she shouted
at me. "They're telling us to stop. We've gone too far.
You must give up your scheme, Hexer. Let it go. These
happenings at the Hall are the talk of the village. There
will be trouble and I will not be part of it."*

*"Well, no," I snapped back at her. "You're already in
trouble here and there, aren't you? Under your many
different names, of course. Oh, yes. I've learned of your
history, Miss Haggstone."*

*She flinched but didn't reply to that. "I am going
to pack my bags," she told me. "When I am ready, we
will discuss how much you will pay for my silence over
these matters."*

Oh yes, I thought. I will agree not to turn you over

*to the constabulary for fraud and blackmail. That is
what I will pay.*

*I stared out of the window at my overgrown
grounds, my mood as sick and heavy as the sky. Then
I tried to think coolly. Suppose she is right. Suppose
opening the doors to the past has let all sorts of bad
things come through to the present time. Well, then,
it is too late to close that door. I may as well get
something useful from the danger. I must hold out for
the book.*

Meg was much cleverer than I gave her credit for.

After a short while, she put her head around the door.

"He's gone to use the pot," she whispered. "But I'm
putting a potion into his wine. I can only put tiny drops
in or he'll taste it. But after a few more cups it'll make him
sleep, heavily enough for you to get out and get away."

I gave her the best smile I could manage.

"When he's in a deep slumber, I'll tell you. Then you
can get the book and go," Meg explained. "Get that potion
too. I'll take care of the serpents. I've got some rabbits
they'll be keen to eat. In the meantime, here. Food."

She threw a bundle at me and disappeared.

Jeannie was happy to eat the food but I couldn't face
it. Anyway, I knew the bread in this place tasted of ashes.
The cheese wasn't much better.

We sat, feeling like we were melting in the sticky heat,
for what I guessed was another hour or so. Jeannie fell
asleep, her fluffy, fair head on my knee. But I couldn't

relax a single nerve or limb. Every time Bess moved at all, just a slight flick of the end of her tail or a ripple across her thick, muscly body, I jumped and felt my scalp prickle and my skin creep. It was the same every time I sensed a movement in any of the glass tanks: I gagged. I was glad the glass was so thick and mottled I couldn't see the creatures in any detail, just their shadowy, horrible shapes. How Meg got used to handling the reptiles, I couldn't imagine. She once tried to tell me Melusina was not cold or slimy, as she looked. She said the serpent was soft and that the softness comes as a surprise. This still didn't make me want to touch them.

But then Meg could also handle that monster of a doctor, I thought. For such a scrap, she was very brave. All the time, I was aware of him grunting and moving about in the room just next door. Meg's soothing voice piped up now and again and there was the clinking of more wine being poured. Was his voice sounding slower and slurred? I wanted to believe it.

It grew darker and much more quiet. Somewhere far away, across those snowy fields, I heard the sound of what must be the monastery bell. Funny time to ring a bell, I thought. I was sure it was the early hours of the morning, well before the sluggish winter dawn. And then, at last, Meg put her head back around the door.

"It's time," she said, under her breath. "He's fast asleep."

Chapter Fifteen

I gently shook Jeannie awake. Meg came in, holding up her apron. She was followed by Melusina, slithering across the stone floor behind her. For a moment I wondered why the beast was following Meg. Then she tipped out the contents of the apron and two blood-stained rabbits fell onto the floor. Melusina went for one immediately. I turned away from the sight of the animal being dragged, slowly and cruelly, into the snake's jaw. Its mouth got wider and wider as it took in the food. Meg bent and picked up the other rabbit, throwing it towards Bess. The bigger snake didn't take any notice.

"Funny," Meg murmured. "Bess has been off her food for days now. Perhaps she's ill."

I hardly cared about that. "Come on," I said, through my teeth to Jeannie, who was watching open-mouthed as Melusina devoured the rabbit. The beast didn't chew, just slowly gulped the animal's whole body further and further in. The lump it made stretched the snake's throat, making me feel even more sick. "We haven't got time to watch the animal freak show."

Carefully, we checked around the door. Huksor was slumped across his desk. One arm was stretched out across his book.

"Oh no," I groaned. "Of all the places for him to fall asleep."

"Don't worry," said Meg. She lifted up Huksor's heavy arm and dropped it back on the desk with a soft thump. Her tired eyes twinkled. "He doesn't know it, but his wine's been flavoured with mandrake, henbane and poppy. You won't be able to wake him up for hours, not even if you play the pipes and drum right next to his ear."

"That's wonderful," I grinned. "You're so clever, Meg."

Meg even found us a large cloth which we wrapped around the book several times and tied at the top into a kind of knotted handle. I put in the lidded pot with Huksor's special cure. I heaved the bundle up onto my shoulder. I was trembling all over again, this time from sheer tiredness and excitement.

I had it. At long, long last I had the precious book. It might be full of good ideas or it might be evil. But that couldn't be my problem. My job was just to deliver it – and leave it in Lady Hexer's hands.

Hexer Hall
11th January, 1899

*Early this morning, before I had even had breakfast, I
became aware of a commotion out in the courtyard. I
went to the window and breathed on it to see out past
the film of cold. I could see several of the servants, two
of my labourers and a handful of the maids, milling
around. They were wearing their shawls and cloaks,
and holding bundles. One of the gardening men held
his sick child in his arms, wrapped in blankets. She
looked barely conscious. Another was supporting
his wife, who could hardly walk. I could hear Mrs
McKinnon's voice and I strained to hear what was
being said. I decided I ought to go down there, so I
went through the kitchen, which was empty, and out to
the back cobbled yard. It turned out that almost all of
my staff – the well and the sick – are abandoning me.
Mrs McKinnon was trying to reason with them and
persuade them to stay. I remained in the background,
unnoticed, listening. The servants were saying they
had "had enough", that they were afraid of the sickness
sweeping through the estate and of the frightening
jungle that seems to be forming across the grounds.
They were leaving, they said, in fear of their lives.*

*Mrs McKinnon pleaded again. "When have you
ever had such a generous, liberal employer?" she
scolded them. I smiled to myself. That was kind of her.
"You will not get such good rates anywhere else," she
went on.*

"Aye," one of the men replied. "Nor will we have to put up with dark magic and ghosts being called from the dead, bringing their cursed disease. If we leave, we may save our souls."

There was a general murmur of agreement and they began to shuffle out of the courtyard, carrying all their possessions with them. I walked away quickly around to the other side of the Hall, before I was spotted. I feared if they saw me, they might turn on me. I found myself on the great front step of my beautiful Hall, my eyes stinging and watering from the pinching cold, clutching my arms around myself and wishing I had stopped to put on a cloak. I lifted the brass knocker, shaped like a noble python with its mouth agape, and rapped for someone to let me into my home.

No one came.

I turned to Meg and grasped her fingers. I noticed patches of her skin had become red and sore. Somehow, I didn't care about any disease any more. It was more important to hold Meg's hands.

"Thank you so much," I said. "All I have to do is find a way back and I'll be safe. And free."

Meg's eyes shifted guiltily. "I still have your blue dress," she said. "It's there, rolled up under the desk. I was going to hide it and keep it."

"You can have it," I said. She looked delighted and immediately dragged the bundle out from its hiding place. Grinning, she pulled it on over her plain tunic. It was far too long for her, but she didn't seem to care.

"But what will you do now?" I asked her, suddenly realising I might actually miss her. "Huksor will be so very angry with you, Meg."

Meg looked up at me. "I don't suppose I could come with you?" she asked. "It seems better ... wherever you come from. I like your clothes. I could stay and work for you instead of Doctor Huksor."

I didn't know what to say for a minute. "You can't work for me, you silly thing. I haven't any money to pay you. On my own, I haven't enough to feed myself."

"I don't eat much," Meg said. "I wouldn't be any trouble."

"I don't even know if it'll work anyway, the other way round," I said. "I don't know if I can bring you with me." I looked at her face and her hopeful eyes, and sighed. "We could try, though. We'll go back out to the passageway and try to find our way back, like we did before. I've never quite worked out how it's done. It's always felt like a bit of an accident or just good luck. Anyway, Meg, you stay with us and keep hold of one of our hands all the time. We'll do our best."

Meg's eyes shone brighter. "Thank you," she breathed.

"Only – listen, Meg," I went on. "It's not that much better, where I'm from. Not if you haven't got lots of money. I really haven't, I'm afraid."

"Doesn't matter," grinned Meg, linking her arm to mine and squeezing it tight. "There's nothing for me to stay here for any more. Whatever I end up doing, it has to be better than cleaning up snake mess."

Jeannie made a gagging noise.

"Let's get going," I said. Then we all stopped and listened. There was some kind of noise going on and getting closer. The sound of people shouting – or was it singing? Yes, some kind of rowdy singing. Not hymns or carols. I looked at Meg. "What is it?"

She shook her head. "I don't know. Wait there."

She let go of my arm and hurried out of the study, into the chilly passageway. Huksor gave a loud snore, making Jeannie and me jump. We looked at him, but he hadn't moved. He was still slumped across the desk, breathing as noisily as an old boar, his mouth open, showing his stained teeth and a sliver of spit trailing off them.

Meg darted back in and shut the door behind her. "I forgot," she said. "It's Twelfth Day. The patients have started early this year. It's not even daylight."

"Started what?" I asked, my stomach turning over again.

"The celebrations, idiot," said Meg, shaking her head at me. "They've chosen their Abbot of Unreason and they're–"

"What's a Bot of Reesin?" whinged Jeannie. "Anyway, I don't care about the stupid thing. I want to go, *now*."

"So do I," I said. "What're you talking about, Meg? Where I'm from they've already had Twelfth Day. All we do is throw out the Christmas holly and have a bit of cake."

Meg sighed. "The Abbot of Unreason is the stupidest, lowest person," she explained. "They're made king for the day. They've chosen Old Will. You know him. He was half-mad before he came here and he's worse now. He's in charge of everything, all day. All the patients are going to be singing and acting daft for the rest of the day. Last year we had a lot of trouble."

I remembered now. Meg had told me this story already, when I mentioned how new parts of the hospital looked, with its clean, golden stone. It was because the patients had started fires all around the yard, as was the custom, and some of it had burned down and had to be rebuilt. Twelfth Day was the one time of the year when everyone was allowed to behave exactly as they liked, never mind how unruly they were. These patients were so ill that it probably seemed they could do as they wish, and that it would hardly matter.

The singing grew louder. I could make out some very bawdy song words. "They won't set fires again, will they?" I asked Meg.

"We'll have to hope they don't." Meg looked awkward. "They're asking to see Doctor Huksor," she said. "I said he's still asleep but they might get a bit rowdy in a minute. It'll be difficult to get past them without being dragged into their wild games."

"Oh, no," I said. "What will they say if they see Doctor Huksor like this?"

Meg scratched her head.

"Let's hide him," suggested Jeannie.

"How can we– wait a minute. That's not a bad idea," I said. We put the book down, still wrapped in its cloth.

Meg and I each took hold of one of Huksor's arms and put them around our shoulders. Jeannie took hold of his feet, slipping off his heavy cloak and boots first. It was lucky he was so small and lean for a man. The noisy band of patients was banging on the study door, shouting and laughing. Slowly and clumsily we dragged Huksor into the snake room, puffing and panting with the effort. Jeannie complained about how heavy he was.

"This was your idea," I grumbled back at her as we laid him on the floor close to Bess, who lifted her head and glared.

Then we heard the study door being pushed open, with much groaning and laughter.

"Where's the old chief, then?" someone shouted. "It's our day today. Tell him to hand over his wine. Twelfth Day, doctor! No rules! Only mis-rule until the sun goes down! Wake up!"

The three of us shuffled out into the study. We must have looked very guilty, standing in a row in front of the entrance to the serpent room. Around nine or ten patients were there, unsteady on their feet, and one or two of the staff, I guessed. It was hard to tell for certain, because they all wore masks and head-dresses made of fur, twigs and horns. I knew some of them couldn't walk too well anyway, but they'd also been drinking. The sour smell of barley ale hung around them, mixed with their usual stench of sweat and bad breath.

"How did they get hold of all that ale?" I whispered to Meg.

"The parish left some yesterday. For a wassail, you know – a special drink. It was a kind thing to do, but I told Agnes to hide it away."

I sighed. "She hasn't done it very well, then."

"Where is he, Miss Meg?" slurred a man wearing some sort of horned mask on his head, like a stag. "In there?"

"That's where he keeps his fine wines," yelled a woman. "Let's get in!"

Meg held up her hands. "No, don't go in there," she begged. "He'll be very angry with you, never mind Twelfth Day."

The crowd of figures burst out laughing again. Jeannie stepped behind me and hung onto my tunic, snivelling.

"There's no wine in there," I said. "Only medicines."

"Well, we could all do with a few of those too," roared someone wrapped in a mangy fur cloak. "Let's see what's on offer, eh?"

"No," pleaded Meg, but they all pushed past us. One of them tripped on the sleeping doctor and gave a loud, rasping laugh. "Looks like he started celebrating without us," he shouted. "Let's see what drinks he's hiding. Anything in these jars, Miss Meg?"

"Don't touch them," screamed Meg.

But someone grabbed a thick glass jar and tipped it over. Out slid a long, slender snake-like creature, the brightest jewel-green I ever saw. I jumped back with a yelp. It slithered rapidly into a corner and hid. The masked patients started shouting and stumbling around in a panic. Jars tumbled to the floor, cracked and broke. To my horror, one serpent after another tumbled out on to the floor. Some were slim and brightly coloured as a hair ribbon: red, poison-yellow, glossy black. Others were thick, darkly patterned with bands and speckles, menacing. The horrid mermaid fell out of its tank, its fishtail flapping on the floor, its wicked monkey-face gnashing its teeth.

The shambling figures seemed to take a few moments to realise what they'd unleashed. Then they began to turn and make for the door as fast as they could, trampling over Huksor's sleeping body in their rush, shouting and yelling. Jeannie joined in their screams. Without a further thought I snatched the girl up into my arms and ran unsteadily out of the room, through the study and out into the passageway. I yelled for Meg to follow us.

Hexer Hall
11th January, 1899
Later

>*I sat shivering on my own doorstep, the cold from the snow-covered stone seeping quickly through the thick velvet of my skirts. I watched as a line of people who were once happy to take my wages trudged slowly out of the grounds, heading out of the estate. They would rather walk into the dead of winter with no job or prospects than stay here. Some of them turned their heads and noticed me, but they quickly looked away again and kept walking. My own face and fingers were burning with the cold. I picked myself up and brushed the snow from my clothes, then walked around to the*

back of the Hall and the kitchen door. I found myself knocking at the servants' entrance to be let in. This may be my Hall but the kitchen is not my territory. Mrs McKinnon opened it. Her face looked tight and strained. She was very shocked to see me, of course.

"No one answered the main door, Mrs McKinnon," *I said.*

She looked down. "No, ma'am. I'm afraid most of the servants have gone. They are too afraid to stay, what with the sickness and– and– everything else."

I sighed and asked her to bring me up some tea and something sweet to eat. She hung her head. "We are rather short on supplies, ma'am. The grocer has refused to come these last three days, because of all the talk about the sickness at the Hall. I went into the village myself yesterday but he would not serve me because of the terrible gossip that is going around. I don't know what to do next, ma'am. I'm sorry."

"Well, then, take the coach into the town," I snapped at her.

She shook her head. "The coachmen have left, my Lady."

"Were they ill too?" I asked.

"No, but they are both very religious. They feared that some sort of evil practices were going on. I couldn't make them see sense, I'm afraid."

I sat down, there in the kitchen, and stared at the whorls in the wooden table. "Then I don't know what to suggest," I said.

Jeannie and I stood, gasping for breath, in the stone corridor. We watched the patients stagger and drag themselves past us, all looking like creatures from a terrible dream. Old Will led the procession, limping along at the front wearing something like a bishop's hat, although it was battered and teetering at an angle, about to fall off. I recognised the stolid figure of Agnes, wearing some kind of feathered mask that was meant to look like a bird. I couldn't help thinking that she was one of the least bird-like creatures I'd ever seen. Some wore masks that looked like skulls, and one had the scorched red face of a horned devil, with mad, black eyeholes and the mouth hole sliced into a grin. Jeannie hid behind me when she saw him. They hobbled, as fast as their failing limbs could take them, out into the white courtyard, where the night was just giving way to a blood-red winter dawn.

"The thirteen fires!" I heard one of them shout. "Fires will put paid to the devilish creatures! Light the thirteen fires!"

As I glanced around the dark corridor on the lookout for serpents, Meg came stumbling along behind them, dragging her too-long skirt. "You're still here," she panted. "I thought you might've gone without me."

"What are the thirteen fires?" Jeannie asked.

"It's a custom," Meg said. "You light one big fire and twelve smaller ones. For all the thirteen nights of Christmas. When they did it last year, some of the hospital burned down. It was a miracle no one was killed."

"Well, they're about to do it again," I warned. Meg

groaned. She ran out into the courtyard, to try to talk the patients out of it.

"Let's go," said Jeannie, tugging at my arm. "Let's just get away, now."

"We can't," I said, even though of course I was panicking inside. All those serpent monsters on the loose – the worst thing I could possibly imagine. The staff and patients running amok, full of ale and Twelfth Day madness. And now we might all be burned alive. "We can't go now. We promised Meg we'd try to take her with us."

Jeannie pouted. "But she's too late, isn't she?"

I frowned at her. She might've looked like a sweet child but she really did have a bit of her sister's nastiness.

I pulled her into Meg's cubby-hole to wait, jumping every time I thought I spotted a shadow moving. Mice, I told myself, or spiders – the serpents would surely not have come this far away from their warm room.

We listened as the shouting from outside grew louder. I heard the crackling sound of a fire getting under way and glanced outside. The patients had pulled together enough bits of wood to start a fair-sized blaze and it was spitting nastily. Still in their head-dresses and animal masks, they started to sing some old song about the end of the winter. *Old King Holly dies away, winter will not leave its mark. Raise a wassail for Twelfth Day, light must chase away the dark.* They moved around the flames in a slow, stilted dance. The song got faster each time they sang it, although they couldn't dance with any more speed to keep up with it.

Meg dashed in. "I can't get a word of sense out of any

of them. Even Agnes laughed at me when I tried to get her help. Of all the days, it would have to be this one. Nothing matters to anyone today."

"What now?" I asked, pulling Jeannie closer to me.

"I begged them not to start any more fires, but I don't think they'll take any notice of me," she said. "We'll try to wake Doctor Huksor up and then we'd better get away."

"We can't do that," I said. "If Huksor wakes up, he'll kill us. That room is alive with snakes and monsters. I can't go back in there, I just can't."

"I can," she said, stubbornly. "I won't just leave him to die. Anyway," she added, with a sly look, "the book's in there. If we don't get it now, it might get burned up."

The smell of smoke filled up my nose. Flickers of orange danced across the slit windows and the stone wall, to the cracked tune of the Twelfth Day song. Jeannie started to cough. "Let's just *go*," she said.

I looked at her and thought, I have to be braver than you, miss. Meg is right.

"Come on, then," I said, with a sigh, sounding much stronger than I felt. "Let's wake the old goat up." We turned and ran towards the study.

Hexer Hall
11th January, 1899
Later

> *Of all my other servants, only Lucy has stayed. When the others left, she was in the gardener's cottage nursing her sweetheart Tom. Indeed, her loyalty lies*

with that young man, rather than with me. Or perhaps it is that she will find it harder to get work, because of the colour of her skin. As I sat talking to Mrs McKinnon, Lucy rushed in, all tears, begging for cool water and anything else to bring down a fever. Tom was getting worse.

"Oh, ma'am, he is unconscious and thrashing around on the bed in great distress," she told me. "And his skin is burning! The heat is coming off him as if he's on fire – I hardly dare touch him!" Mrs McKinnon took pity on her and helped her find a clean cloth and a jug of fresh, cool water. Then she began searching her cupboards for anything else that may help. I felt so useless at this point that I left and went upstairs.

I stood for some time in the drawing room surveying my ruined grounds. Watching all those people walk away from me – taking what is left of my reputation with them, no doubt, to toss around in the shops and ale-houses – has left me bereft. I feel as if I have barely a true friend in the world. I have but one hope: that Annie will bring me the book. Only that can help me heal my broken reputation.

Meg, Jeannie and I all held hands as we crept towards the study door. We checked the floor for serpents as we went. Outside, the blaze grew larger and brighter. The singing and shouting got louder and bawdier. I thought I could hear a crackling sound from one of the rooms along the corridor too, but I pushed that idea away until we did what we had to do. Slowly, Meg pushed the study door open and glanced around.

"I think the serpents are probably all hiding," she whispered. "They're quite nervous creatures, really."

"I can't think why," I grumbled. "I wouldn't be frightened of anything if I looked as scary as they do and if I had poisonous teeth."

Meg frowned. "Something's wrong."

"What do you mean?" I asked.

"I don't really know, it's just– I have a horrible feeling," she pressed her hand to her stomach, "just in here."

"You're scared," I told her. "We all are. Let's get this over with as fast as we can. Jeannie and I will get the book and you wake Huksor, if you're able. Then we'll all run for it."

Checking around her feet, Meg went into the serpent room while Jeannie and I hoisted the book, still wrapped in its cloth, up from the floor. The pot of ointment rolled away. I was about to reach for it. Then we heard Meg give a terrible, high, moaning sound, like an injured pup. Jeannie and I glanced at each other and rushed to the doorway of the snake room. Meg stood there with her back to us. She turned, her face death-white and her hand clapped across her mouth.

"What?" I asked her, looking over her shoulder. "What is it?"

Meg couldn't speak but only shook her head, her eyes brimming. Then Jeannie screamed and jumped back. In the same instant I suddenly noticed the huge, misshapen body of Bess on the floor. Misshapen, in that it was no longer a fat log-shape. It was bulging out with the beast's last meal. The giant snake was eating her sleeping master and her body was swollen with the distinct shape of a small man. Only his lower legs and feet still stuck out of the snake's jaw, which had slackened and grown to get the huge meal in. It was a few moments before I realised what I was seeing. Then I turned away and was shudderingly sick on the stone floor.

Jeannie was wailing like a banshee by now. I wiped my face but I didn't tell her off. Meg too was weeping as if her heart would break.

"It's all my fault!" she sobbed. "I left him in there, half-poisoned with sleeping draught. I as good as killed him!"

I tried to comfort her, putting my arms around her skinny shoulders. "No, Meg, no one could have guessed what the beast would do," I told her, but the very words made me retch again. We clung to each other for a moment. Meg was crying so hard I had to hold her tight, trying to stop her violent shaking. Then the smell of smoke seemed to get suddenly stronger and I remembered the patients and the fires.

"We must try to get out of here," I shouted. "Come on, Meg. There's nothing more you can do for your master now. Save yourself!"

Still sobbing, Meg followed me as I started for the study door. We pulled it open to the sounds of furious crackling and burning.

CHAPTER SIXTEEN

Hexer Hall
11th January, 1899
Later

> *Haggstone marched into the drawing room and had the*
> *nerve to complain because she couldn't get a coach to*
> *take her away from the Hall. I suggested that she might*
> *like to walk, as all my staff had done. She was trying*
> *to bully me into finding her some transport when*
> *there was a loud rapping noise at the Hall's front door.*
> *Voices, shouting in angry, accusing tones. I made my*
> *way to the top of the staircase, overlooking the entrance*
> *hall. Poor Mrs McKinnon was trying to hold the heavy*
> *front door against a small crowd of people who were*
> *baying to get in. It hardly seemed fair on the woman,*

so I walked down the staircase and demanded to know what was going on.

It was Mr Pocklaw, the local minister, some of my own former servants and a handful of self-elected dignitaries from the town. The minister stepped forward to speak for this rabble.

"It has come to my attention," he began, with his usual pomposity, "that unnatural things are going on in this Hall. I hear disturbing tales of séances and unholy magical practices. Your servants have abandoned you but I cannot allow the matter to end there. Your staff believe you are responsible for the spread of sickness among themselves and many of the villagers. We demand answers, Lady Hexer. Just what has been going on in this place?"

I answered with as much dignity as possible, given the aggressive tone of his voice and the poisonous looks I was getting from the whole party.

"Mr Pocklaw," I replied, "these are the wild imaginings of an over-superstitious, under-educated group of peasants."

There was an angry gasp from the crowd.

"I know of no such nonsense," I went on. "It is fair to say—" I glanced behind me at the staircase, where I guessed Haggstone was lurking, "It is fair to say that I have foolishly entertained a woman who claims to be a psychic and medium. I now believe this person to be a fraud. She will be leaving my premises today. As to all your other suggestions, they have no basis in fact.

Now please leave my grounds and stop frightening my housekeeper."

The minister bristled. He was used to people cowering when he spoke, not standing up to him.

"Lady Hexer," he went on. "The servants feel you ought to destroy the exotic plants which are covering the ground. They believe they have sprung from evil roots and may be a cause of the current epidemic of fever."

"Just as soon as I can find the labourers," I replied, "I will do exactly that. Or perhaps you feel I ought to don my gloves and go out there myself? As you know, many of my workers have abandoned their duties. The plants are merely weeds, of course, but unpleasant none the less."

"I'd be happy to torch them for you," muttered one of my old gardeners.

I waited for a moment. "Will that be all?" I added.

My self-appointed judges glanced at each other and then the minister puffed himself up again. "We believe there is a child in the Hall. A servant girl whom you have taken into your care."

I narrowed my eyes at him. "Yes. An act of great charity, would you not agree, Mr Pocklaw?"

"Ah, well," said Pocklaw. "That rather depends on how she fares. We hear that she is locked away, that she may be ill and that she has barely been seen for some days."

I swallowed hard. "She is, as you suggest, unwell at

the moment. But she is only locked in her room for her own good, to stop her from sleep-walking in her present fevered state."

"We demand to see the child, Lady Hexer," Pocklaw insisted. "Her aunt, a good church-going woman, has written to me asking about her welfare."

I shivered as the cruel winds blew into the Hall. "If you imagine," I told him, "that I am going to let a crowd of strangers march into a child's room when she is ill, you are mistaken. It is my duty to protect the girl at the moment."

"She's killed her!" yelled out one of the men, suddenly. "She's murdered her and her ghost is wandering around the Hall! Some of the servants have seen it!"

There was a shocked murmuring and the minister stuck his booted foot inside my doorway. "We must see the child. At least one of us must confirm that she is alive and well."

"Very well," I agreed. "But I refuse to invite any of you inside my home. You may stand in the grounds and I will bring Annie to the bedroom window. You will be able to see that she has not been harmed."

The minister turned to consult with his cronies and I took the opportunity to pull back the door and slam it shut, when he wasn't expecting it. It was rather satisfying to hear him yelp in pain as he jumped out of the way.

Then, ignoring Mrs McKinnon's open mouth, I swept

*back up the stairs. There was nothing for it. I would have
to call Annie back to the present right now. I hurried along
to her bedroom and unlocked the door with trembling
hands.*

The room was empty. Annie was not there.

We stumbled along the narrow, dark corridors, the heavy
book slowing us down. The flickering slivers of firelight,
bright then black, as if some hobgoblin was dancing in
front of us with candles, made me blink again and again.
I was used to the sounds of the hospital: the groaning and
occasional crying of someone in pain, the busy sound of
the kitchen, the lowing of the animals outside. But all we
could hear now were the crackles of nearing fires and the
strains of the singing, which somehow made it feel more
frightening, as if no one cared what happened any more.

"We have to get out of here – fast," I kept urging, every
time Meg stopped to glance back towards Huksor's study
or Jeannie dragged her feet. I was out of breath but the
air was full of the smell of burning, which scratched like
nails at my throat. "I don't know how fast these fires will
spread."

Jeannie was tugging on my sleeve and snivelling.

"Whatever it is, Jeannie, it'll have to wait," I told her,
pulling her along.

"I can smell food," Meg said, suddenly.

"That's all you ever think about," I muttered, but she
was right – there was a smell of something cooking, like
animal flesh. As we reached the hospital kitchen, Meg

leaned against the heavy door and pushed it open. Smoke poured out and I wrenched the door shut again as best I could. The kitchen was alight and every scrap of food in the room was being burned up.

Outside, there was the sound of some of the patients blundering around, panicking and shouting. We edged along the corridor, smoke clogging our nostrils and clouding our sight. I bore the weight of the book, because Jeannie was no help at all. In fact the tiresome child was dragging her heels and slowing us down.

We were almost at one of the doors but we saw that the biggest bonfire in the courtyard was spreading fast towards it.

"I think we can get past it if we're very, very quick," I whispered, trying not to breathe in too hard. I pulled Jeannie towards the door. But the stupid girl came to a dead stop.

"Come on," I urged. "We have to get out, now. Move!"

"I've been bit," wailed Jeannie. She dropped to her knees. "I've been trying to tell you. You've not been listening. One of them snakes has bitten my foot." She started to make a high-pitched keening sound. "I've been poisoned! I'm going to *die*."

I stared at her, helpless. She wrapped her arms around herself and I knew she wasn't going anywhere. Meg wiped her face and took a deep breath, then coughed hard because of the smoke.

"Get that pot out," she said. "There's a cure in there. Hurry!"

My insides sank. "We dropped it," I admitted. "Back in the study. I forgot to pick it up."

"I'll have to go back and get it then," Meg said, sniffing, her eyes watering badly.

"You can't," I pleaded. "There isn't time. There's too much smoke. You won't make it, Meg."

She gave me her wilful look, through the grime left by her tears.

"I will," she said. "You wait here. I'll be quicker on my own. You need me to bring back the special salve or else Jeannie could die. We don't know what bit her."

She turned to head back for the study. I watched her disappear into the thickening smoke and heard her call, "Don't go without me!"

Hopelessly, I sat on the hard floor with Jeannie, and took her hand as she cried and rocked back and forwards with pain. I sighed. Trust you, I couldn't help thinking, you pest. We could have been out of here by now. I knew it wasn't fair to think like this, but really. This girl had been nothing but a nuisance and now we might all meet a terrible end, thanks to her.

The next second, there was a huge explosion and a blinding globe of fire burst out of a room further down the passageway. I jumped up and pulled Jeannie, sobbing, to her feet. The fire was like a mad tiger, making its furious way along the corridor, latching on to cloths or wood or dust or anything, gobbling up everything it passed. I didn't let myself think about any patients who were still in their beds.

"This way," I croaked, and pulled Jeannie back towards the study, even though the smoke was so black and foul that way we could barely see. What fool made windows that were nothing more than tiny slits, so no one could get through them? I pulled my hood over my stinging eyes and tried to cover my nose and mouth from the fumes. One hand was still clutching at Jeannie and dragging her with me. Panic filled my whole head and body with a loud thumping and pounding.

Then there was an almighty crashing sound. Just behind us, a wall collapsed. The fire licked greedily at its newly-found bits of wood. The stones threw up so much dust that we were blinded for a few moments and our heads rang with the noise. I rubbed my eyes and then suddenly I could see out to the courtyard. Several smaller fires were dancing there. The heat melted great dollops of snow, which slid off the roofs and slapped onto the ground. Right in the middle of the cobbled yard stood Tom. He was holding his arms out to me and shouting my name, his face desperate and scorched red. I screamed for him. Still pulling Jeannie, who seemed to be getting heavier and heavier, I stumbled through the broken remains of the wall. I threw myself into his arms. They encircled both of us.

We all clung together, staring round at the blazing courtyard. Patients were shouting and screaming, some limping, some crawling around the square, not knowing what to do. I knew there would be others lying helpless in their beds as the blaze headed towards them. Some, like

Old Will, had got as far as the gates but were too afraid to go beyond them. Agnes sat on the ground in the melting snow and wailed like an overgrown baby. There were terrified bleating and grunting sounds coming from the animals, thrown into panic as the fires raged on.

Then came the worst moment of all. I saw Meg stumbling towards the collapsed part of the wall. It was as if she was being chased by the fire. The blue dress pulled behind her, slowing her down. She saw us all huddled together out in the courtyard and shouted out, "Annie! Don't leave without me! You promised!"

I watched in horror as she tripped over the hem of the silly long dress, falling her full length onto the stony rubble. A tiny pot sailed out of her hand in an arc and somehow, behind me, Tom reached out and caught it. I yelled at Meg to get up and run for her life. But in less than a second, the angry flames whipped their way up the back of the dress and Meg disappeared into a flash of orange-gold, like a Chinese firework.

"Meg! *Meg!*" Screaming and sobbing, I started towards her, Tom pulling me back. But then the flames burst out of the building, enormous, overpowering, blasting me with their wicked hell-heat. I stumbled backwards, hearing Tom shouting, Jeannie yelling. Then all I knew was the dizzying blackness of nothing.

I thought I could see Meg, standing smiling at me in the blue dress she loved. She looked beautiful, surrounded by a soft summer sky and pink blossom. I tried to say her name, my throat raw and stopped up. My words turned into a painful fit of coughing. Meg shrank smaller and smaller. I blinked my sore, dusty eyes. Then I realised I was looking at the painted plant pot with its fancy picture of the goddess of spring, next to the hearth in the drawing room of Hexer Hall. The fire I could smell, though, wasn't the sweet coal and pine logs of Lady Hexer's grate. I could still taste the dirtier, thicker smoke of burning buildings.

I sat up and looked around. It felt very warm, much warmer than usual. Jeannie was also lying on the thick rug, white-faced, her eyes closed. Next to me, slightly charred, was Huksor's great book, still wrapped in the smoking, dirty cloth. There, too, was the pot Meg had thrown.

Meg. I couldn't even bear to think about her. Pushing the vision of her last moments out of my mind, I grabbed the pot and opened it. The distinct, clean smell of lavender hit my nostrils. I looked again at Jeannie. She was breathing heavily. I picked up her bare foot and saw that it was purple-red, blistered and swollen, with two tiny puncture marks near the heel. Without much hope, I dipped my fingers in the pot and rubbed the oily lotion around the wounds. The drawing room door opened and Lady Hexer stood there, staring at me.

"Oh! Thank goodness!" she gasped. "I didn't know where ... but how did you get in here?" Then she spotted the book, some of its leaves sticking out of the greyed wrapping. All thoughts of me and tiny Jeannie lying sick on the floor seemed to disappear. Her eyes became excited and greedy as she bent down.

"You did it! My book!"

Furious, I leaped over and sat on the book, hard. "Is that all you can think about?" I shouted at her.

She stepped back, staring at me in her shock. "Why, but–"

"Jeannie's nearly dead – look at her! We have to do something!"

Lady Hexer stooped down and held out her pale hands. They were shaking like birch twigs in the winter wind. "Very well, then. First we will do what we can for Jeannie. Then you must tell me all you have been through."

She sighed. "No local doctors will come near the Hall. But you have the book! Let's see if there is anything there which may help the child!"

I shook my head. "Oh no," I said, firmly. "Not this thing. I've already put one of Doctor Huksor's crazy cures on Jeannie's snake bite, because it's all I have, but a fat lot of use I expect it to be."

Lady Hexer took a step towards me. "Get up, Annie. The book, please. It belongs to me now."

"You haven't listened to me, have you? Those patients kept on dying. Huksor stopped caring. His experiments took over his mind."

Lady Hexer knelt down on the floor beside me, her skirts billowing out in a silken pool around her. "You are quite distraught. You have been through so much. Let us talk this through, as friends."

"We're not friends," I spat back at her, making her start.

"I'm just someone you've been able to use. I don't really matter to people like you, because I'm just a girl, because I'm poor and I need your wages, because you've put your crazy ideas in front of everything and everyone.

"I almost died in that hospital and my friend Meg is dead, all because she was so brave and tried to help me. I don't know where Tom is and poor Jeannie may not survive. And there is a whole list of patients in that hospital whose names I'll never know, all dead in the name of Huksor's work. It needs to stop."

Lady Hexer swallowed with a tiny movement of her elegant throat. "It cannot stop, not now. It has all gone too far. If I give up now, then everything you describe will have been in vain. I can see that some terrible things have happened. But it all has to be for something, don't you agree?"

For a moment, I was almost swayed. Lady Hexer was very good at talking people into her way of thinking. But then Jeannie gave a soft moan. I realised I had to stop up my ears to Her Ladyship's pleas and remember all the people who'd been hurt. I placed my hands down hard on either side of me, keeping the book held fast.

"Now then." Lady Hexer's eyes were fixed on the book, not me. "You are right, there were times when I should have done things better. I– I hurt you. I underestimated you. But you're wrong to say I don't care about you. I care more than you know. But my reputation, my family's reputation, it all depends on this. If I give up my hope in it, then I have nothing left but a long life during which I will never be accepted, never respected. I cannot bear that thought."

I felt reckless when I said to Lady Hexer, "You'll be all right, whatever happens, because you have money. It's people like me and Lucy who won't be accepted and that's because of the way we were born, because of things we can't help."

Lady Hexer sighed and I thought I saw a ripple of annoyance run across her face. "Really! I'm not going to get into a debate on the ills of society with a twelve-year-old child. I will raise you up so far, and your reward is guaranteed, but do not test me further. Just get up and give me that book."

Behind me, Jeannie's breath seemed to quicken. I slid my gaze toward her but I didn't move.

"The book is mine, after all. It belongs to my family." Lady Hexer stretched out a hand.

"It will end up making things worse, for you and your precious good name," I said.

"That's something you must let me decide. I will not put my fate in the hands of a grubby child whom I've plucked from the streets."

I felt my face go red with anger. I still didn't budge.

"For pity's sake! What is it you want? More money?" Lady Hexer was shouting now.

"More money? You don't know me at all. You certainly don't care, so stop pretending. As for this – it's all madness! This is what I think of it!"

In one quick movement, I rolled off the book and grabbed at it. I heaved it up, cloth and all, and lifted it above my head.

"Now, now," said Lady Hexer, pleadingly. "Be careful, please."

She circled me carefully and I could tell she was going to make a grab for it. I looked around wildly and then, with the last of my strength, I flung it on to her fire. It made a great whooshing sound. The flames chomped at it, crackling and cackling as though with laughter.

Lady Hexer let out a howl. She threw herself at the fire, all the while screaming, "No! NO!" She kept plucking madly at the flames and then jumping back because of the heat.

I suddenly realised there was a lot of noise coming from the grounds outside. It might've been going on since I had arrived, but I hadn't had time to take it in. I ran to the window and saw there were huge fires out in the grounds. They were tearing along the gardens and the dense plants like angry dragons. Thick, green spirals of smoke rose up from the flames.

"Lady Hexer," I shouted, "your grounds are on fire!"

She didn't turn round but kept approaching the fire in the grate, arms outstretched.

"Stupid minister," she muttered, more to herself than me. "Stupid, superstitious peasants. They think they're burning out the magic. They'll pay for this. They'll be sorry."

Tom, I thought. He might be in the cottage. I have to get to him.

But then there was a loud hissing, spitting sound. I turned to see Lady Hexer backing away from the hearth.

Rising out of the fire was the shape of a serpent, formed from greenish-black smoke, its mouth open, its tongue flicking. Arching up, it slid out of the fire and along the carpet. It was followed by a second, thick-bodied snake, no less terrifying because it was made of smoke. Then a third.

"Get out of here!" I screamed at Lady Hexer.

I suddenly noticed Jeannie stirring, rubbing her eyes. I grabbed her hand and pulled her up and towards the door.

"Come on, you stupid woman!" I yelled at Lady Hexer.

She looked frozen for a moment. Then she blinked and with wide eyes she ran towards the fire again, jabbering, "The book! I must try to save the book!"

I ran back to her, and tried to grab at her sleeve and tug her away. She pulled away, back towards the flames.

"Please!" I screamed at her, clutching a hank of her skirts and wrenching at it. "Lady Hexer! You cannot save the book now, it's too late! Your grounds are all alight! You must get out now or you will die!"

She turned and gave me a violent push, sending me spinning backwards into a dazed Jeannie. Then she ran forward again. The smoke snakes were gathering, forming misty knots around her. Then she threw herself at the flames.

I heard her terrible screams but I couldn't stop to think a second longer. I dragged Jeannie away, out of the room and down the back stairs towards the deserted kitchen. From the thundering, rattling sounds and the choking, poisonous smells, I knew we were being followed by fire.

"Becky!" Jeannie yelled, when she found the kitchen empty. "My Becky's asleep upstairs!"

"I'm sorry." I pulled her out of the door. "We have to get out before we get killed too. Hurry up!"

We ran out into the grounds. Panting, I tried to work out a way across the gardens that avoided the worst of the fires. We scurried in a crazy zigzag, heading for the cottage. The heat and smoke stench almost overcame me. Then I heard someone yelling my name. Tom and Lucy were running towards me. I ran at them and tried to hug them both at once. Tom's eyes were streaming.

"I had terrible dreams about you," he said, squeezing me hard and kissing the top of my head. "I dreamed we were stuck in a fire. Then Lucy woke me and the fire was real. We need to get away, all of us. Fast."

Still clinging to each other, we turned towards the blazing Hall. The thick plumes of smoke which rose up from it formed the shape of fat, sulphurous snakes, their hazy bodies swelling to a monstrous size.

We had to edge closer to the burning building to reach the main road out of the estate. Again I could hear the sickening, crashing sounds of the Hall's grand rooms falling in on themselves. I heard a terrible, mad shriek and we looked up to see Haggstone, leaning out of her open bedroom window, the bright amber of the fire right behind her.

"Help me!" she was yelling, her throaty voice alight with fear. "I'm trapped! Help me!"

We all looked at each other, gasping for breath. "There's

nothing we can do," Tom called up at her. "We can't get to you. Is there no way you can get out?"

Haggstone let out another crazy scream and to our horror she clambered up onto the ledge. "No," I whispered. I wiped the sweat and grime from my face. We watched, our mouths open, as she fell, flapping like a shot bird, her wraps and scarves aflame. She landed with a thump right in the middle of one of the fires. We ran towards it but again the flames and black smoke forced us back. In just a few seconds the blaze disappeared, as suddenly as if someone had thrown water at it. We edged closer. Nothing was there but a fat pile of dark, smoking ash.

"Lady Hexer," I said, tearfully, looking back at the burning, collapsing building. "She's still in there."

"Becky! My Becky!" Jeannie wailed.

I stared wildly at Tom. "Can we do anything? Can we try to save anyone?"

No one spoke. Lucy just squeezed me around the shoulders and steered us away.

As we stumbled to the gates of the grounds, a coach rattled up towards us and stopped. Mrs McKinnon got out. She stared at the burning Hall and grounds, her eyes gleaming with tears.

"Get in the coach," she ordered. "Jeannie, your sister has escaped and made it to the village. She's weeping her heart out, thinking you dead. She'll be overjoyed to see you. Lucy, you can stay with my sister in the village for tonight. Tom, Annie, there is a room for you in the Fleece Inn."

As we clambered into the coach, carts carrying men

from the village lumbered up towards the grounds. "Get away from here," one of the men shouted. "We'll do what we can to put the fires out."

The coach clattered us towards Hexendale. Flames were still thrashing out of every window of the Hall and from the tall chimneys the smoke serpents were rising and fading into the bright blue winter sky.

We spent an odd, sleepless night in the village inn. The keeper made a supper for all the people who had fled the Hall, in return for listening to their stories. I didn't tell all of mine, of course. No one would have believed it anyway. Becky came up to me and her pinched face broke into the first proper smile I'd ever seen her give.

"You saved my sister," she said. "You got rid of the snake poison. Thank you so much."

I shrugged. "It wasn't me, really," I admitted. "It was someone else. My friend Meg." Saying her name gave me a stabbing pain in my stomach and I blinked hard, forcing back tears. "She knew what would cure it. I didn't really believe her. But it worked after all."

Becky squeezed my hand. "Well. Jeannie said you were very brave."

I felt myself blush.

Later, Tom came and put his arm around my shoulder. "I'm sorry," he said. "I brought you to that place and put you in so much danger. I didn't know."

I leaned my head on his chest. "It wasn't your fault," I said.

"It looks as if I'm not able to look after you," he said, hanging his head. "Do you want to go back to Aunt Catherine's?"

I made a choking sound. "I do not," I said. "Do you?"

Tom shook his head. "Lucy's going to try to find a position in Edinburgh. I thought I'd go with her."

"And me," I said.

Tom grinned. "And you, hobgoblin. If that's what you want."

He gave me a squeeze. "Hey," he said, suddenly. "Feel that."

He took my hand and rubbed it across the top of my scalp. Underneath the pads of my fingers, I could feel soft, new, baby hairs on my head. Thoughts of Meg still haunted my sleeping and waking moments and I could almost hear her say, "I told you the cures would work." Or perhaps it was something else. Perhaps it was just time for things to grow again.

Tom, Lucy and I made our way back to Hexer Hall some days later, to see if we could salvage anything from our cottage. The fires hadn't reached as far as our home, so we were able to bundle up some blankets, a couple of pots and, thankfully, Tom's leather bag where he'd saved his wages.

"There's quite a lot in there," I said, surprised, fingering the heavy pouch.

He winked. "I told you Lady Hexer paid well. This

should be enough for our train fares to Edinburgh."

"A train?" I couldn't help feeling excited, because I'd never been on one before. Lucy chatted about how she might be able to find work with her old employer, who'd be happy to see her come back. Edinburgh was full of tall, beautiful buildings, she promised, and wealthy merchants looking for staff. There were factories, too; all sorts of places in which to find work. Everyone would speak as if they were singing, just like Lucy.

We walked towards the blackened bones of the Hall. The snow had all disappeared, not just because of the fire and water, but because the temperature had risen and the air felt much milder. The ground was soft and muddy under our feet. Under the lingering smell of the burned-out building and the scorched trees and shrubs was a new, sweeter scent: moist earth, filled with the promise of growth.

But we would not stay here to see it.

"This place is bad," Tom said. "I feel sorry for anyone who tries to build on it or grow anything. So many terrible things have happened here. I'm not sure it'll ever be right. In fact," he shivered hard, and not because of the cold. "Let's just get out of here, as quick as we can."

I agreed. It was important to leave this place. It fooled us, like a pretty face. But I had opened a door to the past and I didn't know if it would ever fully close again. Perhaps, somewhere else, I wouldn't keep seeing Meg disappearing into the blaze whenever I closed my eyes. Perhaps we would find a place where people would not stare at Lucy or call her names, just because of the colour of her skin.

Maybe I could make some good come from all of this. I'd taken something with me: Meg's ointment, tucked into my pocket. I hoped I could use it to help people, just as she would have wanted. We linked arms, all three of us, and started to march away towards a wide, wide, new world.

About the Author

The Serpent House was written during Bea Davenport's Creative Writing PhD at Newcastle University. Her tutors were Jackie Kay, the award-winning poet and writer, and Professor Kim Reynolds, an internationally-renowned expert in children's literature.

In its early, unpublished form, *The Serpent House* was shortlisted for the 2010 *Times*/Chicken House award. It was inspired by the village where Bea lives, which is named after a medieval leper hospital, and the stories of Bea's three great-aunts who all worked in service in the early twentieth century.

Bea has also written a crime novel for adults, *In Too Deep*, and teaches creative writing classes. She lives near Berwick-upon-Tweed in Northumberland with her partner and children.

More titles from Curious Fox

The Spider Sun

When twelve-year-old Jacob's doodles are stolen by a creature from an underground world and misinterpreted as plans to start a war, he finds himself on an adventure to prove his innocence and save London.

The adventures of Rémy Brunel

No one performs on the circus trapeze like
Rémy Brunel. But Rémy also leads another life,
prowling through the backstreets of Victorian
London as a jewel thief. Forced by the evil
circus owner Gustave to attempt the theft of
one of the world's most valuable diamonds,
she discovers an underworld of treachery
and fiendish plots.

*I was holding my breath ... I never
expected what happened to happen*

Stormi, Books, Movies, Reviews! Oh My! blog

Secrets & Spies

Beth Johnson is a talented and beautiful young
actress. She is also a spy. The King's life is in
danger and Beth must do whatever it takes to
protect him, whether it's investigating a ghost
ship or escaping the horrific Plague. But when
she gets the chance to stop the King's enemy
once and for all, can she leave her life as an
actress behind and journey to the New World?

For more exciting books from
brilliant authors, follow the fox!

www.curious-fox.com